Love Labors & Won

A 'Pride & Prejudice' and 'North & South' Variation

NEY MITCH

Hello readers!

Welcome to the official second to last entry of the Austen Gaskell series.

Readers, I acknowledge that I was wrong in assuming this installment would be the conclusion. After the story is an Afterword to explain why that has occurred, and that I hope the reader will forgive me for making this series one book longer than expected.

With any luck, this next installment will be satisfying, and worthy of your attention.

I dedicate this book to you all, who have stuck out enjoying this series and have been there for me. I'd be lost without you lot!

Also, I give another round of thanks to my family, publisher, Helyn Guy-Roberts, A. Madison, and all who helped bring this book to life.

Cheers, Friends! Cheers.

Chapter 1

Childlike News

Everything always looks better when you wake up from a lovely previous day.

Naturally, there is the anxiety that awaits you when the sun rises. For you must accept the possibility, the grim possibility, that the present day could never be as promising as the day before.

Yet it was not this day. When my eyes opened, all prospects seemed possible. Removing the blankets and sheets from me, I rushed to the window and looked out at the sky.

The sun was rising on the horizon, and it was too early for the smoke from the factories to fill the atmosphere. Through the clouds, I saw the promising hues of blue that was the true sky color. It was daring to burst through the clouds and provoke the smoky chimneys, willing to show that mother nature still had a hand in the North.

When looking downward, I still saw the gray and sordid aspect of Frances Street. And yet, it was as if I was seeing it with new eyes. Here was the constant application of work, the painful aspect of labor, but the honor of knowing that one is making a living for oneself.

This was humanity, by and by!

And I was a woman in love. Therefore, the whole world took on a brighter aspect. It all felt anew, refreshed, and touched by the morning grace.

For one interesting moment, the streets of Milton Common transformed and captured the same feeling that I once witnessed when I managed to walk along Longbourn just as sunrise occurred.

Naturally, I assumed that when I was in the thick of it all, when I sat on the omnibus and was being tossed about among the passersby on the street, reality would become *reality* again and lose its dreamlike quality. But for the moment, I would give into the fantastic and see the romance that secretly filled Milton and found its way into the hearts of those who knew where to look for it.

Good morning, Milton! May you always be as lovely as you are now.

On the ride on the omnibus, I was not alone.

Kitty and Rasby were with me, because we had caught it at the same time. While I remained with them, I was silent the entire time, but not out of a desire to be sullen. On the contrary, I was elated and allowed Kitty and Rasby to talk amongst themselves as I looked at every person who was sitting down around us.

They were either resting their eyes, looking at their laps, exhausted, or looking around at the walkers along the street. Most of them were wearing plain clothes, and one man even had his chimney broom with him—the dear lad was a Sweep.

It was strange. So terribly strange. I thought that, when I had to integrate myself into society again, my fascination with the mundane would die. A quick death, I imagined. However, that was not the case at all.

Rather, I found the gray and the smoke of Milton to be a reminder of reality itself, and that there was beauty through it all. And with the hard and iron look that they all had on their faces as they prepared for work, they were an image of England that I wanted to be forever etched in my mind. I viewed the people of Milton as a portrait of Britain, laid out as just another painting that accurately displayed our history.

In my mind, every person sitting on the omnibus became an outline and transformed into a series of pastels, shades, and hues from the paint of my imagination. The sky had streaks in it that were manifested from a steady paintbrush.

The Portrait of the North, through the eyes of a Southern Woman.

I could never draw myself but let the mind create art where it will. And when it shall.

Eventually, I arrived at Granger Hall and the first person that I came across was Mr. Dennison.

"Still hate me?" I asked, merrily.

"I don't see why you smile at that," Mr. Dennison responded.

"Because I realized something about you," I said, walking past him as I went to arrange my things.

"And what is that?" he called after me.

I stared at him squarely.

"That you are not my problem anymore. It's very liberating, I can assure you."

I didn't stay to see his reaction. Rather, I went into the

storage room and got my desk, to be met by a bustling little creature rushing up to me.

"Miss Bennet!" Little Molly Gibson cried, racing up to me and jumping into my arms. Naturally, my alarm died quickly, to be replaced by excitement at seeing Little Molly again. I put my desk down to embrace her properly.

"Oh, there she is!" I said, twirling her around. "How is our little Molly doing today?"

"She's doing well!" Molly cried as I put her down. "No, pick me up again and twirl me around again. Please, please, please! That was so much fun!"

"Very well. Just for you."

I picked her up and twirled her around again.

When I set her down, I sat on the floor to be on her eye level.

"Well, you are looking smart."

"Thank you," Molly said, holding her bonnet, "the Kirkpatricks bought me this new bonnet. Do you like it, Miss Bennet?"

"I think it very fine. And how do you find yourself getting on there?"

"I like it very much."

"And you are not letting dear little Roger take liberties, are you?" I asked.

"I do not like it when he gets in trouble because of me. He is so very good to me."

"I know. But you must always tell Mrs. Kirkpatrick if he gets too familiar. Always be his friend. You can be nice to little Roger, but do not become a creature of deception. Promise me?"

"Very well, Miss Bennet."

"Good."

Raising out my hands, we began to play a hand game, with me making the first mistake.

"What can I say?" I questioned. "I'm out of practice."

Little Molly giggled, and I sensed a person watching us. Not surprised in the least, I turned my attention to the doorway and saw Mr. Hanley standing there, with his notes wrapped under his arm. When seeing us, he grew insecure and adjusted his spectacles.

"Well," I said to Little Molly, wickedly, "we have a spy, Molly."

"Yes, we do. Are you watching us, Uncle?"

"I was...well, I simply didn't wish to disturb you both," Mr. Hanley said.

"Whatever shall we do with him?" I asked Molly.

"I'm sure that I do not know," Molly replied.

"Nor do I. I suppose that we just have to forgive him. What do you say to that?"

"I say 'yes, we should'."

"Well, Mr. Hanley, we have decided to execute mercy rather than harshness. You are forgiven, sir."

"I trust that I am," Mr. Hanley replied, "and my crime was one that I would repeat again. You both looked so happy. It would be a shame for me to have interrupted that."

"A worthy defense. So, will Molly be my companion for the next class?"

"Yes, I will be," Molly replied, "the Kirkpatrick carriage will not come to summon me till after the class. But don't worry." Molly raised up her two dolls. "I have enough to occupy me."

"Two dolls. Two friends. May they aptly do their service." I looked at Mr. Hanley. "Are you prepared, sir?"

"Yes, I am," Mr. Hanley replied, smiling gently as he helped me carry my things to the class. "Into the fire, we go?"

"Yes, into the fire," I echoed. "Onward ho."

With Molly bouncing in between us, we walked to the lecture hall and the class began.

Once more, Mr. Hanley delivered his lecture with gentle sincerity. Despite the prowess and power of Mr. Dennison and Mr. Hunnicutt, Mr. Hanley perhaps might always be the most favored of the teachers. We all have flaws. But he... was real. In a very different sort of fashion.

Eventually, the class ended, and the Kirkpatricks were true to their word.

We both escorted little Molly out of Granger Hall, and the carriage was already waiting for her. When Mr. Hanley helped her inside of it, I leaned in and reached out my hand. Taking it, she looked at me curiously.

"I only give you this gesture for fear," I said, "that we might not see each other after this."

"What do you mean?" Molly asked. Then her face filled with dread. "Miss Bennet, are you leaving?"

"Yes, I am. Soon, I will be leaving Milton."

"Why?"

"Because it's time for me to return home. Home is in the South, Molly."

"Must you leave?"

I knew she would react this way, so I still tried my best to soften my news.

"Molly, we all have to return home eventually. It's my time now."

Her expression changed from sadness to childlike wrath.

"I hate you," she spat.

My subtle coaxing was all for nothing as my expression

drooped to shame. Mr. Hanley, having heard what his niece said, leaned his head in and his tone turned harsh. He spoke in a way that was quite unlike him.

"Molly, what could possess you to say that?" he declared, passionate. "That was rude, cruel and very wrong to say. Apologize to Miss Bennet at once!"

Molly's eyes filled with tears.

"I never taught you to act thus," Hanley continued, "nor did your parents, or the Kirkpatricks. I am ashamed of you."

"Thank you for defending me, Mr. Hanley," I said, but since I knew the source behind Molly's remark, I sought to establish the reconciliation that I wanted to find. "Your uncle is correct to chastise you, but what prompted this? I suspect that I do know. You do not really hate me, do you? You hate that I am leaving, and that, in some way, I have let you down? Am I right?"

Molly, so terribly in agony, nodded as she looked down at the carriage's floor.

"I just don't understand why people have to go away," she said. "Why people have to leave."

"I know," I assured her. "But not everyone has to. Your uncle is not going to ever abandon you. The Kirkpatrick family will stand firm, by your side, if you stand by theirs. Not everyone in life will let you down. I do not leave you. I simply go home. Come, Little Molly, let us part as friends. If you leave here, hating me, I shall be heartbroken for a long while. Be kind to me now. If you still hate me, you may nod, and not say anything."

She did not nod.

"If we part as friends, please nod once."

She nodded.

Now, I could be happy.

7

"If we do not see each other again, then dear one, be safe and happy. And do not forget me."

Molly nodded again. The carriage took off, and Molly gave me a backwards glance through the window. I waved to her. Fortunately, she exerted herself enough to wave back at me from the window until the coach disappeared down the street.

Chapter 2

Heartbreaking News

M r. Hanley and I walked back inside, we went to the library, and I began to copy his notes. He sat on the other side of the room to give me the space that was needed.

"You were right," I said over my shoulder, as I wrote.

"Beg your pardon?" he asked. "What was I right about?"

"To chastise Molly but also give me the time to coax her into a better way. Sometimes the maxim 'spare the rod, spoil the child' is quite true in such circumstances. Discipline is one of the best lessons to teach one. However, thank you for giving me the chance to encourage her out of her glum state. She needed that as well."

"You propose that we both worked well as a team, do you?" he asked, hopeful.

Oh dear! I offered encouragement where it was not profitable for either of us. Oh well, I could not change who I was.

"Yes, we were. But my compliments were primarily to you. You knew the delicate balance of discipline, but also of understanding. It's a difficult balance for a parent to achieve."

"You flatter me."

"I speak as I find."

"And I wonder if I am happy that you do, or am unhappy if you do?"

"Why this confusion? Do you fear being told of your accomplishments for fear of becoming self-conceited? I do not think you are the sort to fall prey to that sort of flaw."

"It's not that. It is merely that I worry that your kind words will affect my heart—more than it has already."

Closing my eyes, I lowered my pen. Finally, we arrived at the conversation that we both had no choice but to experience. How I dreaded this moment.

I was not alone. As soon as he uttered the words, Mr. Hanley grew agitated, and he stood up.

"I'm sorry," he rushed out, "I should leave you to your work."

Quickly—or as quickly as such a sturdy and steady man could walk—he went to the door.

However, I knew my duty. To leave him with such unease and discomfort would not do. The only way for him to move on from this experience was for me to give him the conclusion that he needed. Catharsis is always necessary, despite how hard it is to distribute.

"Mr. Hanley," I said before he could open the door. "You and I both know what you were referring to. Come. Sit down and talk with me. I cannot say that my words will cause you no pain. But I can say that I care enough about you to not leave you so much in the buff."

"Hurt me?" Mr. Hanley asked. "Perhaps I do not wish to remain for that."

"I can neither command you, nor convince you. You may remain or leave as you wish. Do what you will, sir. Do what you find to be best."

Returning to my writing, I continued to copy his notes.

From behind me, I heard no movement.

None at all.

That indicated that Hanley was still deliberating of what was the correct response to my request.

I remained writing.

No movement.

I had to fix my pen.

No movement.

I finished a page.

At last, I heard footsteps. But they were not from exiting. Rather, they drew closer as Mr. Hanley passed by me, pulled up a chair and sat down opposite me, so that we could face each other.

"Would it be easier if I looked at you?" I asked him, stopping my work, and placing my pen on the paper, next to the ink.

"I do not know. Maybe, if you don't look at me, it would be easier for me to say what I have to say."

"I can understand that."

Out of the corner of my eye, I saw Hanley fidget again, his fingers kept balling into a fist and then releasing.

"Go on," I insisted. "I am not afraid of anything that you have to say."

"I know that you are not. You are fearless. That is one of the things that I loved about you."

"Mr. Hanley," I said, "I am grateful to everything that you have done for me. You have always been a great friend, a chief ally, and my defender."

"But I am not the man that you want. Nor that you prefer."

"It is not that I don't prefer you."

"Then what is it?"

His question was not venomous but spoken with gentleness. He was merely curious.

"The man that I have chosen is an old acquaintance of the family. He loved me soon after we met, and I did not know what I was about for so long. When our relationship went from a stage of professional to friendly, I was already softened toward this gentleman."

"Oh," he said, less pained. "Then, what you refer to is that you felt for this gentleman long before you and I became warmer to each other."

"Yes," I insisted, finally looking at him. "There was never a sense of competition, nor of you being inferior to anyone. It is merely that..."

"I came into your life too late."

Even if that were true or not, I felt this was the best way of going about the matter. For sometimes, the truth is not enough. At least, where it comes to the easing of grief.

"Yes," I answered, "you did. When you began to feel toward me, I was already a woman who was falling in love elsewhere."

"Then maybe, it appears...that the fault is mine. I was hesitant and I took my time. Fortune favors the bold, as it was. Or the speedy."

"Do not forget," I assured him, "that it also has been set down that slow and steady does win the race."

He looked deeply into my eyes.

"But not in this circumstance. For now, I have quite defeated myself."

"We shall never fully know."

"No, we perhaps shall not. But I must ask..."

"I am here. Go on. Ask me."

"Is everything really quite settled between you and this

Mr. Darcy? It is all final and your engagement is a certain prospect?"

"I do not say this to hurt you, but to give you peace over the closure of certainty. All is quite final, definite, and I will marry this man."

When hearing this, he looked down, swallowing his pain.

"Then all that there is left for me to do is wish you joy."

"You don't really, do you?" I asked.

"I admit that maybe I don't."

"I understand. But thank you all the same. Mr. Hanley, please, believe this. Not only did I never intend for you to get hurt, but since I first saw you, I wished you joy."

"I know. That was another thing that I loved about you."

Standing up slowly, he walked to the door. I followed his expression and wished that I could soften that look. But I admit that I was at a loss of what to say or do. I could not encourage him, but I also did not want to put him down.

A miracle came my way when Mr. Hanley turned back to me, one last time.

"Perhaps I am undergoing a sense of self-torture at the moment, but that's what happens when sensibility takes over," he uttered, "so I cannot help myself. I must ask this. If you had never met Mr. Darcy, or he had not fallen in love with you—would you have ever considered me?"

The poor man. He needed comforting where he could find it. This was the one comfort that I could exert on him. I did not find this impertinent nor unwelcome.

Looking at his graying hair, his ageless face, and his defined features, I hoped to soften his look.

"Yes," I said, "I would have."

His whole posture slackened, as the pains of rejection lessened.

"You would have?" he repeated, still trying to believe what he had just heard.

"Yes," I said, "I would have."

"As vain as this sounds, you have made me very happy."

"I am glad that I did not leave this conversation only hurting you."

"Thank you."

Finally, he left me alone.

For today, he might be happy in hearing that I would have considered him.

But tomorrow, he might become morose, for to some 'almost doesn't count'.

My second class was with Mr. Hunnicutt. His class came and went very amiably.

At first, I wrote down his notes with ease and as fluid as ever.

However, amidst his class, I began to feel glum in some way. I could not account for it, but somehow, the page in front of me became blurred. Blinking, I worried that my eyes were failing me. But soon, I felt my stomach tighten, my chest began to throb violently, and I began to feel ill.

What could account for it?

I continued to write on, however, trusting that my disturbed state would soon pass.

Unfortunately, it didn't.

It wouldn't be till the end of the class that, after confronting the inner workings of my heart, that I discovered what it was.

I felt the pains of breaking a worthy heart. I was not in love with Mr. Hanley. Never had been. Never would be.

Although, I was aware that he deserved my love. Such great characters are always worthy of a happily ever after. I suppose I feared that he would never find his.

To my surprise, this all disturbed me in ways that I did not foresee.

When Mr. Hunnicutt's class ended, I was copying his notes in the library, when I stopped writing.

Once again, the paper blurred in my eyes. This time, I was aware of the source. My eyes began to swell with tears that I was trying to suppress. This is what it meant to break a heart of someone that you respected.

To my utter shame, Mr. Hunnicutt entered quietly and walked past me with some books in his hand.

"So," he began, "how do my notes—"

He cut himself off when he saw me quickly wiping tears from my eyes. How humiliating!

"Miss Bennet?" he asked me. "Are you ill?"

"No," I assured him, "I am quite well. Thank you."

He took one look in my eyes and grew still.

"I saw Mr. Hanley earlier, and his eyes looked a little similar," he observed. "You would not know anything about that, pray?"

I did not respond.

"I know that I ought to mind my own business," he continued, "but you must understand that when a woman is crying, abandoning her does not seem to be the most chivalrous thing to do. Do you want me to leave?"

I looked at him, unable to control my emotions.

"Why does this hurt so much?" I asked him, at a loss of how to govern my sensibilities. "I am in love with another man. So why am I so upset for hurting Hanley, and for feeling like I have committed something awful?"

Mr. Hunnicutt pulled up a chair and sat down beside me.

"The only assumption that I can make on that score," Mr. Hunnicutt said, "is that you feel awful because you admire Hanley. It hurts to reject someone that you adore. But know this. You have committed no wrong, no sin, and you have not drawn him in. His love for you was his choice, and his alone. There was nothing you could do."

"I want him to be happy, Mr. Hunnicutt. I really do."

"I know. He will be heartbroken for now. But we men are such complex creatures. Some of us do not recover from such devastations of the heart. But others of us do. I cannot know if Hanley is either sort of man. That's the one thing that us men cannot always read about the other. But what I can say is that he will be broken now. But over time, the pain will lessen and lessen. And he must make a choice which path that he will walk down."

"I hope he chooses the right one."

"I do as well. But what I can tell you is that it is all out of your hands."

"Do you know what it's like to never intend to hurt someone, but you do anyway?"

"Yes, I do. That's why I know what you are feeling."

He placed his hand on mine and squeezed it.

"But what Hanley knows is what I know. And what Mr. Hale knows. And maybe even what Dennison knows. Women like you are a joy that we had but were never meant to hold. We could not have you in our lives forever. Now it is time for us to let you go and progress onward. We, here at Granger Hall, are a stagnant sort. But you are young. It is your right to shift, bend, fall, then rise, and then fly. Fly to new horizons, Miss Bennet. We will be happy for you."

Giving into my sensibilities, I rested my head on his shoulder and wept. Closing his arms around me, Mr. Hunnicutt became the father that I lost and offered the paternal embrace that uttered peace, tranquility, and genuine support.

Chapter 3

Good News

"Ah," Margaret Hale told me as we walked back to Crampton. She had met me at Granger Hall, and I escorted her on her walk back home. As we did so, I told her everything that had transpired that day. She had much to say on the matter. "I suppose that we should have talked about it earlier than now. But I worried that it might be too delicate of a subject."

"You think that I did not handle the situation well?" I asked her.

"Oh, no. You handled it perfectly. It is merely your reaction that is the part I refer to. If we had talked of Hanley's growing affection for you sooner, then maybe it would have given you time to adjust to the pains of breaking his heart. I agree with Mr. Hunnicutt; you did what you had to do. But the feeling of rejecting someone that you admire is painful. It is something that you are not accustomed to. You feel like a villain over time, even when it was necessary. When you rejected Mr. Collins and Mr. Darcy, you did not feel a tenderness for either gentleman. As such, you didn't fear wounding their heart. It's easier during those circumstances. But now... things are more complicated. And so, it hurts."

"You sound like you know precisely where my heart lives. You did not tell me that you felt such pain when you rejected Mr. Lennox."

Deliberately, I had asked that question. If my declaration that she was hurt over Lennox was correct, then it would say one thing. But if she was not referring to Mr. Lennox's proposal, then she was referring to something else that was closer to the Northern home.

"In truth," Margaret responded, "no, I didn't feel much pain over rejecting Mr. Lennox."

"I see," I said. "Therefore, your rejecting him really was on the same level as when I rejected Mr. Collins. But with Mr. Darcy, I did feel an immediate headache afterwards and I was a little disconcerted. If I had read into the workings of my heart correctly, I would have known what that hinted of. I suppose, deep within, I was aware that there was goodness there. However, you understand me too well for it to be mere empathy. It must be experience. You know the pains that I felt today, and therefore, it had to have happened to you before. Margaret, did you grow to feel this way after Thornton proposed to you?"

"He is my father's dear friend."

"Yes, I know."

"And therefore, that had to be considered. It hurt to reject someone that my father adored so very much. There was that initial reservation. Also, I felt gratified that he cared for me."

"And it hurt to hurt him? You discovered that eventually."

"Yes, I did."

"Margaret, are you sure that it is not something more?" I pressed. "Are you certain that it is not something else?"

Margaret looked ahead, more preoccupied as we crossed the street.

"Margaret," I pressed.

"We were talking about you."

"And now we are talking about you. Remember, I promised that I would not let you neglect yourself."

"Yes, you did. Lizzy, this is hard to confess."

"Then say it quickly. Speed helps hard confessions."

"It's just... I do not regret that I rejected Mr. Thornton. It is merely that I do not like making him unhappy."

"Yes. I suspected as much."

"I don't know why that is."

"Because, whether you love him or despise him, you respect him."

"Yes. I do. Even when we disagree, I suppose that I have grown to understand him. I wish that I did not feel the grief of disappointing him. But it must be done."

"Yes, it must."

I took her arm in mine, to show solidarity.

"Well, onward we go," I said, "always looking for a clearer tomorrow."

"Yes. If only it wasn't so cloudy in Milton."

When we reached Crampton, we entered to find Charlotte and Maria assisting Dixon with everything.

"Finally," Dixon said, "the proper amount of help to allow me to host a small party to come in here."

"Our home may not be large enough to hold a dinner

party," Mrs. Hale said, sickly and in her chair, "but at least we can have some friends over for coffee and cakes."

"A house in Crampton will do as much as any house in Town," I offered her.

"You are too kind, Lizzy," Mrs. Hale said, coughing. Margaret poured some water for her and had her drink it. "Oh, I remember when my father hosted the greatest dinners on our street. It was the likes of which you would not believe."

We let her talk for quite some time about the joys of her youth. For when one is wasting away, the beauties of their youth and health offers a greater bloom than ever and you cannot help but reminisce. Even so, we liked it when she mentioned earlier times in her life. Older individuals are always more interested in storytelling than us younger sort.

After a while, Mr. Hale joined us as we assisted Dixon in making preparations. He had been teaching one of his pupils and had just finished. Therefore, when coming down to see us all bustling about, he couldn't help but feel the compliment of it all.

"My mother once told me," Margaret whispered as Mr. Hale held Charlotte's and Maria's hands, thanking them, "that father appreciates charity. Also, that he loves help, and that when one starts to help him, you can never stop."

"I never feared a gentleman asking a lady for help," I said. "For that's where unity truly is found."

"I know. I like that he is that way."

"So," Mr. Hale said as he sat down by Mrs. Hale, taking her hand. "How many are coming for coffee?"

"It's a large sort," Dixon answered for us. "When you have a lot of us women in your life, we can over-invite, is what I've learned."

"We could not help it, father," Margaret said. "We had to

invite all the Bennets, Rasby, Plato, Colonel Fitzwilliam, Mr. Darcy, Mr. Bingley, and Mr. Thornton."

"Yes," I said, "there is some news that Mr. Darcy has to share that he was hoping to inform the whole company of. Him and I decided together that it would be perfect to do it here, for you are such friends to us."

"And afterwards," Charlotte Lucas assured Mrs. Hale, "Mr. Bingley made arrangements for us to dine at the hotel."

"I wish we were better dressed," Maria Lucas whined.

"You look perfectly fine," I assured her. "Our men are at the stage where a fancy dress does not make or break their respect for us."

"Well," Mrs. Hale said weakly, standing up, "I think... that I am excited."

We all smiled.

"Dixon," Mrs. Hale instructed, "And Margaret, help me up. I may be very ill, but I will not have myself look anything else but presentable. I wish to change for the party."

Margaret and Dixon escorted her to her room. That left the Lucases and I to entertain Mr. Hale. Being a proper gentleman, we passed the time most animatedly, and soon, it was time for the rest of the company to arrive.

With our help, Dixon was able to display her skills to good measure. Despite the size of the living quarters, it was naturally cramped, but since we had managed to squeeze in more individuals in our house on Frances Street, this was easy to maneuver.

We had pulled out enough chairs from the upstairs bedrooms and placed them accordingly in the parlor, by the fire.

Soon, Mr. Bingley and Mr. Darcy arrived, bearing Jane, Lydia, and Denny. No more than five minutes after their arrival, Colonel Fitzwilliam, Plato, Kitty and Rasby appeared at the front door.

We served them their coffee and all that was left was Mr. Thornton. This gave us the time to distribute the coffee and cakes around, and we were actually a rather merry gathering when Thornton did finally arrive. When he entered, he bore a collection of flowers from the hothouse to offer to Mrs. Hale.

Thanking him, Mrs. Hale had Dixon put the bouquet in a vase and placed it on the mantel over the fireplace.

When he entered, I drew near Margaret.

"How are you feeling?"

"I am determined to make myself agreeable to him," Margaret said, "but not falsely so. If I were to suddenly start smiling and laughing, I would not only betray myself, but I might make him die of fright. He is used to me hiding my feelings."

I chuckled.

"Well, good luck," I offered.

"I shall need it."

Breathing deeply, Margaret approached Mr. Thornton.

When seeing Margaret accost him, Thornton was very still, formidable.

"Mr. Thornton," Margaret said, sedate but friendly, "welcome to our party."

"Thank you for the inclusion," Mr. Thornton responded, his brow quite heavy.

"He will always have the eternal scowl," I whispered to Mr. Darcy. "It will not do."

"I scowl as well," Mr. Darcy responded, his tone equally as quiet.

"Yes, you do. But I know how to soften that look. Can Margaret do the same, I wonder? It would take a bloody miracle."

Mr. Darcy squinted. "Did you just say *'bloody'*?"

"I've been in Milton for long enough. I suppose that it had no choice but to have some sort of influence on me."

"The sooner we get you to the South, the better," he jested.

"Ah, you joke, you joke, you joke."

"Indeed, I do joke. I think I am finally gaining the skill of being in jest, while also being serious all in one."

"A fine quality to obtain."

Despite our tendency to fall into our own world, we spied everyone around us.

Kitty and the Colonel were engrossed in each other's conversation, like Bingley with Jane. All of us couples had quite abandoned all common civility, to the point of appearing rude, and that would not do. Fortunately, Lydia, Denny, Plato and Rasby spent much time conversing with Charlotte and Maria, who had fully developed their 'Milton legs', as it were.

Meanwhile, Margaret had arranged for Mr. Thornton to be seated next to the fire as she got him some coffee and cakes. When she had done so, she placed herself next to him. She sat down and while he didn't smile at her, his expression softened.

A little unnerved by their close proximity, and aware of his history with her, Margaret found herself unable to do anything else but blush and look down at her lap, where her hands were folded.

"Forgive me," Margaret said, "I make poor company of myself, don't I?"

"It is well," Thornton responded, "we must start somewhere, mustn't we?"

"We always do seem to be starting somewhere," Margaret responded, "and then we find ourselves in the fishpond. Do you mind if I try my hand at being friendly? I know that I shall make poor work of it, but I am determined to make a better effort at getting along with you."

"I would like that."

At last, she looked at him.

"I am trying to enhance a better way of being," Margaret said, "and therefore, I am willing to listen to your side of things on all matters. It is important to me that maybe I ought to try and understand you as well. But I must ask that you also understand me and see my point of view."

"I do want to understand you, Miss Hale," he responded, turning his body more toward her. "I confess that, certain things that I may have said in my past—that I may have offered—were done so without taking the time to get to know you better. You must understand that in the world I live in, time is money. And I see that, once more, I am saying the wrong things."

"I am listening. Pray, continue."

"What I mean by that is that, despite your father's teachings to enhance my perspective into that of a gentleman, I am still a pert and direct sort of businessman. I am used to speaking of my life through my work, but not always in a way where I connect to others. It is a... fault of mine."

"I can understand. We both met, very set in our ways."

"What was it like for you?" he asked. "To be uprooted from Helstone to Milton?"

Margaret looked at him, with hope in her eyes.

"I just realized that I never fully asked you about that, did I?" Thornton asked.

"No, you never did. But it was not your fault. When we first met, it didn't render itself easy to becoming further acquainted in the proper style. But we can rectify that. If you like, we can try again. I am not implying that we can ever fully go back and start from the beginning."

"But—and I am not wishing to be disagreeable in this matter—yet, can't we try?" Thornton asked. "I am neither ordering you, nor wishing to be contrary. I merely wish to be direct for the sake of not being misunderstood. Can we not attempt to start over? Perhaps, with a little compassion on each side, with the experiences of knowing how each other are, can we not go back to the beginning?"

"I see the appeal of that, Mr. Thornton, but I have one reservation on that score."

"And what is that?"

"The more that I look back on our experiences, the more that I am certain that I do not want to erase our history. It, perhaps, was vital to our experiences. Those experiences do not have to be forgotten. They can be used as learnings to help us turn the page of our lives. Rather, can we not look on that all *as* the end of a chapter, and then, when the page is turned, a new chapter begins?"

"You wish to start a new chapter."

"Yes, I do. I would like it for us to do so. I am not asking for any promises or assurances on your part. I just want to be able to start anew, while also remembering the old."

"Very well. I can oblige."

Mr. Thornton breathed a sigh of relief.

When he finished sipping his coffee, Margaret continued their discussion as she made him another cup.

"I know that it seems like we form a sense of camaraderie," Margaret said, "and then we undo it all, only to try again. And then fail again."

"Our discord and then harmony is not our fault," Thornton said, "for I have noted that the world has a habit of constantly getting in the way of any attempt we have toward friendship. I do—well, I do mean to please you, Miss Hale."

"I am aware of such. Believe me, that I am." Margaret sat up in her seat, more direct. "When I first heard that we were to come to Milton, I confess, that I was shocked, horrified, and so terribly frightened. You see, Mr. Thornton, in Helstone, I had finally found the life that I felt I wanted all that time. Yes, I was raised as my cousin's companion in London, but I never fully wanted that life. I wanted to be among the simpler and provincial folk. To be part of it all, and to be among people with no pretense, and aristocratic lifelessness. I wanted to be amidst the great world of contribution and differences being made. It was the perfect sort of world for me. Thus, losing all of that was hard. To obtain a haven, and then to know that one is being cast away from paradise." Margaret looked at Thornton directly. "Imagine, Mr. Thornton, to be told that you shall be cast out of Milton, torn away from it for, perhaps, forever. And that you shall never see the inside of a mill again, that you will never get the chance to run a cotton factory again, that you would be severed from the world of your acquaintances. How would that make you feel?"

Thornton leaned back and looked into the fire, reflectively.

"I would be horrified. I would feel so utterly lost."

"Precisely," Margaret responded, "you would hate every moment of it."

"Yes. I would. And what's more, I would rebel against the edict that forced me away from the world that I have built up so much."

"Exactly. You are proud of your mill, your factory, and the house you have placed your mother in. You pride yourself on the contribution that you make that runs Britain. And your pride might very well not be incorrectly placed. Therefore, take that feeling you have, of rebelling against the force that compelled you away from the very life that you loved, and transfer it to my heart. That's how I felt when coming from Helstone. I felt as if a part of my heart had been quite torn out. But I could not rebel, as you felt that you had the right to. After all, I am a daughter. I am a woman. The province of rebellions are not often bestowed upon us."

"Oh, I am not so certain of that."

Margaret looked at him and smiled. This small admission swelled Thornton's pride, and he felt comfortable. At last.

When seeing Margaret and Thornton getting along, I breathed a sigh of relief. I merely hoped that it would last this time. The world always seemed to be getting in the way of them both, as well as themselves. Perhaps the breach could finally be yielded.

"Well," I said, "at last, they are getting somewhere."

"It makes me happy," Darcy said, "Thornton needs friends now."

"Why?"

"I thought it was obvious. Soon, I shall have to leave him."

I looked at Mr. Darcy, and I was seeing another aspect of his character. And an old one of my own.

"He puts great stock in your advice and your company, doesn't he?" I asked Darcy.

"Yes, he does."

"Him and Bingley both depend on you."

"Yes, they do."

"And it makes me wonder, who do you have to depend on? Everyone must have a shoulder to lean on when the time comes for solace."

"For the longest time, I had Colonel Fitzwilliam. And now, I have you."

"Now that is a comforting thought," I said, "but you and I are in the same situation again. You are to leave Thornton, and I am to leave Margaret. My mother once had a saying: there is nothing so bad as parting with one's friends. For one seems so forlorn without them."

"I cannot believe that I am saying this."

"Hm?"

"But this might very well be the first time that I actually agree with your mother."

I laughed heartily. It led to the party turning from what they were saying and direct their attention towards myself.

Oh, the awkwardness of life!

"Well," Darcy said to me, encouragingly, "I can use this opportunity to finally make an announcement."

"I am happy that my laugh was for something," I said as he stood up.

"Oh, I know that gesture," Mr. Bingley said, "that means that Darcy is about to tell us some fortunate news."

"How did you know?" Darcy asked him. "I could be delivering bad news."

"When you deliver good news, your posture is different. When you deliver bad news, your countenance is heavier, graver."

"You know my moods too well, friend."

"I cannot help it."

Mr. Darcy addressed Mr. and Mrs. Hale first.

"Before I proceed further," Darcy began, "I want to thank the Hales for allowing this crowd to enter their home and give me the opportunity to deliver this announcement."

Mr. and Mrs. Hale thanked him, and Mrs. Hale did her best to be agreeable, despite her ailment.

"Well," Darcy continued, "this news has a slice of the sweet as well as the sour about it. My dear Elizabeth and I have been contemplating the matter, and we thought this was the best way to deliver the news." He looked at Colonel Fitzwilliam. "Richard, I hope that when I deliver this news, you shall understand why I committed to this. I just felt this ought to be news that you would like to share immediately when hearing it, so it seemed best to do it from the very first."

Colonel Fitzwilliam looked a little surprised as well as disconcerted.

"Me?"

"Yes."

"Well, this is altogether interesting, isn't it?"

"And it is about to be getting even more so," I noted. Then I shifted my look to Kitty, who immediately gave a 'what is this all about' sort of expression. Oh, I could barely wait for the outpour of triumph and exhilaration.

"Well," Colonel Fitzwilliam said, "Miss Elizabeth smiles. That means that good fortune has come to town."

"It has, in a manner of speaking," Mr. Darcy said. "Before I tell you such news, first, I shall inform everyone that it is concerning my aunt, Lady Catherine de Bourgh."

"The poor woman who lost her child?" Mrs. Hale said.

"Yes."

"I wish that I could comfort her. It is hard to lose one's child."

"And what's more," Mr. Hale said, "one's only child. That must be the most overwhelming thing in the world."

"It is," Darcy continued, "and she has born it with fortitude as well as displaying all the true maternal instincts. My late cousin, Anne, deserved all the best in life. She was a young woman with a bright future—but was not given good health. Life dealt her a very unfair blow. I am heartily sorry for it. However, we must all press onward, especially in such circumstances. My aunt needs family around her, more than ever. I have promised so many things to accommodate her. She deserves our love and company now. And so, her desires work in perfect alignment with another part of family."

Now, he turned to Colonel Fitzwilliam and Kitty.

"First, she welcomes all our marriages. From my own, to yours, Richard, and yours Mr. Bingley. She is eager to see us all...and have us wed at Hunsford Parish, on her estate."

This news alarmed everyone in the company.

"You all will marry in Kent?" Margaret asked.

"Not up here, where many friends are?" Thornton asked, a little unnerved by the sentiments he displayed.

"That's what I worried over," Jane said, "for the Kirkpatricks would wish to attend. Mrs. Kirkpatrick has long been eager to see us wed."

"That's what I had assumed," Kitty added, "for after

31

losing Bessy, Nicholas and Mary Higgins needed something to look forward to."

"Yes," Margaret added, "this is a complicated sort of situation."

"I know that I was perhaps too ill to attend," Mrs. Hale said. "But the idea of you all dining here after you wed seemed like such a very appealing prospect."

"I suppose," Mr. Hale added, "that we have to oblige you all, despite our hopes for the contrary."

"Ah," I said, "I see that this predicament has made the lot of you a little upset."

"Perhaps," Colonel Fitzwilliam said, "despite our desires to marry in Milton, our aunt does require some tending to. She is in a despairing place, and like Darcy said, she does need family."

"Yes," Mr. Hale added, "I am sure that she does. I will lament the prospect of not being able to attend, but the great lady does deserve your devotion."

"Well," Kitty said, "if we cannot oblige our friends here, then hopefully our wedding will bring the dowager some cheer. I just...well, I was hoping that you all would be there."

"We can always visit Milton again, after we wed," Jane offered, to show consideration.

"I never suspected that Milton would be the ideal visiting place for newly-wedded couples," Mr. Thornton voiced.

We all looked very forlorn when he said that. Despite herself, Margaret gave him a look, to which Thornton read it very well.

"And now I can see that I have made the situation feel dourer, I suppose," Thornton added.

"Not your fault, Thornton," Darcy administered. "You are just being very realistic. I know that this feeling does give one a sense of a great divide. But I hope that in the light of making my poor aunt happy, that we may oblige her." Darcy looked at me. "I am a man who is eager to marry, but also eager to maintain family ties. I hope that this news will appeal to us all over time."

"Well," Jane said, "I thank your aunt for caring for us."

"Has a date been set?" Rasby asked. She smiled, but the happiness did not reach her eyes. I think she was becoming very aware, day by day, moment by moment, that the distance of her friend marrying in the South didn't just present a geographical divide, but a potentially permanent one.

And what was one friend without the other?

"Lady Catherine de Bourgh wishes for us to be married in Kent within two months' time."

"Then we ought to be happy for you," Mr. Thornton said, taking on a lighter tone. Standing up, he raised out his glass. "Forgive my selfishness. It is merely that we have grown very fond of your company here in Milton. It is to the point where we feel that you all have become vital to the place. But I propose a toast! To a triple wedding to three deserving couples! Everyone, let us raise our glasses and wish these six worthy souls all the joys of domestic felicity. To the six fiancés of the South!"

"Cheers!" We all said, drinking to the wedding that we hoped would occur sooner than later.

"Oh," Mr. Bingley said, "we feel like a dull lot. Not going to lie," he said, taking Jane's hand, having her stand up and twirling her around. "I have the great desire for a dance, myself!"

Jane laughed as he twirled her about.

"We all do feel like more merriment is worthy," Mr. Hale said, laughing. "If only our drawing rooms were large enough for a set to be laid out. Maria, wouldn't it be nice to see the younger folks in the middle of the waltz?"

"Every young lady deserves such at their special time," Mrs. Hale said as Dixon poured her some more coffee. While her face was pale and a little sweaty, the joys of the moment did reach her, and she rose above her ailment. "Do you recall, my dear, when we first danced together?"

"Oh, I never forgot it," Mr. Hale said, animated, "I was dazed. I felt as if I had been struck by a thunderbolt. I am sure, Mr. Darcy, Mr. Bingley, and Colonel Fitzwilliam, that you felt the same thing when you first beheld your belles of the evening."

"I can assure you, sir," Mr. Bingley said, "that when seeing Miss Bennet, I felt like that of a moth drawn to a flame."

"Oh, Mr. Bingley," Jane said, blushing and looking at her lap.

"You better have done so as well, or I will never forgive you," Kitty said to the Colonel. "But I jest, for how could you adore me when I wore my maid's uniform? I doubt anyone could get passed that gruesome outfit."

"On the contrary," Colonel Fitzwilliam responded, "I liked that gruesome outfit on you the best."

We all exclaimed at that comment.

"Did you really?" Kitty asked, dubiously amused.

"Yes. It gave me the sense that you were like me. Born high but brought on the level of profession. It gave me hope. Intense hope that maybe you were on the same plain as myself, and therefore, I had a chance with you."

"Pretty words, sir. Pretty words. There, everyone, I went fishing one day and came back with a trout that knows how to speak. What a fortunate hunt that was, was it not?"

"You compare me to a fish, my love?"

"I dare anything. Despise me all that you like. I've got you for a husband, therefore, I have won. And there is no getting around me."

"I am happy that there is no way of getting around you, in any direction, dearest." He kissed her hand. "You love me, yes you do. You poor, poor, creature."

"Oh, you pity me. How delightful."

Darcy gave me a look that said 'they think they are the adorable ones. How quaint.' I quite agreed.

"Well," Darcy compiled, "I have more news to add to this evening."

"More news?" Colonel Fitzwilliam asked. "Good or bad?"

"This is a dinner party celebrating our upcoming wedding, Richard. I promise that no ill news shall reach us. On the contrary, this is a turn of fortune that can be drawn from the tragedy of losing our cousin. My aunt had two children that she clung to fondly: her dear Anne, and Rosings Park. She sadly lost one, but she still has the other. And Rosings Park is like any other grand estate led by landed gentry: it needs an heir." He turned to Colonel Fitzwilliam. "Richard, when I went to visit my aunt, the tragedy of Anne led to her also understanding that she didn't want to leave the world without her fortune, title and estate being lost. And she is still very fond of you. As such, between the grief of loss, and the desire to have family close to her at this troubling time, Aunt Catherine has done all, upon legal binding, to pass Rosings Park and all that it entails, to you. Therefore, Colonel Fitzwilliam, I congratulate you, cousin, for you are the new heir to our aunt's home."

With all the joys of seeing reward being offered to the one who was most owing of it, I looked to Colonel Fitzwilliam, to see his reaction.

In fact, we all focused our attention to the weatherworn soldier, and his reaction was precisely what was expected.

First, he sat there, frozen.

After a few seconds, he leaned forward.

"The heir of Rosings Park? Me?"

"Yes, cousin. You are now risen to the point of knighthood and the proud inheritor of all of Rosings many fortunes and delights."

Colonel Fitzwilliam breathed out and in, very heavily. As he raised up his arm, his hand was trembling. It truly was a humbling sight.

"It cannot be? I am never lucky."

"You are now. I swear it, Richard. This is all true. Lady Catherine cannot wait to see you returned to Kent, and to begin your duties as the future master of her home."

"I..." Colonel Fitzwilliam stood up, turned away from us, and went to the window. At last, he turned back around.

"I really am the new Master of Rosings?"

"Yes, you are."

Colonel Fitzwilliam's constant repeating of his good fortune was understandable. To go from being a man who depended so heavily on the salary that he earned, with no hope of ever achieving wealth, to inheriting a great house and a grand fortune. From the very moderate of livings to the most illustrious, it must be beyond belief.

"I just..." the Colonel extoled, his tone breathy and his masculinity unwinding as he fell before the great Goddess called Fortune. "You must understand that I feel as if I am in a dream. That soon I shall wake, and all of this was not true. Good fortune doesn't just appear from the sky, nor when the wind changes. It doesn't gust my way, so it all feels like a super-reality. An unreality. Something so fantastical that it cannot be true. But is it?"

"Yes, it is."

Colonel Fitzwilliam's eyes filled with joy.

"If you say it is... then all my worries are over. All the anxieties that I had will fall away—to be replaced with new ones, of course. But those are cares that are not wearisome and do not make one age with a sense of being tossed among the strife of contrariness. My aunt has saved my life, and my love."

Suddenly, he rushed up to Darcy and hugged him with a burst of intense affection. This public display of familial regard took Darcy quite by surprise, and he was initially alarmed. Soon, it gave way, and he understood that Richard needed his love. Therefore, he wrapped his arms around his strong cousin's shoulders and even found a sort of enjoyment out of it.

"It is too wonderful!" Colonel Fitzwilliam responded. "Too wonderful! I'm an independent creature now."

"And a knight. You're of the peerage now."

"Do my mother and father know?" he asked.

"Aunt Catherine has written to them. Soon, you will receive of letter with their effusions of your good fortune."

"Then it's real," Colonel Fitzwilliam expressed, sighing. "It's all real. And..." he turned to Kitty. "Kitty, dearest."

"You roaming son," Kitty said, "you thought you would never get credit for being a good man your entire life, did you?"

"No, I did not. Fortune does not always favor kindness."

"Providence proved you wrong. And amen for that. No one deserved it more than you."

"And now you as well. Kitty, you will now be a Lady."

This revelation struck Kitty, who had not thought of herself in this case. She was so amazed at all that Colonel

Fitzwilliam had gained, that she must not have thought how it affected her in the process.

"Me? A Lady?"

"You will be the future mistress of Rosings Park," Jane professed. "Now, that is remarkable!"

"A Lady to an estate," Kitty declared, equally as overwhelmed as Colonel Fitzwilliam had been. "Me? Could it really happen?"

"Yes, it does." Colonel Fitzwilliam walked up to Kitty and took her hands. "We are the new inheritors of one of the greatest houses in Kent."

"Oh, my stars!" Kitty both cried and laughed, as the Colonel lifted her up and embraced her. "It is too good to be true."

"That's how I feel!" Colonel Fitzwilliam laughed.

"I share your doubts," Kitty said, "but if Mr. Darcy says it is so, then it must be. Richard, life has been kind to us." Kitty turned to us. "Everyone, behold, the new heir of Rosings Park!"

"Well, I may not know of the grandness of this Rosings Park, but I detect good fortune when I hear it," Plato said, raising his glass. "To the Colonel! And to the future Mrs. Fitzwilliam! I trust this new slice of fortune will make you happy."

"Oh, it will Plato," Colonel Fitzwilliam said, "it will."

Once more, a toast was rendered, but this time, with more exhilaration.

"Now we are sounding like a proper merry party," I whispered to Mr. Darcy, who sat down beside me as we watched many people clap the Colonel on the shoulder, and the ladies went to Kitty, to offer their congratulations. "Our wedding announcement was the dourest thing imaginable."

"I suppose we never realized how much our presence was meant here," Darcy said. "It was strangely flattering."

"Yes, it was. But now, when all things are considered," I noted, "Kitty is going to be higher in rank than Jane and I."

Mr. Darcy considered this.

"I never thought of that. But peerage set aside, nothing could be higher than you."

"I like that you flatter me," I said, content with his buttering me up in such a fashion, "but there is no need. My self-assurance is not puffed about because of a title. I know your self-worth, which is incredible, just as I know my self-worth." I smiled. "I just marvel at the turn that life takes with us all. At home, not much was ever ado about Kitty. Jane was supposed to be the one that had the best marriage."

"To be sure, your mother boasted of it often. And your father seemed to agree, despite that he never said anything. And now, Kitty will be a Lady, and her husband will own Rosings Park."

"What would mama say? In truth, I am quite sure that she would forget every time that she declared Jane's beauty to win the best catch of all and declare that she always knew that Kitty would be the one to make the best match. Just like she believed that I was going to make the worst match."

Darcy and I exchanged a look that said 'ah, yes!'. Then we chuckled.

"A part of me wished that she was here now, just to see what she would say."

"Like you said, Lizzy, she would take the credit."

"Yes. She would take the credit of it all."

The cries of true happiness! Now that the Colonel's life had been changed utterly, Colonel Fitzwilliam and Kitty were very verbose.

When we left the Hales, and went to dine in Bingley's hotel quarters, they still were talking of their good fortune. Kitty wanted to know everything about Rosings Park, for she had never been there.

Now that the reality of his good fortune had truly felt sincere and properly earned, Colonel Fitzwilliam was all too willing to explain it to the company. He described Rosings Park in exquisite detail, and we could see the love that he had for his new home.

"To marry a man without seeing his house first," Colonel Fitzwilliam joked to Kitty, "why did you accept me?"

"Because you were like me," Kitty said, "you were a roaming badger. Besides, you and I could not disparage the other for not owning a home, because we never actually had a home that we owned."

Everyone laughed.

"That's the wonder of it," I considered, "we went from Longbourn, to visiting family, to Frances Street, and we had to learn to adjust to a smaller life. And now we must learn to adjust to a grand house, where Kitty and I have never even seen the grandeur of it all before."

"You will love Pemberley," Darcy assured me, "of that, I can promise."

"Will you be there with me through all the days?" I asked.

"Yes, I will."

"Then, of course, I shall love it."

Darcy's face grew gentler.

As we sat down to dinner, Mr. Darcy sat on one side of me, and Margaret sat on the other. On her right, sat Mr.

Thornton, and they found themselves able to converse with each other with an ease that I had hoped they would obtain before we left them to find their way in Milton.

"You were very thoughtful," Margaret acknowledged, "to encourage us to overcome our anxieties of losing our friends to the South again."

"Thank you," Thornton responded. "It was my attempt to be selfless. I worried that I had not done it very well."

"You did the best that anyone could. I suppose that, no matter how much I have prepared myself, I am still unprepared."

"Unprepared? Do you refer to being unprepared for when Elizabeth, Jane, and Kitty must leave for Kent and Derbyshire?"

"Yes."

"It will be hard. But hopefully, the Miss Lucases will prove to be sturdy and reliable company."

"They are delightful girls, and I am certain that they would be pleasant to be around. But one cannot force a bond or camaraderie between individuals. It must occur organically or not come at all. Lizzy and I became friends quite naturally."

"I can empathize. It was the same between Darcy and I, despite the social divide between us. We never intended to be friends, but fate had other plans, took a little turn, and now here we are."

"Oh, I never got the chance to observe."

"Observe?"

"Well, I was so occupied with trying to adjust to the possibility of life without Lizzy, that I never got the chance to reflect more about that you and I are in the same predicament. You feel the same about Darcy's leaving, don't you?"

"He is as sure a friend that I have ever had, excepting

your father. Perhaps, when Darcy leaves, I might make the mistake of clinging to your father more when they all go into Kent to wed. Sometimes, it truly hurts to part with one's friends. But yes, you and I are in the same situation. Our comrades are leaving us. We will do as we always have: shift and endure. But a part of our souls will be missing."

"That is the first time that we have ever had a discussion about the workings of the soul."

"Yes, we never talk about it. Do we?"

"No, we don't. I suppose that we are more like Aristotle and often talking about the workings of man, from harmony to discord, as opposed to being like Plato sometimes, and wondering about the cosmos. Am I getting too philosophical for a dinner party?"

Thornton chuckled.

"No, I do not think so."

"That is very well, because I know no other way to be. Well, Mr. Thornton, whatever happens after this, we will shift as we may and continue to thrive in the way that we know your mother would always know you to, and that my father expects me to. Well, it shall be that way until we receive that letter in the mail where we are invited to travel from one great house to the next."

"Darcy knows me, and that I cannot travel to any great house for leisure."

"Not even to Pemberley? It's not far. He is your friend."

"And I must run a factory that is behind in all its orders, due to an unwanted strike that lasted for weeks. I have debts that are meant to be owed to the bank and worry daily about how I shall sojourn from one month's end to the other. Leisure is meant for the fortunate, not for the industrious and eternally enduring."

Margaret looked at her food and continued to eat.

Seeing that Thornton had quite broken the spell that was between them, I saw his face slacken and be replaced immediately by remorse.

"I am a dunce, I know," Thornton said. "We are at a dinner party, and I speak of business. I must be a tedious sort of character that you must regret sitting next to."

"Why do you think so? I am not for the veneer of false charm. You were speaking plain and frankly about a situation that causes distress to you. Perhaps you read my expression incorrectly. I was not looking at my food out of boredom, but out of something that was like regret. Bessy said that the strike would kill her, you see. Then the strike itself caused no change, but only set everyone back even further, including yourself. I cannot help but sympathize with the workers, you must understand. I do not do it out of a slight towards yourself, Mr. Thornton. Believe me that I am not wishing to blame you for any of this. I see how, in Milton, life can be quite complicated. It is just... I know that, when it comes to both sides of this matter, there is a level of complication to always consider. I cannot help but understand both sides of this dilemma now."

"I can understand. For so long, I have been trained to consider how it is so often, us versus the workers. Then you come along, and your father, and you have no choice but to be torn between both worlds. It took me a while to discover this."

"Do you really feel like it is often you masters versus the workers?"

"We have no choice but to consider it as such."

"Is there any way that...perhaps, you can ever find a delicate balance; an equilibrium as it were? A peace between the laborers and the masters. There must be some way that it can be done."

"I fear that it is unlikely."

"Well, I cannot give up so very easily. I may not be as learned as you are, but time has always taught temperance and eventually harmony between both sides of a conflict. I will not lose hope in your enterprise, Mr. Thornton. It's just my nature."

"Miss Hale?"

"Yes?"

"Did you just say that you will not lose hope in my enterprise?"

Margaret looked at him, at last. His repetition of her words evidently affected him in a comforting sort of fashion. It was obvious that he was flattered by her consideration of his craft.

"Well," Margaret rushed out, "what I meant was... I see the importance of your factory. I acknowledge that industry does serve a vital purpose to the running of English society. It is a professional interest, as it were. I just—well, I needed time to learn."

"That is all that I ask for. I just wished for you to under-stand me."

"But I ought to be clear. Everything that I say, I do it out of a general sort of respect. I am not attempting to establish any sort of tenderness."

"Yes," Thornton said heavily, seeing her implications. "Yes."

When looking at him, Margaret saw that she might have hurt his pride.

Ah, the trappings of being on two different sides of heart-break. For, one wishes to be kind, but it is hard to be so without giving encouragement. Although, if one is mean and cruel to the other, for the sake of making them understand that the rejection is permanent, one does feel the agony of being harsh. Either way, there is a sense of profound disappointment somewhere.

Margaret was not blind to her behavior, nor was she blind to seeing the effects that it caused. In her eyes was a sense of guilt, a regret for the truth distributing such inner disquiet. She was now beginning to experience, more than ever, the problems of learning to care for one's past antagonists.

For one cannot spend one's life hating someone when time had proved them undeserving of that contempt. Time forces a hope, as well as an attempt to heal bonds strained through discord. Margaret may not prefer to display emotion very much, but she still was not stone. Over time, her emotions would have no choice but to be stirred, while she considered the thoughts and feelings of others...and she was doing so now.

"Have I hurt you?"

Margaret's question made Thornton become sharp and alert.

"No," he responded quickly. Too quickly for me to believe that he was sincere at all. Rather, it was the actions of someone who had raised their defenses, and was equally wishing to suppress their true emotions, locking them away from public display. "Not at all."

"Mr. Thornton...are you certain? You can tell me the truth, you know."

"Can I?"

"Yes."

"Very well. Perhaps I am distressed."

"I admit that I cannot help that. However, what I can do is perhaps soften things. I have grown to think of us as friends now. Please, if you would be so kind, can you find it within you to think of me in that fashion? We have spoken of it before. But now, I wish for more certainty. Can you think of me as a friend now, Mr. Thornton? And soon, we shall lose some of the best of our company. We are the last ones left of the original set. If you would be there for me—then I shall be there for you as well. I realize that now I did not phrase that particularly well."

"You phrased it perfectly well."

"Then, what do you say to my supplication?"

"I can agree to it," Mr. Thornton said, warmly. "I should like to be your friend."

Margaret smiled at him, and he continued to eat.

The evening ended very well, and carriages were drawn to convey us all home.

While one was arranged to return us Bennets and Lucases back to Frances Street, and Rasby back to her lodgings, I remained next to Darcy.

As we drew near each other, with the express desire to speak the sweet nothings that fiancés share, we noticed that we had a spy.

Turning around, we saw Jane eyeing us, suspicious.

"She gives us the wary eye," I whispered to Darcy.

"Yes, she does. I never thought your eldest sister could ever be intimidating a day in her life."

"I had never suspected as much either. Believe me when I tell you that I was equally as shocked as you. I daresay that she does not trust us, within an inch of our lives."

"And she is correct," I acknowledged, my eyes twinkling, "Darcy, dear friend, you and I are not to be trusted. And what's worse, we perhaps are not ashamed of it."

"True," he replied, his eyes equally as alight with the

passion that stirred in between us. "We are not. This is the first time that I despised your sister's watchfulness and obedience to propriety."

"Oh yes. When it came to Lydia, Jane was correct to be as vigilant as ever. But with us, it is inappropriate that she allows propriety to be the order of the day."

"Yes."

Aware of my own nonsensical thoughts, I was amused.

"Mr. Darcy, we are such hypocrites."

"Yes, we are. Hypocrites of the highest order!"

"Oh, we are wicked."

"Possibly."

"Whatever shall we do with each other?"

"Oh, I thought it was simple."

"Is it?"

"Yes, it is."

"What is this simple solution? Go on then, o' magistrate of Derbyshire, humor me. What have you observed that I have overlooked?"

"We must return to Derbyshire, submit to all our passions, and never leave the bedroom."

My mouth dropped open slightly under the wantonness of his last statement. What a provocative and vulgar thing for the Master of Pemberley to admit. And how much it made me love him all the more. For, very rarely in life, does someone share your passionate confessions, your sensual side, and justify it with their own. For someone else to voice it first, to give credence and plurality to your desires—well, in such cases, it is unpardonable to feel so very alone.

"Is that a promise, sir?" I asked him.

His eyes grew even darker than the sky above. His heart was awake. His desires were alive. And so were mine.

"Oh," he assured me, "it is a promise in every sense of the word."

"Then I shall hold up to it. My innocence commands me to be inexperienced, but I will rise to the challenge. When you make a haven out of the bed we share, I will seek out every desire of yours and match it."

His face fell from the heaviness of me having to leave him, so terribly unsatisfied.

"Yes, I believe you will. And each time, I will rise higher and find more desires to stimulate you. Your form, your figure—your bare skin shall never feel the cold. For I shall cover you with my own form, and you will feel on fire. And the fire shall never leave you."

"Lizzy!" Jane called. "Sister, it is time to depart."

Propriety! Once more, it knocked upon our door, barged its way in, and dared to sit at our table and lord its horrid face over us.

And this time, once more, it did it with the ultimate disguise; it did it with my favorite and beautiful older sister.

"Mr. Darcy," I said, curtsying to him. "We must part."

"Yes. Alas we must."

"I hate it," I whispered to him.

"I hate it more," he responded.

We got into our carriage and were off. Kitty, still amazed with her good fortune, talked the entire way home, wholly ignorant of the quiet pain that Rasby felt.

Chapter 4

Beastly News

"Friends," Thornton groaned, "she wants to be friends."

After the dinner, Darcy and Thornton had returned to Marlborough Mills. When they arrived, the lateness of the night did not lure them to bed. On the contrary, they felt as awake as ever, so they retreated to Thornton's library, had the fire drawn, and Thornton told Darcy about Margaret's words while they poured wine from the decanter.

"Ah," Darcy said, sitting down on the other side of the sofa, with his wine in his hand. "Friends, eh? Yes, the 'f' word."

"Yes, *that* word."

"Yes."

"Yes."

Both men drank.

"It's a word."

"Yes, it is a word."

They drank again.

"It's a wonderful word."

"It is a wonderful word."

They drank again.

"But it's also a painful word."

"Yes, a very painful word."

They drank again.

Their wine glasses were empty, and they were too lax to move to pour anymore. Rather, the warmth of the fire had lured them into a sense of serenity, and they had no desire to move.

"Is there any way," Darcy said, "that I can convince you that this is a good thing?"

"I know that it is, but..."

"It's a step in the right direction, Thornton."

"I know it is. But why do I feel as if it is no better than when she had despised me?"

"Because it is still not what you want. You want to have her, to have her love you."

"I do not want to ever feel as if I could make her love me, because that is wrong. Although..."

"You wish that *you could* make her love you."

"Yes. I know," he groaned, rubbing his face. "I sound horrid."

"Every man has a beast within him. You do as well, Thornton. It's better to know about it, in advance. This way, you can defeat it. It's the side of you that wishes to possess her, aggressively, to wrap your arms around her, and to never let her move from your embrace. To never let her walk where you cannot see her. To moderate her movements—to feel as if you can regulate it all. Almost as if you are a savage that must own her, possess her. Even breaking down her own self-will, her autonomy, because she is what you must have. Your basic animal instinct."

"We men are not allowed to acknowledge such things."

"Of course, we are not. It's not proper. And it's also a

shocking blow to one's ego that we are no better than the warriors of old, who ran among the trees, wearing skins and taking as one wishes. To know that, deep down, we are mere barbarians."

"Yes, I suppose it is." Thornton leaned forward, staring into the fire. "My desires are more savage than anyone's."

"But you keep it under good regulation. It could easily rise up, overwhelm you, you force your attentions on her, and you would become that beast. But you do not."

"You felt as I have felt before, haven't you?"

"Oh, yes. But I am more fortunate than you. Elizabeth knows about that part of myself."

Thornton turned to him, surprised at this.

"She does? You told her?"

"In my own way, yes. I have."

"And she doesn't turn from you."

"On the contrary, she welcomes my desires, my savage passion for her. She understands the monster that is in me. Because she trusts me. Whatever my faults, I am trustworthy, and she knows the monster will always be under good regulation."

"And what I am doing now? I am upset that she wants to be friends, despite not coming to me—despite not coming into my bed—even when she has done everything to improve her opinion of me. I should be grateful. Why am I not?"

"Because of the wolf that lies within. The wolf that wants everything and anything."

Darcy leaned over.

"Now it's time to take that beast within and rise above it. She wants to be friends with you. Be good friends with her. Just by doing that, the monster within will lose."

"I hope so. I don't want to hurt her."

"You won't, Thornton."

"I know that I won't. I just still love her more than ever. But I want to be good for her. Yes, I will be."

"Good. See? The beast now sleeps."

"Yes," Thornton said, self-assured. "Now, I am no longer scared."

Eventually, they felt their eyes drooping and they retired to bed.

Chapter 5

Neighborly News

"So," Nicholas Higgins said, "this is what is to happen?"

The next day, I realized that it was better to tell him the news of our changed wedding plans, and how it would signify our departure from Milton society. When I finished, it was needless to say that he was not very excited.

When I arrived, I had brought a basket, and Mary was taking the items and putting them away.

"Yes, it is," I said. "How are you, Mary?"

"I am well, Miss," Mary said. "Yesterday, I was at the Hales. I helped clean things for Dixon throughout the day."

"And you did good work of it," I said, "for when we had an evening party, the house looked very clean, and Dixon had nothing to complain about."

Mary smiled but had nothing else to say. I always wondered how much else was going on in that mind of hers, but I knew not to ask.

Turning back to Nicholas, I realized that maybe he deserved better answers.

"You do not look happy, Nicholas."

"I am well."

"You are lying to yourself, neighbor."

He groaned and then grinned gently.

"Very well, yea, yer be righ' bout that. I was lyin'. Beggin yer pardon. I hope yer can understand why I was."

"Yes, I can. Whether you like it or not, can you entertain the possibility that you might miss us?"

"Why mus' yer be so plain and frank about that?"

"I profess to not doing that out of being self-conceited, but out of all that we experienced. I never meant to leave people behind."

"But that's what 'appens when two people choose to be fallin' in love and all that. People leave, tha's plain and flat."

"Yes, I suppose it is."

Nicholas sat down.

"Do yer lot be thinkin' that maybe, yer might come back to Milton?"

"I'm not sure, Nicholas. I want to say that we will, but I am not the only one that I must think of now. I will soon have a husband, family that I must look after, and if I am fortunate, children. All bows when it comes to accommodating family. But, if things come to my power, then we will return. But what can be certain, is that we shall miss you."

"Yea," he replied, "who would miss me?"

"We would. And we mean it."

"I'll not forget yer lot," he said. "I wouldn't, no matter how much it hurt."

"I know."

There was a knock on the door. Mary moved to get it, but I assured her that I would get it for her, while she tended to her duties. Walking to the door, I opened it and came face to face with Margaret Hale, with a basket on her arm.

She chuckled, surprised to see me.

"Did we have the same thought?" I asked.

"Close to it, but not so much so," Margaret said as she entered. "I brought a basket for the Bouchers and thought to come and visit Nicholas and Mary."

"Well," Nicholas said, "seein' yer both together will be somethin' that I can't enjoy much of anymore, eh? Especially since one of yer will be gone soon."

Margaret gave me a sympathetic look.

"Yes," I said, "I thought it would be best to convey all sooner rather than late."

"Ah," Margaret said, "well, Mary, you did a fine job at cleaning yesterday."

"Thank you," Mary said, "how was the party and all? The one las' night?"

"We had a delightful time," Margaret said, "but Nicholas, I see that you are still out of work."

"I don' work because I choose not to."

"But Nicholas," I said, "you know as well as we all do that you are a person of industry; you cannot bear to be idle for long."

"Yer right, tha's plain," he said, "but even if I wanted to work, I doubt anyone would have me. Boucher's influence still falls over me' head like a shadow."

"And that's what I came to talk to you about," Margaret said. "Last night, I have been thinking. Have you applied for work at Marlborough Mills?"

Nicholas turned to her, a little disgusted and stubborn.

"What? Work for Thornton?"

"Yes."

"What rubbish is tha'? Work for him? He's the one that broke the strike. He called in the Irish."

"Who deserved better than how the workers fell upon them," I said. "And Nicholas, think of what Thornton was undergoing. He had many orders to fulfill and no workers to fill them."

"That's what I came to realize last night," Margaret added. "Both master and laborer were acting out of desperation. You all went on strike because you were desperate for a better life. Thornton, out of desperation not to fall behind on his orders and ring up further debt than he has accumulated, brought the Irish in to fulfill those orders."

Nicholas's face became distorted as he considered something.

"Debt?" he repeated.

"Yes," Margaret continued, "Nicholas, I don't want you to repeat this to anyone. And Mary, please, for me, do not."

"We won'," Nicholas said, "speak yer piece, Miss."

"When the workers went on strike, Mr. Thornton had many orders in hand, and they went unfulfilled. As such, he needed to complete the orders to maintain supporting his family. Well, something was confessed to me that indicated that Marlborough Mills suffered terribly, due to the strike. Now, he needs help. Also, he is becoming more open to the common laborer's problems. He is showing signs of not looking on them so meanly. Can you not go to him and consider asking him for a job? Everyone mentions how you were a fine worker. Maybe Thornton needs that."

"And when you think of your own need for employment," I said, "Nicholas, you might need this as well."

After hearing our advice, Nicholas sat down, a little vexed at having to be lectured.

"He wouldn' listen to me knowhow," Nicholas uttered.

"You have to try," Margaret said, "and when you succeed, perhaps you can help Boucher return as well."

"Boucher!" Nicholas grunted.

"Nicholas, it's time to forgive."

"I know the truth," he spat.

"What truth?" I asked.

Nicholas looked squarely at me.

"I know that he never saved yer sister's life."

I blinked. How, in god's name, could he possibly have known that?

"I..." I began, "I can't think what you mean."

"Boucher is thin. Too thin to pull anythin' out of any water." Nicholas leaned forward, intent on bearing the truth. "If he tried to save anythin', he would have needed help. But I don' think he would have even gotten tha' far. Yer lot lied. He never saved Mrs. Denny, did he?"

Margaret and I looked in between each other.

"No need to say nothin'," Nicholas continued, "yer silence says it all."

How humiliating it was to be discovered. Honestly, I thought that I had planned it all so perfectly, and to be found out so easily was pitiful. Oh well, it did not do to dwell.

"Nicholas," I said, "Boucher needed to be given a new name. And when I say a new name, I mean that he needed all offenses from his name to be wiped clean."

"How did he get wet? What? Did he fall into the water, or somethin' like tha'?"

"Well, yes, I suppose that he did," I lied, as did Margaret.

"Tha' fool! He can't even walk straight, but no! He has to fall in and wait for someone to pull him out. Good god, he can't do anythin' right!"

"Nicholas," I stressed, "you both must promise us that you will not tell anyone."

"Think of Mrs. Boucher and the six children," Margaret stressed.

"Ah," Nicholas said, "he lucky he got them six childer. If it weren' for them, where would he be? Very well, for the childer. For them, I will keep me mouth closed on the subject. And no more of that."

Margaret and I breathed a sigh of relief. Some truths had to remain hidden.

Nicholas looked at Mary, and then at the rest of us.

"I've only got one left meself," he noted, still very cast down. Once more, he delved into the very depths of despair from being a father who expected to leave the earth before his children did. Knowing that there was nothing else that Margaret and I could do but have a moment of silence, we just sat there and let Nicholas feel the weight of Bessy's absence again.

Without even thinking, I turned my eye back to where Bessy was known for sitting at. An empty chair by an empty side of the table, where she would smile no longer. How long would her ghost haunt us, from a metaphoric standpoint, I did not know. Yet, what I did know is that, for a woman who was born, lived, and died low, her presence was mightier than she would have ever suspected.

"Not we three," Nicholas continued, "naw, I can't say that now. Only can I be sayin' that there be the two of us. And with so many friends gone, I say we all done lost somethin', I reckon." He looked at Margaret and me. "If I go and see Thornton, his overseer will turn me out. That'll be good for a laugh."

"All I do know," Margaret finalized, "is that it will be futile if you never try."

"A man doesn't like bein' a laughin' stock, yer know? But I suppose, people have laughed at me already before."

"No one's laughing at you, Nicholas," I declared. "That's

just your frightened side playing tricks on your confidence. Don't let that side win."

He smiled slightly.

"Very well. Jus' for yer two, I'll give it a go."

Margaret and I left together and made our way to the Bouchers.

"What about Boucher?" I asked Margaret. "Yes, there is the chance that we can import his family back down South and give him a tenancy there, but I suspect that he might not know how to uproot his family so easily."

"I doubt Thornton might want to rehire him," Margaret admitted, "but perhaps...well, let's just see how this goes."

We knocked on the door.

"What are the chances that the children will knock us over when the door is opened?" I pondered.

"Lizzy, some of them are small. Besides, you overvalue our importance."

The door opened and Mrs. Boucher appeared, her face lit up as her more active children rushed out at us, and jumped on top of us, happy to see the basket.

"Of course," Margaret said, a little humble, "I've been wrong before."

We embraced the children as Mrs. Boucher told them to let us go. Holding their hands, we entered the house and was met by Boucher stoking the fire in the fireplace.

"Miss Hale and Miss Bennet," he said, a little embarrassed to be in our presence. He still felt that he owed us a great deal. As such, when a man feels that he owes a woman something, sometimes it leads to him being a little distant or depressed in her presence. "How do yer both do on this fine day?"

"We are well, thank you, Boucher," Margaret said, handing Mrs. Boucher the basket, "we come with some food."

"My childer love yer for it," Boucher said as he moved some chairs aside so that we could sit down by the fire. Accepting the invitation, we took the seats.

"How are you doing?" I asked.

"Have you managed to find work?" Margaret asked. "Or do you still need to uproot your family to the South?"

"If the opportunity finds itself to that, and there is work for me down there, then yea, I would do that," Boucher said, giving me a look. Knowing that I would be the means through saving his family's reputation again, now he felt doubly heavy. The man was like a useless lithe; he didn't know how to begin to move on his own but needed to be carried. And he knew that. The poor man. "I don' fear a slower way of livin'. In fact, sometimes I be wonderin' if maybe I was made for tha' sort of life, and I jus' was born in the wrong place." Leaning into us conspiratorially, he lowered his voice so that only we could hear. "Also, goin' down South would give me a chance to start over, yer see? However, this is what my family knows. Milton is their only home. Before I think about movin' down there, I should give the mills one last chance. Especially since this is the only work that I understand."

Suddenly, I had another thought.

"I am a fool," I uttered.

"What do you mean, Lizzy?" Margaret asked.

"Margaret, the idea was staring us in the face, and we didn't see it at all. Boucher, while London is not Milton, I still gather that you could find your way into the workings of city life in the South. It's my uncle. Uncle Gardiner. He runs a textile factory, and it's a very successful one. If you need help with the rent at all, I'm sure all your friends on this street can assist you for the week, but can you give me time to write to him? He might have the space for a new spinner, or someone to help in the sorting room."

Boucher's eyes lit up.

"That would be a jolly good thought," Boucher said. "Miss Bennet, please write to him. Please believe me when I tell yer this: I never shirked from me work. I was always on time, and I never was accused of failin' on the job. It's just that—well, yer know what happened. I don' think I'll get any good references."

"Boucher," Margaret said, "I can help in that regard. If you promise to always be considerate, never allow yourself to be swept up so much that you commit to violence, then I will see if Thornton can give you a good reference."

"Yer would do tha' for me?" he asked.

"We've already done a great deal," I noted, "so what's a little more?"

His eyes filled with the pathetic appearance of humility that made a person always forgive him, ultimately.

"I cannot say that it will all be fruitful for you," I said, "but give me a fortnight. If nothing occurs by then, then try your luck at getting work her in Milton again."

"Yer both mus' understand," Boucher said, his voice frail from the eternal supplication that he usually exuded, "I can't repay yer both for any of this. I don' ever know how to, so I never can."

"Boucher," Margaret said, "we never expected repayment. You can put that sense of obligation out of your head."

When hearing that we were aware that he would never return our favors, it didn't lessen his woes. On the contrary, it seemed like it made him more despondent. Boucher looked at the fire that he helped blaze.

"Childer look to their father for the support," he uttered, still looking away from us and into the flames that flickered along the coals. "That's our job, yer see? To look after them, and when we don't, we fail." Once more, he looked at us. This time, I could tell that he was fighting back tears. Of course, he would master that feat, gaining victory over his emotions, and no tears would be fully produced. But, for a moment, there was something there. "A man must make his own way. He must ride the ways of economy and reign it in, yer see? And that ought to be the beginnin' and end of it. But this—what am I?"

I groaned inwardly. Quite frankly, I didn't have the patience with generalizations. Maybe it's because I was getting married, and I felt that so many things were getting in the way. Or call it my constant tendency to rebel against old ideas. I don't know what, but I have never been very patient when a solution is so close in sight.

"Enough," I declared. "I don't know what you experience or how others look at you, Boucher. But what I do know is this: there is no such thing as a man who has gotten far in life without the help of a woman who supported him somewhere in his life. For what was the man but the woman who helped raise him? I know that sometimes you are told such harsh lessons, but so are us women. You must accept help sometimes. Not expect it—for if you do that, then you will never learn independence. But you must accept it. And just continue on. Economy, in a country, functions on the thriving of both the man and woman of that industry. So, there is nothing to be afraid of anymore."

Looking over his shoulder, he watched his wife as she began to cook the food that Margaret brought.

"When I first met her, she was beautiful," he said about his wife. "Time and childbirth wore her down." At last, he looked at me. "Yer uncle will get back to yer in two weeks?"

"Yes. Can you wait that long?"

"Is there a chance that yer can often bring us food every now and again?" he asked. "Please?"

"Yes, we can," I said, not worried any longer, for now I knew that I had nothing to fret over. Economy was no longer something to fear when it came to my purse.

"Then I can wait that long."

"Very well. I'll write the letter and have it sent today."

His eyes were lighter. He no longer felt the guilt of owing someone something.

"Thank yer. I suppose I can enjoy the day now."

When we left, Margaret gave me a look.

"If I keep dealing out offers without getting permission," she said, "then, I daresay that I will have to start calling myself a busybody."

"Margaret, I have some sad business to tell you."

"And what is that?"

"You have always been a busybody."

"I am not."

"Are too."

"Am not."

"Are too. So, tell me, will you go to Thornton and ask him to give Nicholas a fair chance for work?"

"Yes," Margaret said, "I might just have to. Oh dear, I am a busybody."

"You care, Margaret. That's a good thing. Besides, life starts when people start making decisions. And if someone doesn't decide to help someone else eventually, there will be nothing left on earth, excepting birds or fishes."

When we reached my house, the door opened, and Maria Lucas emerged from it. Her face was white with shock.

"Lizzy and Margaret!" Maria cried. "It is the most shocking thing."

"Maria?"

"I can't believe it."

She was so much in a flutter that it was hard to get her to calm down.

"Calm yourself, Maria," I said, "and breathe." Suddenly a scary thought occurred to me. "Does it have something to do with Mr. Darcy?" When she didn't answer my question after only one second, I grabbed her shoulders. "Maria, has something happened to Mr. Darcy?"

"No," Maria rushed out. "It's not Mr. Darcy."

"Kitty? Jane? Lydia!"

"No. Kitty is inside with me now, and for all that I know, Jane and Lydia are well."

"What about Charlotte?"

"She is inside as well. There is nothing the matter with anyone here in Milton."

She opened her mouth and then covered it, in grief. It could only mean one thing.

Releasing her arms, I stood there, a little embarrassed that I didn't think of it before.

"Oh, no," I sighed. "Is it your father or your mother? Maria, I am sorry that I did not think of it sooner."

"It's not that either, Lizzy. It's just... I spoke so ill of her for so long. Now I feel heartily stupid."

"Maria," Margaret said, "please tell us what it is that troubles you?"

"It's Mrs. Collins."

"Mrs. Collins?"

"Do you mean Mr. Collins's wife?" I asked.

"Yes. Lizzy and Margaret...she's dead. Mr. Collins's wife is dead."

Chapter 6

Shocking News

"Mr. Collins's wife is dead?" I repeated.

"Yes," Maria Lucas confirmed.

"How do you know this?" Margaret asked.

"Mary Bennet sent a letter and Kitty just opened it. Come inside and you will see for yourselves."

Grabbing our hands, she pulled us inside of our house. There, Kitty was, with Charlotte Lucas. Charlotte just sat there, as calm as ever, and Kitty was holding the letter.

"Kitty?" I began, "is this true?"

"Yes," she said, handing me the letter, "our cousin lost his wife."

Taking the letter from her, and with Margaret leaning over my shoulder, I began to read:

> *Dear Jane, Eliza, Kitty and Lydia,*
>
> *I write with a tale of woe.*
> *Before I begin unfolding some very grievous news, I must assure you all that I am well. Everyone on*

Gracechurch Street is also healthy, and we do our best to be quiet and productive.

Work at the factory is also successful and Uncle Gardiner's business is very profitable. In fact, each of us workers have been given a raise in our wages this past month.

Therefore, be not alarmed at reading this with any apprehension on our family's part—excepting Uncle Philips, who I heard is still brought low by recently losing our aunt. I am told that he still wears black clothes, in tribute to her death. I never knew he loved her so much.

On that same subject of Hertfordshire, that is where the sad business has occurred. I just received a letter from Mrs. Long saying that our cousin, Mr. Collins, has recently suffered a tragedy. His wife, Mrs. Collins, had recently taken ill with a cold that proved to develop into a high fever. From what I recall of her she never appeared as being delicate.

Therefore, you can imagine the shock of everyone when the fever took her, and she died.

Mr. Collins is now a widow, with an infant on his hands who he is at a loss of how to raise. From what I have been told, he is breaking apart, for lack of a better term for it.

Mr. and Mrs. Collins, who may not have been a popular couple in the county, still were a productive one —in the sense that they were properly suited. From what I understand, they got along tolerably well. Who knows? Maybe he did love her a great deal.

For, from what I have heard, Mr. Collins has been taking to the bottle a little too much, out of a desire to drown himself in his woes.

When hearing this in Mrs. Long's letter to me, I could not believe it. Yet, when I wrote to Uncle Philips, he confirmed that Mr. Collins is falling apart, and he does not tend to his child at all but leaves the infant to be taken care of by servants.

Despite our history, he is our cousin, and his child should not be punished for the crisis that rests between us.

Out of a desire to show solidarity, I wrote to Mr. Collins, to offer my condolences. Without thinking anything of it, I submitted my services if he should ever need my help. Truly, I thought nothing would come of it. After all, he did not part ways as friends with us.

Although, imagine my surprise when I received a response from him, requesting me to come to Longbourn. He felt that he needed family beside him, as well as a female family member to assist him in tending to the child. Then he also requested to see the rest of my sisters as well, in this troubling time.

Of course, I know little about tending to children, but it is not the Christian way to avoid helping others. My uncle has been very kind to me and has allowed me reprieve to go and visit Mr. Collins. However, I do not know how long I shall be able to be away from my work before Uncle Gardiner might have to replace me.

I shall leave for Longbourn tomorrow. Jane, Lizzy, and Kitty, I am aware that Lydia cannot come, due to her marital position. However, I think I shall need your help in this venture. I feel a little lost. I know that I must help, but I worry that I am not the correct choice. Therefore, can any of you please return to Hertfordshire within a couple months? I daresay that, with us all together, we *can make the right decision on how to help our cousin recover.*

When sending me a response, please direct it to Longbourn.

Please, come when you may.

MB

Closing the letter, I sat down.

"How old was Mrs. Collins?" I asked Maria and Charlotte.

"I am not certain to her exact age," Charlotte answered, "however, she could not have been older than twenty-five years old."

We all looked in between each other.

"Whatever she was like," I said. "That is too young."

"Yes," Charlotte added, "too young."

"I am sorry," Margaret said, "for the tragedy of it. Though I suppose that my words carry flimsy condolences, since I never met the woman."

"And we barely had a chance to have a wider acquaintance with her ourselves," I said for Kitty and myself. "We can offer our prayers, but we never gained any intimacy with her."

"Lizzy," Charlotte said, "while it is wrong to speak ill of the dead, in truth, you would not have liked her."

"So, I have been told."

"Well," Maria said, "it was a general consensus that the Collinses were the least liked couple in Hertfordshire. I know that I must sound like the worst for confessing all. I didn't mean to speak ill of her."

"No one is judging you, Maria," Kitty said. "Not here in Milton, at least."

We all sat down at the table, silent.

"Will you go?" Margaret asked us. "Back to Longbourn?"

"Mary needs us," I said, "but this was all so unexpected. We already had a difficult job of having to plan everything. And now this? I can't leave just now. My work needs a note-taker, and I didn't orchestrate it in such a way where there would be no one to take up the task. Also, I cannot put off this wedding. Mr. Darcy is correct; Lady Catherine does need our company right now."

"I can help," Charlotte said. "I know the duty and I can do it. I shall take the notetaking position sooner than expected."

I looked at her, grateful beyond words.

"I cannot ask for that."

"No, but you never did ask me. I volunteered."

"We arranged for you to return to your parents, to tell them the news in person, and have your whole trousseau brought here to help the adjustment."

"And you and I both are aware, that whenever humanity makes plans, Time and Mother Nature throw a tempest into it, and all unwinds. Eliza, my moving here was never going to be smooth. It was never going to be gentle. And who knows? Maybe it was better this way."

"How so?" I asked.

Charlotte looked at Maria and they both looked resigned as well as a little pale in the face. I knew that look. Within their faces was a hidden message; they were secretive about something.

"Charlotte and Maria?" Kitty asked, equally as aware of this. "What is it?"

Charlotte bit her lip and then she turned to me.

"Before anyone judges me, I need for you to understand me. I needed to get away. I needed to leave Hertfordshire."

Kitty, Margaret, and I looked in between each other. It was obvious that we had never been told the whole history of the Lucas sisters.

"We never actually told our parents why we came here," Maria announced abruptly, talking swiftly, as if the speed would help her deliver the news.

"What?" Kitty asked.

"We were afraid that mother and father would not understand the concept of us moving to Milton for work."

"Or for us to gain any sort of employment at all," Charlotte elaborated. "We weren't raised to work, and especially not to do so in industrial towns in the North. Even when we were taught a trade, it was done just for the sake of being accomplished."

"So," Margaret stressed, "Sir William and Lady Lucas have no notion that you came here, with the prospect of staying?"

"Yes," Maria said heavily. "I suppose, maybe even I wished for a change as well. We were heartily sick of Mr. Collins and his wife looking down on us."

"Mr. Collins never did forgive me for rejecting him," Charlotte said. "And I couldn't bear even the mere thought of his society amongst us. So, we did everything we could to give you the impression that our parents were amenable to your request. Even down to writing you letters with their agreement on the matter. However, if I remain here, start my work, and Maria takes over for Jane, then we do not have to return home and face our family. We can write the letters to them, explaining everything in a manner that shows that we were helping you all the entire time, that we are substituting for your helping Mr. Collins."

"In a perverse sort of way," Maria realized, "this has helped us."

"As terrible as it is for a young woman to pop off, as it were," Charlotte said, "Mrs. Collins's tragedy is the perfect sort of way to force you to return to Longbourn and have me take your place. And I cannot be here alone, so Maria must remain as well and take Jane's place while she also travels down South. And when it becomes very evident that Maria and I are to remain here permanently, our parents will have no choice but to accept it. Because, at that time, you all would have gotten married."

"And we would need someone to have taken over for us permanently," Kitty concluded. "So, in their eyes, you never deceived your parents."

"But rather," I finalized, "you came to save us from the family crisis, and it accidentally led to you having no choice but to take over for us completely. This forced you both to be heroes at the last minute, sacrificing your comforting place in the country for working in an industrial town."

Maria and Charlotte did not answer, but they might as well had said yes.

"Well," I said, "doesn't that just beat everything?"

"Yes," Charlotte said, "who would have thought? I never knew that being deceptive could be that profitable in my life."

"Actually," Margaret inferred, "that is a more common maxim than you might think."

"Mr. Collins wants you all to come and see him!" Lydia declared. "Odious man!"

Once being told the news, my sisters, the Lucases, and I knew that it would be best to tell Lydia about this new development. Since the regiment were to leave Milton in three days, we knew that what ought to be done cannot be done too quickly.

Therefore, we went to pay her a visit at the officers' headquarters, and her reaction was as to be expected.

"Well, that is most unfair," she remarked, as we paid our visit in her rooms. "Why couldn't he be the one that died?"

"Lydia!" Jane cried. "That is a horrible thing to say."

"I know. And I don't care. Honestly, why are you all so surprised by anything that comes out of my mouth, at this point?"

We all gave each other a look, and perhaps we were not as surprised as we wanted to appear.

"And the woman has left this earth with an infant," Lydia continued, "and it's left to a man who probably has no notion of how to raise a child."

"Oh," Maria Lucas said.

"Oh?" Charlotte repeated her words. "What did that 'oh' mean?"

"Well, the more that I think about it, the more that I think I might know what happens next. Mr. Collins has an infant who he had no intention of raising all on his own. Servants can only do but so much, after all. Knowing him, as well as knowing his natural inclination to maintain the standards in his life, he either will be looking to remarry very soon, or he will have to pass his child off to another relative to raise. That is a common resource for widowed men who find themselves wholly lost."

"And Mr. Collins is perhaps more lost than any other man in this case," Lydia commented. "I cannot see him having any notion of what to do."

"Nor can I," Kitty said, leaning back in her chair and rubbing her neck. "And knowing him, he will expect us to come and assist him." Jane gave her a look, but Kitty was firm. "I mince neither words nor judgments now. He will find himself very ill-used during this all and then forget how he mistreated us. He shall be the ONLY victim in this case and forsake all ideas when he inflicted that sentence on others."

"No, he won't," I vowed. "For I will not let him."

They all turned to me.

"For the sake of the child, I am happy that Mary will go and tend to the family. And despite all desires for the road to our weddings to be soon, I accept the fact that we must accept his invitation as well. After we marry, we must go to Longbourn and have our honeymoon afterwards. For the sake of seeing how Mary fares, how the infant is, if for nothing else. But make no mistake. I will not allow Mr. Collins to believe that he can employ our help, as if it is his due, and to forget how he treated us before that. I am not in the mood to let him believe that he is above any reproach. Even when we all age, we still need to believe that there is a repercussion to our actions."

"Precisely," Lydia whined. "I don't want him thinking that about us either. We must not take this lying down. We must not!"

When she said this, she viciously had placed a log in the fire.

This sudden rash act made us all blink at her sudden burst of anger. We were used to Lydia being very verbose, and loud, but not in so harshly sincere of a way.

What brought more surprise to it was that she didn't turn to us. Rather, she remained crouched down, looking into the fire. There was a rage in her eye, that was unlike any I had ever seen.

"He turned us out," she uttered. "He turned us out of our own home. He was offended that you didn't accept him,

Lizzy, just because he expected that you would accept him no matter what. I understand that he meant well, that he thought it best to marry one of us, but he didn't see any of the matters clearly. He should have seen that you didn't love him, Eliza. He should have considered that Mary was better suited for him. And when our parents died, he should have remained at Hunsford until we were all safely secure in our future. If Denny and I hadn't fallen in love, I don't know where I would have fallen in life. I was not meant to work. I knew that I was not. And when we had to shift where we could, did he care? Did Mr. Collins care?"

With this last question, she looked at us. Intimidated by her willful speech, we did not answer. Perhaps it was because we knew that, deep down, Lydia was having another true and sincere emotion. She loved Denny and was serious about him. That was certain. She was serious about loving us. Of that, I was also certain. But since there was little else that she was serious about, it always made it more alarming.

"No, he didn't," she answered for all of us. "Now tragedy has befallen him. Now he knows how it feels. But many of us are selfish in our woes; we act as if we are the only ones who have it. He won't learn." She looked at me. "Lizzy, make him learn. Give him some sort or manner of hell. Make him learn."

Standing up, I walked over to her and sat down next to her in front of the fireplace. Slowly, I raised my hand and held hers, out of solidarity. I didn't say anything, but that was confirmation.

Lydia looked at me, leading to a remarkable sight. There were tears in her eyes.

"I loved Longbourn," she said, her expression filled with intense emotion. "I know that I never made it look like I did, but I did. Sometimes, it's not until you lose something that you realize what you had all along. I loved our home. Our parents' souls were in that place. Our mother's laugh, our father's library. Whatever mistakes they made as parents, they loved us. And we were all happy together. And he came along and took Longbourn from us. He took our parents from us! He took it all, Lizzy. He took it all!"

I placed my arm around her shoulder, and she wept into it. Ignorant of everything that had been displayed before me, I never knew that Lydia felt these things.

How much of the human soul is kept a profound secret? I suppose, when considering the childlike experience of a parent's departure from this world, it was perfectly reasonable. Lydia had always been happy and spirited beyond words. When she married Denny, she did not lose her spiritedness, but maybe it manifested itself even more to help her recover from the pain. A hidden pain that she kept to herself —where she discovered just how many things she sincerely cared about.

As Lydia continued to weep on my shoulder, I looked at the rest of us in the room. We all didn't look away but continued to reflect on Lydia's pitiable state.

We knew.

All of us knew.

Despite her vulgar speeches, we were proud of Lydia. For we knew that even though her words could be indelicate to the ears of some, it had been spoken as an act of love.

Chapter 7

Ghostly News

When returning home, I immediately began writing a letter to my Uncle Gardiner, asking him if he would be willing to hire Mr. Boucher, of the North, in case Mary's absence would be prolonged. I explained his true history to my uncle, remarked on how he had been initially against the strike, but was driven mad for love of his family, and that he was a soul in need. Despite understanding why strikes occur, I knew that Uncle Gardiner did not need my impartiality. I also explained Boucher's history with factory work, his experience and dedication to work ethic, and stressed that he had a wife and family of six children who needed a home immediately. I also asked him if any of his workers were aware of lodgings that were vacant, close to his factory, and could house a lower-class family of eight.

When sealing the letter, I waited for Darcy, who arranged for a visit.

When he arrived, I explained the new development on the rise. It was needless to say that Darcy's reaction was not dissimilar to Lydia's.

"You have every right to sever that man's acquaintance from your life," he insisted. "In fact, it's outrageous for him to request any sort of assistance from the five of you. I cannot deny, Elizabeth, if he were here, I would have the impulse to throttle the fool."

"Do you know what is strange?" I asked. "And what shows just how perverse I am?"

"What?"

"When you speak like that, I find you to be a marvel of a man. In fact, I think I've never seen a handsomer creature in the whole of my life."

When hearing me speak as such, his temper relented and was replaced, altogether, with an amiable look.

Slowly, he came up to me, sat down, and placed his hand on the table in our parlor. I reached over and placed my hand in his, and we remained that way. For a second, he closed his eyes. When he opened them again, his eyes were filled with the wantonness that we too often fell prey to. There was lust in his eyes. And, to my utter shame as well as defiance, I would have been willing to give in to every desire that he had... if it weren't for one thing standing in our way.

"I would do more," he uttered, implying that he wished to fully consummate our union, "but..."

"You are afraid that, at any moment, Jane will come through the front door, and we would be found out."

"Yes!"

His sudden answer made me laugh. Growing bashful, he blushed and rubbed his forehead and eyebrows. Over time, I would learn that it was a nervous habit of his.

"Well, it is just—Jane frightens me a little."

My eyes widened as I barely could contain my giggles. "She what?"

"Not in the traditional habit. But for some reason, after

that experience, I am scared to say anything to her. To contradict her. To defy her. I don't know why, but for some reason, I am just so utterly unnerved by her. Maybe I just don't..."

"Want to disappoint her?"

He looked at me, his expression like that of a schoolboy who upset his favorite professor.

"Yes. Perhaps I don't."

Sighing, I admired him all the more.

"Jane has a way of forcing us, to always be better than how we are. It's her chief talent. Welcome to being as vulnerable as the rest of us."

"I don't like being vulnerable."

"Of course, you don't. For you are Mr. Darcy. Mr. Darcy is not frail, and bends or buckles so easily to the wills and ways of others. He is an elm! Rising into the sky, strong and true. But, when staring into the face of the gentlest and kindest creature in the world, such as Jane, you have no choice but to be so terribly humble. It's a good thing."

Suddenly, he rushed to me and kissed me passionately. The action had come on so suddenly that I had no time to prepare or brace myself for the exhilaration of the act.

But for the love of a man whose passions were so overpowering, for a kiss of such depth and not of the flimsy sort, perhaps the rush of it was the most exciting.

When he did so, he placed his body over mine, and I felt shielded from the cold that often seeped in through the windows. Wrapping his arms around my waist, he clung to me possessively. If one is truly in love, then the instincts will always take over, and win. Placing my arms around his back, I ran my hands through his hair, and fell into his beauty, his warmth, and his trueness.

A kiss is a good kiss when it lasts forever, but it never actually does.

The same would be now.

After a minute, he released his lips from mine, but I clung to him.

"That's all I can give you," he uttered, desperately. "For there's the front door, and it can be opened at any moment."

"And a protective older sister can come charging forth," I said.

"Yes, she can."

"And Jane must be obeyed."

The moment of lovemaking had come to as abrupt an end as it had begun.

He removed his body from my person and stepped back.

"Must you all really go to Hertfordshire after our wedding?" he asked.

"Sadly, yes, we must."

Standing up, I went to the mirror to see that I was presentable. A few strands of my hair had come undone, so I had to rearrange some pins.

When doing so, I looked at myself in the mirror.

Every now and again, there comes that one moment, where you look at your reflection, and it's as if you are seeing yourself for the first time. As if you finally see what you really look like.

Often, when looking in the mirror, one can see what one wants to see. Yet, every now and again, we see our true selves, and all the revelations that come along with it.

"And it's more than that," I said.

"More?" he asked, as I saw his reflection, out of the side of my eye.

"Yes. More."

"What else is it?"

"Mr. Darcy, I never had a reason to return home. I wanted to have one but never did. And then, I *never wanted* to return home. Seeing Mr. Collins there, with his bride, I would feel as if the whole world had completely changed. As if...something had been taken from me. Lydia was right. Our parents' souls are in that place. Maybe I have to return and face that."

I watched Mr. Darcy in the mirror as he stood up, walked over to me, and placed his arm on my shoulders.

"Very well. I suppose my parents are also wrapped up in the walls of Pemberley. If I were to lose that, I would not only be losing a place that I love more than any other, but I would be losing them. And I cannot lose them."

"No, you cannot and always ought to have it. I cannot wait to make more memories at Pemberley. But maybe I do have to return, more than ever."

"Very well. Of course, I get to join you."

I smiled.

"I would have preferred it to be no other way."

Handing the letter to Mr. Darcy, he promised to mail it by way of express, and soon, he left. After I saw him depart, Nicholas Higgins came walking down the street.

Raising my arm, I waved to him. He waved in response, but the light never hit his eyes. The poor man. He still missed Bessy.

Chapter 8

Professional News

Bracing herself, Margaret Hale stood in front of Marlborough Mills. Wholly aware of how indelicate it would look to request the help of a man whom she had rejected, she knew that she was preparing herself for a difficult discussion.

Although, she had promised Nicholas that she would assist him. And she had every intention of giving it all her effort.

However, she had one chief ally on her side: Nicholas Higgins's history as a worker. He had always been declared as a fine laborer, and until the strike, nothing ill could have been said about him. Yet, he was also honest. He had that quality on his side.

All around her, workers and wagons were coming and going, the street beneath her had some fluff and dirt underneath. Standing there, looking at the mills, Margaret took in the grandeur of it, as well as the magnitude of the master who ran the establishment.

And no one likes a coward!

Therefore, Margaret gathered her strength and met the

overseer. She asked him if she could arrange to meet with Mr. Thornton. Understanding that he must be very busy, she offered to wait in his office.

Since the overseer was accustomed to her and was aware that Mr. Thornton might be eager to see her, he accepted and went to Thornton immediately.

While Margaret waited, she looked over everything in the office and wondered at it. It was a proper study for a man of industrious business, but there was something personal about all the items that were there. Everything felt as if they were items that spoke volumes about the man who owned them. For reasons that she could not explain, she felt as if the room reflected the man, rather than the man merely existing in the room.

As she went to a bookshelf, she discovered some volumes that she recognized. She became so engrossed at the thought of them that she didn't even notice that she was not alone.

When being told that Miss Hale was there, Thornton felt the need to see her immediately. He handed his task to his overseer and walked briskly to his office.

When he got there, he saw that Margaret was looking around his office. For reasons that he could not determine why, he felt that he didn't wish to disturb her.

As such, he just stood there, watching as she moved to the bookshelf and looked over all the volumes. Her figure was so light, well-made, and healthy. Her form was hand-some, her face was elegant, and she always dressed precisely as he preferred: simple but very lovely. The darkness of her hair was done up in a pleasing style. It was neither ostenta-tious, nor base. And she was wearing a unique hat, that was the latest fashion of modernity.

In her appearance was the greatest contradiction: the past and old ideas nipped away at her heels, like a shadow, but the future and modern customs also loomed over her, like the air above. She was a woman who was perpetually torn between two worlds, two ideas, and two ideals. Perhaps, in the grand scheme of things, it made sense for her to be so utterly confused. Too many different aspects were thrown at her, and she wasn't given time to adjust to them properly.

He was a fool to have proposed to her when he did. He saw that now. He would have had her jump from being his tense acquaintance to being his wife. It was too extreme a jump, too drastic a change to a woman who Change had not always been kind to.

'I still love her,' he thought, but dare not put words to it. 'And I will always love her.'

Accidentally, he shifted in his place, and he made noise. This forced Margaret to rise out of her musings and turn to him abruptly. When seeing him, she jumped, and Thornton cursed that he had disturbed her.

"My apologies," he said, entering his office, "I disturbed you."

Bashfully, Margaret looked down at the floor.

"It is your office, and I sought you out," she responded, "you have nothing to apologize for. I should have anticipated you."

Casually, Thornton approached his desk, sat down, and asked her to be seated.

She did so.

"Can I get you anything?" he asked. "A glass of tea, perhaps. Forgive the lack of accommodations, but I am not used to receiving ladies' company when at the mill."

"I do not require anything, thank you. I understand that this is a place of business, and I do not wish to discomfort you."

"You do not disturb me. A day at the mill is like any other."

"In fact, I come with business in mind."

"Do you?"

"Yes. Mr. Thornton, I am going to do something very presumptuous and very inconsiderate, in light of our history."

The tone in her voice and her words made Thornton lean forward. Was she about to ask him something that would hurt her heart, or further hurt his?

"Inconsiderate?" he echoed.

"Yes. Mr. Thornton, I am about to ask you for a favor."

A favor? Despite being wholly ignorant of what the favor was, her appealing to him could not help but make him feel flattered. To ask him for a favor meant that she respected his abilities, at least. That was better than nothing. After all, he must start somewhere.

"A favor? What do you require of me?"

"I know that the strike has set your work behind, and I regret that things have been more difficult for you. However, there is one man, another factory laborer, who can assist in the work. He is strong, sturdy, and steadfast. The strike did make him wild from the circumstances, but if you were to employ him, then it would enhance the output of your product."

"You need me to employ someone?"

"Yes. I do not wish to force your hand in any way. I merely ask this, as a favor."

Thornton leaned back in his chair. Rubbing his eyes, he made a deduction.

"I suppose, you are referring to Nicholas Higgins."

Margaret looked surprised that he would know that.

"Yes," she answered. "It's for him that I come."

Thornton's familiar scowl returned to his features. Margaret prepared herself, aware that she had her work quite cut out for her.

"I am aware," Margaret continued, "that I have no right to ask you this, but I know that you are his best chance."

"Am I? There are other factories."

"Those factories will not employ him even if he did apply. There is a matter of pride with him."

"Pride? If there is such, then I wonder he would have a woman make an appeal for his side, as opposed to coming himself."

Despite her initial desire to say only kind words to Mr. Thornton, she was not altogether ready to abandon her pride.

"Why?" She declared, bitter. "Why is a man weaker for needing a lady's assistance? We are the ones who bring you into the world, are we not? Yes, we are. Therefore when, while you grew up, do you all forget how much fortitude we possess? Is your mother not strong, Thornton? You have often told me so. She has been your foundation on what you placed yourself on. Well, isn't she?"

Thornton blinked, having no choice but to realize that he did three things: hurt her pride, forget his past, and did not improve his suit.

"Yes, she is."

"Then why can't I be on her level? Mr. Thornton, whatever our past, I thought that you respected my strength. Am I to be wrong about you?"

Despite himself, a very small smile escaped him.

"No, you are not. I spoke hastily, Miss Hale. Please

believe me, that I do respect your strength. It has been on display many a time. And if I ever forget it, I give you leave to remind me of it."

Now it was Margaret's time to allow a smile to escape her. When seeing her display some happiness in his presence, Thornton could not help but take that as encouragement. If he could make her smile, then maybe, she could grow to like him. How quickly the mind can jump from hopelessness to hope.

"I do believe that you are generous of heart, Miss Hale," Thornton continued, "but I cannot feel comfortable with the idea."

"Why not? Is it because of Mr. Higgins's dealings with the strike?"

Thornton did not respond, at first. Rather, he looked sullen and looked down at his desk.

"I am right, aren't I?" Margaret pursued.

"What if you are?" he asked, stoic. "What then? I know that your sympathies lie with the workers, and not with us masters, yet..."

"I am not here to take sides when it comes to this matter. I am willing to consider all sides when it comes to this. For the workers, the loss of a higher wage must have felt like an ultimate disgrace and to feel so let down like that—well, I can see their desire for a better life. However, from your perspective, it must have looked altogether different. It must have looked like your workers had quite abandoned you, without caring for your orders, for the output of your cotton, and leaving you in the delicate place that you are now. Did you feel like your pride had been hurt? I know that, between the master and the worker, there is a merry war that goes on. But it must have felt painful to see them turn out on you in that fashion."

"I felt nothing," Thornton said abruptly.

Too abruptly.

Margaret was not intimidated, nor was she willing to change the subject. In fact, she was quite interested in what they had to say to one another.

"You said that too quickly," Margaret deduced. "Too quickly for it to be true."

Thornton stood up and went to the window, leaning his hand against the windowpane.

"And now you are trying to steady yourself," Margaret furthered. Despite himself, Thornton turned back to her. Standing up, Margaret went over to him. "That must mean that I am right. Aren't I? Your pride was hurt by the strike, and not just your purse. You felt as if you had been abandoned."

"Very well," Thornton admitted, "I was. I am not stone, whether anyone believes so! I am not. Their turning out felt like ignorance and indolence was rising against me and swallowing me up. I hated what they had done! They put me in the position where I had to import the Irish. They attack the Irish, and they attacked you. And then, when their rebellion was crushed, they do what all roaches do: slink back to those they despised and ask to feed off the fruit from the hand that they bit! They have caused disarray, ruined their own lives, and now expect me to save them! I cannot help but admit that I despised them. And perhaps I still do!"

He was about to rant further when he felt Margaret Hale place her hand on his shoulder. The touch of her hand on his person steadied him and quieted his temper.

"I am not telling you to not be angry," Margaret offered. "From your perspective, perhaps you were heartbroken, and you needed to voice your frustrations."

"Could it be?" he asked gently, "that after all this time, you begin to understand me."

"As long as you begin to understand me. No more talk of a man, be he named Nicholas Higgins or yourself, being set down for needing a lady to speak for you. We have voices, therefore, why are we not allowed to use them?"

"I was being pigheaded, wasn't I?"

"Yes, you were. But there is nothing to worry over. I am accustomed to such talk; therefore, I had grown better at giving a proper defense. You have been raised a certain way, and so have I. We have argued before, and we shall argue again."

"Yes, perhaps we shall."

Margaret removed her hand from his shoulder. Thornton missed her hand upon him immediately.

Now that he was in a more rational state, Margaret moved away from him and sat back down. Thornton watched her progress the whole time and only looked away when she turned to face him.

"You are so beautiful," he voiced, unable to control himself.

When hearing his compliment, Margaret breathed in sharply, unnerved.

"I am sorry," Thornton rushed out. "I did not intend to say that. It must have been very disagreeable to you to hear me speak such nonsense."

"I know that you are sorry. And you have not offended me. I am passed being offended by your preferring me to be in your life. Perhaps, I was being foolish myself."

Thornton walked up to her slowly, unable to control

himself. Seeing the intensity in his eye was going too far, however. It was too much, and now, sadly, Margaret had to put an end to it.

"Mr. Thornton," she said, "please, sir... remember yourself."

"Yes," he said, blinking. Removed from the spell that he cast on himself, he moved back to his seat on the other side of his desk. "We were talking about this Higgins fellow."

"Yes, we were. Mr. Thornton, I am not asking you to hire him, but only to give him a chance to be heard. If I were to suggest that you would see him, would you give him the chance to apply at Marlborough Mills? And if he proves to be a good candidate, which I believe he will, then will you give him a chance? I will not ask for anything further than that. What you choose is your own province and I have no power over your judgment. I only have the power to ask. But hopefully that is a power, in its own right."

"Yes, it is. Very well. I shall consider him."

Margaret was happy at this but was a little uneasy when she realized that she had to mention a second favor.

"And there is no chance of you considering Boucher as well, is there?"

"Oh," Thornton said, shaking his head, "that I will not abide."

"Boucher didn't even want to join the strike, initially. In fact, I have it upon very good authority that he was against the strike, because he believed that his children would starve on the strike money that the union was going to pay. He was forced into it."

"Men are only forced into things when they are easy to break."

"You and I both know, that when many men are pressing their faces upon you, it's easy to be persuaded to commit a wrong. Mobs are dangerous things. The pressure can be immense."

"He caused the strike that hurt you, the Bennet girls, and Rasby. Then he wanted to attack the Irish. There were women in that bunch as well. Miss Hale, I just cannot consider the idea just now. I know that he has children, but some of the Irishwomen were pregnant. Did he think of them?"

Margaret did not respond at first, because Boucher was like most men and women in the world: there was a duality in his nature. He had great qualities, but he also had gruesome ones.

"There is much truth in what you say," Margaret acknowledged. "I am not going to pretend otherwise. He was starving and it made him wild from circumstances. But that is no excuse." She started, surprised at her own confession. "Indeed...there is no excuse. But I must think of the children. Lizzy has written to her uncle Gardiner, to see if he will employ Boucher in London, and if so, then he will remove his family from Milton."

"That is a better idea. If Boucher is gone, and he is in a new town, he has no chance of stirring anything up."

"But if Lizzy is not successful, and Mr. Gardiner does not require a new worker, will you consider Boucher? Please?"

"Would this make you happy?"

"My happiness doesn't matter in this case."

"I know. But still, would it make you happy?"

"Yes, it would. And I suspect that you know that."

"Perhaps I did. Very well. Tell this Higgins fellow that he can apply. He must be on time, mind you."

"He shall be."

Feeling that all her efforts had come to fruition, Margaret Hale exhaled, fully relieved.

When seeing her more relaxed, Thornton felt his body lose its tenseness. On the contrary, as she felt better, so did he.

"You look happier," he noted. He was rewarded with a gentle laugh on her part.

"It's because I am."

He stood up but remained behind his desk.

"You thought that I was going to say no, didn't you?"

"In truth, I didn't know what to expect."

"I can see that as well. I am not an ogre, Miss Hale. Occasionally, I can be reasonable."

"Never fear, Mr. Thornton. My opinion of you has changed a great deal, and I am aware that you are a good man. You have had much to overcome, and you have. And I must remember that your history has led to you, perhaps, thinking very meanly on the lifestyle of those under your employment. Since you have risen to such heights, you feel that the others have not the will to be as disciplined."

"That's precisely how I felt," he said, relief filling his voice.

"Yes. And therefore, perhaps it may take time for you to see what they are truly undergoing. Time helps us all, doesn't it?"

"Yes, it does."

She smiled and then she stopped.

"No," he stressed, "none of that. I rarely get to see you smile. It is a wonderous thing."

"I have always been a little apprehensive of emotional

displays," Margaret confessed. "I often found it to be a sign of weakness."

"So have I," Thornton responded. "But in my world, it truly is indicative of weakness."

"You have had to be strong to get ahead in life."

"Yes."

Without apprehension, they both looked at each other. In their eyes was a mutual understanding that was food for them both.

For Margaret, it was the joys that came with peace.

With Thornton, it was the joys that came with knowing that her opinion of him was improving. He couldn't ignore that, but feeling the selfishness of emotion, he could not help but press his suit.

When realizing that they had been looking at each other for too long, Margaret suddenly grew apprehensive. Despite their past, she had begun to feel something. Her stomach grew upset, and her heart felt as if it was pounding for some strange reason. It was altogether a new sensation that she didn't like, in the slightest.

"I should go now," Margaret said, "much to do."

"Yes," he said, "yes, of course. Please tell your father that I shall see him tomorrow evening, for our lessons."

"I will. He will be glad to see you. Especially since Mr. Bell has returned to London, my father will treasure your company now more than ever."

"I am glad of it."

Going to the door, he stood there to receive her as she left. Nodding, she walked past him, but Thornton called out to her.

"Yes, Mr. Thornton?"

Silently, he raised up his arm, reaching his hand out, for her to shake it.

"The first time we did this," he said, "we made terrible work of it."

"Yes, we did. Believe me, I was wholly ignorant of the offense that I had caused. I was merely flustered."

"I know now."

"Yes, yes, you do."

At last, Margaret placed her hand in his, and he covered his other hand in hers, to show a union. A tense union. Margaret did not meet his eye, because she feared what she would see.

"Good day, Mr. Thornton," she said.

"Good day, Miss Hale."

At last, he released her hand, and she walked down the hall, fully aware that he was watching her as she left.

As swift as one's feet could go, hers did progress. As soon as she left Thornton's office, Margaret Hale walked quickly down the hall, out of the mill and through the courtyard.

Further and further, she walked, without any sense of where she was headed.

The people who moved around her were like waifs, as if they were no more than puffs of smoke, mingled with the same fumes that were released from the mills' chimneys. They felt no more or less corporeal than as if they had been ghosts.

This nonsensical outlook remained with Margaret until her preoccupation drove her to such a level of blindness that she collided with a worker who had just entered the courtyard.

This sudden impact with a person gave her the jolt back to life that she needed. She returned even further back to the world of the living when she looked up and saw that it was Colin, the Irishman.

"Miss Hale?" he said, removing his hat. Instinctively, he held her arms to steady her, but when he noticed how disorientated she was, he did not release her immediately.

"Mr. McFlannery," Margaret said, breathing a sigh of relief.

"Are you quite well, lass?" he asked, looking into her eyes. "You look out of sorts and all that."

"I, I am well."

"Miss Hale, with respect, you don't look like it."

"What do I look like?"

"Like you can't find your bearings. Did something hit you hard?"

"No one has hurt me. I mean that."

"I'm not saying that something physically hurt you. It looks like it has to do with your mind, that's all."

Margaret looked up at him, horrified that she had allowed her emotions to be so easily readable. This was everything that she didn't want.

Doing her best, Margaret closed her eyes, swallowed her emotions and when she looked at Colin again, her face was calm and unreadable.

"Never fear, Mr. McFlannery, I am well."

"Now you are," he replied, keenly. "But a second ago, you weren't. You're a game one, aren't you?"

"I can't imagine what you mean, sir."

"You know perfectly well what I mean. You are good at overcoming yourself, aren't you?"

Margaret looked down.

"Yes," she admitted, "I do not mean to compliment myself, but I am."

"I like a gal with a good open temper, so that don't suit

me well. But if that's what you prefer, then good for you. But I saw what I saw, and I know what I know. I know that, a second ago, you were about to cry."

Margaret looked back and forth, worried that someone would overhear them.

"No need to worry," Colin assured her, "no one thinks our conversation is worth overhearing, so you're safe."

"But I do not know that for sure," Margaret pressed. "Please, Mr. McFlannery, if you have any respect for me, do not mention this, will you? To no one."

"Aye, lass, I won't. And that's for certain. But at least let me get you a cab. I don't want you to be walking when you're flustered. I need to set you straight, right and proper."

"Very well," Margaret said, willing to give in. "Maybe I have walked too far today."

"Yes," he said, his eyes shrewd and discerning, "we'll just say that, shall we?"

"That's all I wish for it to be said. Thank you."

He led her to the public road, and they were not left waiting for long. A couple minutes went by, and a cab turned down the street. Colin hailed it, it stopped, and he helped her inside. When he closed the door for her, Margaret reached into her purse to give him something.

"No, Miss Hale," Colin said, "don't do that. We're both too classy for such a gesture, aren't we?"

Margaret smiled.

"Yes, we are. May God bless you, Colin."

"And you as well, Miss Hale," he said, tipping his hat to her. The cab took off, Colin waved, then turned around and he met John, where they walked into the factory together.

Now that she was alone in the cab, Margaret removed her hat. Suddenly, there had been too much pressure on her head, and she felt the confinement of her clothing. Everything felt as if it was out to suffocate her. Her own clothing and shoes rebelled against her.

Yet the hat removal offered no easing of comfort. Her head still ached.

Her stomach still churned.

Her legs felt as if they had transformed into jelly.

And the cab felt as if it was a prison that was locking her in.

Ah, to be home again in Helstone! There was all the air there, all the liberties.

But then, for a moment, she wondered if she did want to return there. For what would she get if she were to return? Her mother was not there. Her father's heart was no longer there either. No matter the present circumstances, her father loved being in Milton, despite all the upheaval that they had experienced.

Also, she had been raised in Harley Street, in London. She had been, in all essentials, a child of three worlds.

Of London, among the higher levels of London society.

Of Helstone, in its simpler ways and provincial manners.

And now of Milton, under clouds there was the constant toiling of industry and power.

Now that she was here, Margaret realized that she didn't have one home, not one set identity. She had always thought so, but now she was not certain.

And Nicholas and Mary Higgins!

They were here and she had become a part of their lives.

And what of Mr. Thornton?

No, no, no! She must not think of him. But she had to. No, she mustn't. But she must.

'What is happening to me?' She asked. 'What is happening?'

At last, the cab dropped her off at her home, she paid him, and she dashed into her house.

Rushing past Dixon and Mary, she quickly gave her excuses that she needed time alone and to tell her parents that she had returned.

Going to her room, she closed the door behind her and once more, felt the confinement of it all.

The room was so small and provoked her.

Her clothing was terse and inconvenient.

She removed her shoes.

Still not enough.

She removed her stockings.

Still not enough.

Then she undid her petticoat, throwing it on the chair. Next was her blouse, which she was fortunate to have been able to remove on her own. She undid her stays, and finally, she removed all the pins from her hair, letting it all fall down to her shoulders and rest along her back.

There, standing in no more than her chemise, she raised out her arms and breathed deeply.

This was the only freedom that she could find. The world was outside. From within, she could rise into the sky and soar wherever she wished, released from the burdens of all earthly cares.

Then suddenly, she realized that she had no notion of where she wanted to go.

She did not wish to return to Harley Street.

She missed Helstone, but her parents weren't there anymore. They were in Milton.

Everyone that she loved was now in Milton. And some she loved were leaving. She did not want that.

The same could be said of Thornton, who would lose Darcy's company as well. They were all going back to the South.

And that left Mr. Thornton. But what of him?

Suddenly, her soul didn't wish to fly anywhere. Rather, it was more content with coming to crash back down to earth, among the dust and dirt in Milton Common. There, she felt that she would rise, not happy, but hearty, and willing to endure it all.

Why did she feel this impulse?

Once more, her mind turned toward Mr. Thornton. In her mind's eye, she could see his face. Every line on his brow and every gesture that he made.

Why did her mind wander to him?

No, it couldn't be?

Suddenly, she felt cold. Pulling back the covers, she got into her bed and folded the blankets over herself.

Thornton's image still intruded her thoughts, and she couldn't release him.

Once more, she drew the covers around her neck, as if it would protect her.

How did this happen? At what moment did she grow to feel for him?

But it didn't matter how, but only at what.

She felt a tenderness for him. It had come on gradually, but it was true, nevertheless. She was growing to finally feel for him, romantically.

And it was everything that she didn't want.

Chapter 9

Departing News

News of Colonel Fitzwilliam's good fortune had spread throughout the regiment, and many toasts were involved. It was a day of rejoicing indeed.

Kitty was able to revel in the popularity of her beloved, for the men were truly happy with his ascension to greatness. Colonel Fitzwilliam, while happy to maintain his title, was equally profuse in his pleasure of relinquishing his duties.

In those three days, many letters were sent out.

Mr. Bingley wrote to his housekeeper in Hertfordshire, to make sure that their house was open to receive us there as his guests, after the wedding.

I wrote to inform Mary that we would be in Hertfordshire soon after we wed.

Colonel Fitzwilliam wrote to his aunt, acknowledging his gratefulness for everything and his vowing to be a good heir.

"There is the possibility," Colonel Fitzwilliam announced to us, "that Aunt Catherine will try to persuade us into choosing her wedding arrangements when we will be there."

"What are the chances," Kitty asked, amused, "that she will get her way?"

"In Kent, there is a saying: anything is possible."

"Would you believe," she asked, taking his hand, and kissing it, "that we have the same saying in Hertfordshire? In Britain, there is room for many places with miracles."

"Well," Mr. Bingley announced, "let us prepare ourselves for a quick meeting and a swift marriage."

"I would prefer it if our friends saw us married," I said, "but maybe, in this circumstance, the great lady ought to be indulged."

"My fiancée wishes to indulge my aunt?" Mr. Darcy asked, surprised. "Now that is a sight that I'd never thought I'd see."

"Miracles," I pressed, "I was born in a place where they exist, remember?"

"Yes," he smiled, "you were."

Mr. Darcy wrote to his sister to meet us at Lady Catherine's. That was the final thing. After all of this, I would finally be meeting my fiancé's sister, Miss Georgiana Darcy.

At first, Colonel Fitzwilliam was worried that he would be forced to remain in his duties for two fortnights, out of a desire to not give quick notice of his release.

Yet, Colonel Forster had assured him that he could soon disperse of his obligations. Captain Carter would take over the Colonel's duties until a proper replacement could be found. It would not take long, because the upper-class were always clamoring for openings of the captaincy in Her majesty's service. The Colonel's new station in life allowed a proper transfer for another rich man's younger son who needed somewhere to fall in life. And thus, the equal balance of English society, and the successful flow of transference, was complete.

Colonel Fitzwilliam was amazed at how well it all had worked out for his situation. He could leave his older life behind, with friends and family ahead, finally feeling that a kind disposition and a generous nature could very well be rewarded in life.

He had his Kitty Bennet.

He had land.

A wonderful house.

And a proper inheritance that was maintained due to his aunt's economic hand.

Finally, the day arrived when the regiment was to leave, without the Colonel. The officers and their wives were all packed away and ready to travel to Newcastle, where they would be stationed for the season.

Once more, the regiment would leave with as much pomp and circumstance that they had when they arrived.

Yet, before all that, the wives had to be properly put up in their carriages and to depart with the luggage.

When they did, Jane, Kitty, Margaret, Rasby, and I had come to see Lydia and Plato Pitcher off.

The Lucas sisters wanted to come. However, they were unable. Since it was time for them to prepare themselves for work, they knew it was better now than later. The only way for them to adjust to their new employment was to dive in. Therefore, Charlotte was at Granger Hall, taking notes for Mr. Hale. Meanwhile, Maria was undergoing her first day as the governess for the Kirkpatrick family.

"Well," Lydia said, before she entered the carriage, "I daresay that Milton has given us many adventures. We can say that for it."

"Lydia," I said, "I just realized something."

"And what would that be?"

"That, out of all of us, you are not only the first married, but you are the first to be a mother."

Lydia laughed.

"I know, and I actually like my husband. Forgive me, but there is something to say for that, with me being the youngest and all."

"And I think you really might be a good mother."

Lydia gave me a look.

"You're just noticing that now?" She shoved my shoulder, playfully. "How can you, a woman who is so intelligent, be so slow to realize that?"

She hugged me.

"Unleash hell upon Mr. Collins, Lizzy."

"I will. That is certain."

Lydia embraced Jane.

"Give Mr. Bingley all the children that he can endure."

"I will," Jane said, chuckling.

Lydia embraced Kitty.

"I will always miss you."

"And I with you," Kitty replied.

Lydia offered Margaret Hale her hand.

"I know that you do not like such public displays of affection."

Margaret shook her hand.

"You understand me, at last," Margaret responded.

"Not really. But I accept you nevertheless."

She turned to Rasby, raised out her arms and Rasby hugged her fondly.

"Because of you, Kitty was not alone when she came here," Lydia said, "and I owe you for that. I never meant to leave her, you know. But she fell in the right direction."

"I never thought anyone noticed."

"I'm the least intelligent one in my family. That leads to me being the most observant."

Having finished arranging the carriages for the wives, Plato approached us.

"And what of me?" he asked. "Will you miss me, I wonder?"

We all assured him that we would, as we all hugged him.

"I know," he answered our assurances, "something tells me that I left a strong impression, whether you like it or not."

A joker, he was, to the bitter end! First Mr. Bell left. Now it was Plato, and then it was Lydia and Denny. And then there were few of us left, and then there would be fewer still. How strange, and how provocative.

At last, Lydia stood back and looked on us all.

"Three of my sisters are soon to become some of the richest women in England." She stepped into the carriage, next to Mrs. Forster, and then she leaned out of the window. "And don't forget your unapologetic sister!" She raised her arm up and shot her fist in the air. "Woooo!!!"

Her carriage drove off, with her cackling all the way.

"Now that is how you leave a city," Rasby commented.

"Especially if your name is Lydia Bennet," Margaret Hale added.

"True," I said. "So true."

As we walked back home, Kitty and Rasby strayed behind us

all, but I was still able to overhear what they were speaking about.

"You really thought no one noticed that you have been a loyal companion to me," Kitty said to Raspberry.

"Well, I did notice a little, but never in such an overt way. I just thought that people accepted me in your company because I was convenient."

"They never thought that way."

"I know. It took me a while to become wiser." Rasby looked ahead. "I will miss you," Rasby whispered. "I perhaps was not as happy for you as I ought to have been. Perhaps I was being selfish. I was afraid of being alone. But I am happy for you now." Rasby chuckled. "Better late than never, eh?"

"I understood why you were upset with how things worked out. Especially since I knew that you did truly appreciate my good fortune. Rasby, I know that you are used to the North. You have always been fiercely independent that way. But if it were possible, could you see yourself adjusting to life on a Southern estate? Great homes like Rosings Park are not the most interesting of places, but you deserve some rest, don't you think?"

Rasby looked at her.

"Are you saying that you would consider taking me with you?"

"Would you be amenable to the idea of it? I need a companion, with such a place. Especially since I will be quite out of my natural element and habit, at first. I will need someone to run to when Lady Catherine will give me an imposing look or make me feel like I quite fail at being a mistress to the place."

"Why would she do that?"

"I've heard all about her. She is a strict woman, and I am

not used to such strict ways. I will need someone to turn to when she makes me upset."

"But would she be upset with my coming? Is she amenable to the idea of it? I should be pained, for myself and for you if she were to take one look at me and turn me out of the house. I don't want you to experience that. Nor do I wish to experience it."

"But if she does agree to the idea, would you come?"

From behind me, I heard Rasby chuckle and then weep.

"Yes, yes, I would come."

"Well, this will be interesting, won't it?" Kitty said.

"Yes, it is. I'm just so very scared at the idea of it all not working out."

"Remember what we said about Kent. Anything is possible."

Chapter 10

Welcoming News

We returned Margaret back to Crampton Street. We thought it best to pay a visit and inquire after Mrs. Hale's health. She might have been active when we saw her, but her pale complexion and whooping cough gave all the indication of Doctor Donaldson's diagnosis. Unless some miracles were to find its way to Milton, perhaps it was not for long now.

On our way to Rasby's home, Mrs. Hale's health soon became the main subject of our discussion. Yet, it proved not to be frivolous or flimsy. On the contrary, an interesting topic was brought up from an unlikely quarter.

"Lizzy," Kitty said to me as we walked, "I have another thought."

"What thought was that?" I asked.

"Well, Richard and I have been talking about Mrs. Hale."

"Yes," Jane said, "these next few months will be hard on us all. The poor woman."

"Poor woman, indeed, but that's what I've been thinking

about. I told Richard about how delicate Mrs. Hale was, but she didn't fall ill till she came to Milton."

"If you suspect that there is something about the air that does not agree with her," I said, "I have considered that as well."

"It's not just the air," Kitty said, "but the living quarters. Richard is terribly clever about this. He doesn't just believe that it's the air, but it's something that he has begun to notice about people with weak constitutions. Now, he may not be a constructer, but he is shrewd and observant. He believes that sometimes, houses and lodgings can be constructed from objects and equipment that can be dangerous to someone who is not accustomed to it."

This idea surprised me, but the more I thought of it, the more that I considered the prospect that there might be some truth in the matter. After all, if you transfer from one living condition to another, without being fully aware of the change in the quarters, there always can be something foreign to a person—something that does not agree with their health altogether.[1]

"That is a wise deduction," I observed. "The Colonel impresses me. Especially since Doctor Donaldson did not think of it himself."

"It would make sense that he didn't, though," Rasby pointed out, "Donaldson is a medicine man, but not one who would be expert in Mrs. Hale's full health history or living

---

1. Homes in that era were not always constructed properly or were maintained. Many homes actually contained asbestos in them, and slowly affected its occupants, easily causing diseases including lung cancer. Also in Victorian era, most homes would easily contain lead-based paint, which caused serious health problems. The only thing that could have prevented Mrs. Hale from getting worse earlier was the wallpaper. That could have stunted the lead's progress.

conditions. Also, there are many problems now that our doctors still are not fully aware of. Remember how long it took doctors here to acknowledge the Moorish healers and that bloodletting was a terrible idea?"

"Yes, that revelation took too long to realize," I said, rolling my eyes. "Moments like that make one determine that maybe a meeting with one's own grandmother can be just as good as the doctor, or better."

"Let's not disparage Doctor Donaldson or his profession just yet," Jane pressed, "for Colonel Fitzwilliam's theory, though intelligent, has not been proven."

"Very well," Kitty said, "but I still trust my fiancé."

"Oh, you had better. Believe in him even when he is wrong. That's my moral medicine for the day."

"Well," Kitty suggested, "when he said that I had a thought. Yes, she is very ill, and yes, it is determined that it cannot be very long now till she...but if that's the case, then there should be nothing to lose."

"Nothing to lose?" I repeated.

"Should we ask Mr. Hale if we could transfer Mrs. Hale to Rosings Park with us? Maybe something in the houses here are making her worse. If we take her there, the rooms are larger, less cramped, and we can have her spend most of her days outside. For, the more that I recall, the country air might help."

"So did the sea air," I noted. "When we went to the seaside at Heston, she looked to be in perfect health. Oh, if only we had time to take her there."

"Of course, for nothing could be cleaner than the sea breeze. And a little bit of sea-bathing could cure her, perhaps. Or give her a little more time."

"Well," I acknowledged, "then I suspect that you are

proposing that we must try and convince the Hales to come with us, to Kent, and see if there is any change in her health."

"It makes sense," Rasby noted. "If Mrs. Hale is already destined for death's door, then what is the error of trying? After all, there *is* nothing to lose."

"And when we marry," Kitty said, "we have the right to enjoy our honeymoon. I fancy that Lady Catherine would not like it if we enjoy a holiday away from her for too long. Therefore, why not go to the coast, and enjoy one of the bathing places in Kent. There's Ramsgate, Deal, Margate, Broadstairs and others. I know that we are planning so much, and thinking we can put it into practice, but since we are planning to save a life, what can be done cannot be done without an attempt, can't it?"

"Precisely so," I said, "tomorrow when I see Darcy, I will ask what he thinks. He likes Mrs. Hale; therefore, I don't see him disagreeing with the notion, especially since you and the Colonel have already discussed it. The main obstacle will chiefly be if Mr. and Mrs. Hale will agree to it. Often, when one is ill, they refuse to move."

Turning to her, I grinned.

"But since fortune has been so fortuitous for us," I said, "I've become very good at not taking 'no' for an answer on things that I know to be right. Brave heart, Kitty, we shall make quick work of this in less than twenty-four hours."

Kitty grinned.

"Two!" She stated.

"Two what?"

"Two very good and charitable thoughts that I have had in less than two days. I don't care what anyone tells me; I have the right to feel good about myself now."

We escorted Rasby home, returned to Frances Street, and were still filled with the natural merriment of bringing things together, while still losing the lovely company of the regiment.

It was strange, but I still felt Plato's departure as well as Lydia's. It's always monstrously unfair when someone latches themselves onto your company so much that you feel the loss very quickly.

Poor mama! She was right about one thing: there is nothing harder than parting with one's friends. One seems so forlorn without them.

Well, sometimes people are meant to walk out of our lives. Some to return, and others to be parted forever.

Those are the two different meanings of friendly departure.

The next day, Darcy and I were walking together in the park. I had told him what Kitty, and I discussed, and he was eager to help.

"But do you really think Mr. Hale will want his wife to be moved?" Darcy asked. "Especially since his work is here."

"His students will still be here when he returns. Everyone has the right to take a holiday, especially when considering his wife's health. He would do anything to keep her alive. Whatever measures that he made when leaving the church, he still loves her and depends on Mrs. Hale. He never did it to be contrary to her or to deliver her into a situation that made her ill. Also, Mrs. Hale was originally Maria Beresford, a woman who was raised to wealth. Maybe, she could be lured back to the South by knowing that she will stay in a place that she once was accustomed to when she was young. That might cheer her."

Darcy looked at me.

"I like Mrs. Hale. I understand her. Or rather, she understands me. Besides," he said, giving me an affectionate look, "no man of true feeling, ever wants to lose his wife. As selfish as it is, we always wish to pass away first, so that we don't have to live without you all. Even when your fate is uncertain as a widow."

"Forgive me for being vulgar again, but selfishness can go to the devil," I declared, "I will do everything I can to stay in your life. If I die first, leaving you alone, I shall never forgive myself."

Laughing, he turned toward me and started walking backwards.

"When we marry, yes, you shall have to adhere to the restrictions of a great mistress to an estate, but for now, might I say that such base talk really becomes you?"

"Truly? Does it add a blush to my cheeks?"

"And a sparkle to your eyes. It also makes you walk quickly."

"And teaches you how to walk backwards," I said, giving him my hand. "There? We are in agreement."

"In every respect," he said, taking my hand.

I skipped around him, kissing his cheek.

"Then shall we about it?"

"Why not?" he answered, "But let's not waste another moment talking of it? To action?"

"Yes, to action!"

Once we agreed, we went to the Hales, and stood at the door, preparing to argue in favor of Kitty and the Colonel's suit.

When the door opened, it was to see Dixon, looking flustered.

"Dixon?" I inquired. "Good day. Is something wrong?"

"Miss Bennet and Mr. Darcy," she said, preoccupied. "To see you both again, that is flattering, and we'd all be very pleased. However, I must inform you both that there is a matter that compels me to inform you that we are not allowing visitors at this time. Rather, we would be happy if you were to visit tomorrow."

Unable to suppress my feelings, I was hurt. When, during our acquaintance, did the Hales ever banish me from their company? I felt a sudden pang of offense, and it must have shown all over my features, because Dixon's traditional strong demeanor gave way to embarrassment.

"Us?" I could not help but utter. "The family does not wish to speak to us?"

Dixon bit her lip, unnerved.

"This is the last thing that we would ever have you believe, missus, I am sure. It is just that there is a delicate matter that prevents me from allowing anyone to enter."

"Is there something the matter with Mrs. Hale?" I asked.

"No, it is not. It is something else altogether. When Miss Hale sees you again, she can explain better than I can."

"I suppose we must go, Lizzy," Darcy said, his tone serious and indicating a sense of being offended. This obviously made Dixon feel even worse.

She made her apologies to us and closed the door.

Breathing heavily, Darcy took my arm, we walked down the stairs, prepared to wonder at what could have occurred to have us barred from the Hales residence, but we were not left to be cast down.

Margaret must have seen us from the window and rushed out of the house to intercept us.

She apologized for Dixon's refusal to give us entry and offered us excuses. She informed us that Dixon had been told to not allow anyone to enter, but as Margaret whispered under her voice, 'I trust you, therefore, please do not let me down'.

She took us inside the house, closed the door immediately, and there was a sense of dread about it all. It was as if she was trying to keep the world outside.

Now that she bolted the door, she went to the windows and made sure that the curtains were properly closed.

"Margaret?" I voiced, watching her mania, "what are you doing?"

"Making certain that there are no prying eyes."

She turned to Darcy and me.

"Lizzy," Margaret said, "I know that I can trust you. Dixon knows that as well. It is just a matter of you, Mr. Darcy."

Mr. Darcy looked somewhat alarmed, and I could not help but find myself offended for his sake.

"For myself, pray?" he asked.

"Margaret," I said, "Mr. Darcy has proven, time and time again, to be a chief ally of yours."

"I know," Margaret said, "but this time, it is different. This time, it is a matter of conscience versus the law."

"The law?" Mr. Darcy echoed, perplexed. "What does this circumstance have to do with the law?"

The law!

Soon, I realized what this was all about. If that was the case, I realized that I had been quite remiss in explaining Margaret's situation. I never prepared him for what had laid in store for us all.

"Mr. Darcy," Margaret implored him, "what I do

pertains to family, and the loyalties that follow. There is no evil in this house. None. It is simply that the matters of naval law allow no room for hearing out a fallen sailor. I know that you are an upstanding man who respects the law, and the order that we live under. Yet, I must ask you to please make allowances for this situation. I want to allow you to see the prodigal side of my family, however, I must ask for you to keep this visit a profound secret."

She looked on us, imploringly.

"Do I have your word that you will please keep a secret and not speak of this at all?"

"Yes," I said, placing my arms in Darcy's. "Believe me when I tell you this, Margaret. You may depend on our silence. If I am correct, I am happy that he is here."

Margaret smiled at me.

"So am I." She looked at Mr. Darcy. "Do I have your word as well?"

"I don't know to what you are referring," Darcy said, "but if it is a matter of family, then I can assure you of being discrete."

"Then I shall be content with that."

We followed her upstairs and were met by Dixon.

"I know you both must be offended," Dixon said, "but mind, I was doing what was best for the family."

"I understand, Dixon," I said, "this is a delicate business. Sometimes, one does not know who to trust."

We both progressed upwards, and each moment filled me with wonder at how I was to receive the gentleman.

I was not left to wait for long before we entered the parlor and a handsome young man stood up and faced us. At first, when he saw us, worry was etched on his features, but soon, it gave way to familiarity and ease.

Frederick Hale had come to Milton.

Chapter 11

Brotherly News

"Mr. Frederick!" I cried. "You are Mr. Frederick Hale, are you not?"

"Miss Bennet!" Frederick replied, equally joyous. "Unless I am wrong, and do not have your identity correct."

"It is correct. You know me well enough by sight, sir?"

"If we met before, that would not account for it. The reason that I know you is because Margaret described you so well in her letter to me. As such, I suspect that I would know you anywhere. Well, is this not something to be amazed at?" He turned to Margaret. "Margaret, you never told me that Miss Bennet was your companion in Milton?"

"I did not wish to speak too much news in a letter," Margaret said, "for fear of it going astray."

"Very wise," Frederick responded, "my actions should not implicate anyone else other than myself. But Miss Bennet, I am happy to find you like my sister: so robust and handsome. If it's not too bold, but you are looking remarkably well."

"Thank you. I am amazed. I thought you should not know me."

He pointed to his forehead.

"When it comes to faces, my mind is like a vault. When it comes to names, that is another matter entirely."

Turning to my left, he looked on Mr. Darcy.

"Oh," I said, "forgive me. Mr. Hale, this is my fiancé, Mr. Darcy, the Master of Pemberley, Derbyshire. Mr. Darcy, this is Mr. Frederick Hale, Margaret's brother."

Apprehensive of this stranger in his midst, Frederick Hale offered his hand to shake. Mr. Darcy, equally apprehensive, shook it.

"Sir," Mr. Darcy said.

"A pleasure to make your acquaintance," Frederick said.

Margaret and I saw the tenseness between them, and I knew that I had to do something to end the awkwardness. Margaret's skill was never in easing tension or misunderstanding. Sometimes, she seemed to prefer to allow awkwardness to build, or to create it herself. I did not acknowledge such to slight her because I did not think anything that she did not think of herself already.

"I suppose explanations are due," I said, "but Mr. Hale, I can assure you that Mr. Darcy understands the importance of secrecy. You can depend on him."

"I confess," Mr. Darcy said, "I would prefer to hear all that I ought to know on the matter."

"Dixon," Margaret said, "please tell father that Mr. Darcy and Elizabeth are present."

"I will, miss," Dixon said, then she turned to Darcy and I. "Mrs. Hale took a turn for the worse this morning and must keep to her bed."

We nodded our understanding, and Dixon went off.

Now that we were settled into the company, Frederick was aware that he owed an explanation to Mr. Darcy, who was the chief stranger to his life. Since I could not remember if I told Mr. Darcy this history or not, I thought it best to elaborate. Better to repeat oneself, rather than make assumptions.

"Darcy," I began, "Mr. Frederick was a sailor who found himself to be against the law, due to circumstances."

"Circumstances?" Mr. Darcy repeated.

"Miss Bennet puts it delicately," Frederick said, "I sailed under a Captain Reed, and due to his abusive tendencies, I assisted in leading a mutiny."

Mr. Darcy raised an eyebrow.

"A mutiny?"

"My brother had no choice," Margaret supported, "please, Mr. Darcy, I know that it appears as erroneous. However, Captain Reed was insane."

"I know that I must appear as accepting chaos and defying the rights of a subordinate," Frederick responded. "But Captain Reed would beat the children who worked under him within an inch of their lives, for the smallest mistake. He would make it impossible for them to perform their duties without fear of the lash, even threatening those who did not perform swiftly enough. Sailors died under his employ, for no reason at all. Sir, I could not call myself a man if I stood by and allowed it to happen. None of us could. As such, I am one of the few men who did not hang for his offenses, because I fled England for a time. Yet, I return, upon hearing that my mother was ill. You understand that I had to return. What son would I be if I did not?"

Mr. Darcy did not have time to respond to this plea because Mr. Hale came downstairs, giddy at the prospect of his son being amongst us.

Of course, he was sad over his wife being ill, but naturally the joys of seeing his child again, after so many years of separation, had no choice but to be the predominant emotion.

"Miss Bennet and Mr. Darcy!" Mr. Hale called, walking up to us eagerly. "You have finally met my son."

"We have," I said.

"I confess that I was quite amazed myself when I saw him." He looked like a proud father. "I declare, I forgot how handsome my son was."

"Oh, Father," Frederick replied, bashful. "You exaggerate."

"He does not," Margaret said, equally impressed. "It had been so many years since seeing you that the difference from the time that you visited us on Harley Street to now is remarkable."

"It is the wonderful sun that I have experienced in Cadiz," Frederick said, "that is what accounts for the transformation. There, we see the sun more than you all do here in England."

"And the North more than anything else," Margaret answered, "here in Milton, the sun is not a friend we see as often as we would like."

"I can imagine such," Frederick looked around, "when I last saw you all, it was either in Harley Street or Helstone. Therefore, to see you all here, in such a different environment, was altogether a change. Then again, I changed myself, haven't I?"

"How is Mrs. Hale?" I asked. "Did you find your mother to be able to recognize you?"

"When I first arrived," Frederick said as we sat down, "she was sleeping, so I knew that it was better not to interrupt. When she woke this morning, I was able to meet her." His eyes became remarkable in the variety of emotions that ran through it. First, there was wonder. Then there was sorrow. Next, there was regret, and finally resignation. "How I missed her. After all, you only have one mother, you know? I don't know how I was able to endure for so long without seeing her."

"We both were separated from her for too long," Margaret said. "I was sent away, for my cousin needed a companion, and you had to go away to make a life for yourself."

"And what a life it was," he said, "while I confess to being happy to be in Cadiz, and Spain is the perfect place for my current condition, it doesn't change the fact that I am banished from my home country."

"Oh, Frederick," Mr. Hale said, apprehensive in our company, "perhaps it is not best to talk of such matters now."

"I wish not to do so, but I suspect that Miss Bennet and Mr. Darcy shall want me to fully explain myself, since they are not very well acquainted with me."

"I confess, I am starved from curiosity," Mr. Darcy said, "you have any evidence of your captain's tyranny?"

"That is the very problem with life on a ship," Frederick said, "there is a saying: what happens in a sloop remains in a sloop. The children that he tormented bordered on torture, and the sailor's death that he caused was attributed to his own negligence. Very few of us officers who took part in the mutinous act escaped the viciousness of the courts. Those who were caught pleaded their case, but it did not matter. Captain Reed's insanity will always be protected and shielded by the law, due to his rank. Rank scares everyone.

So do those sorts of men because they conceal that evil so well. It's as if those sorts of men are very good at mesmerizing the world."

"It is their position," Mr. Hale stressed, "and the strict edicts of obedience that they demand."

"I still wonder that we cannot assist in getting you acquitted," Margaret said.

"Especially since it had been so long ago," I stressed, "does the law still chase you?"

"Alas it does," Frederick answered, "to my dismay. The fact is, that no matter how awful and disreputable the captain was, the courts will always vote in support of him rather than the mutinous crowd. For, no matter the circumstances, order must be maintained, especially on the seas."

"Precisely," Darcy confirmed. "No matter the reasons for revolt, the legal system can never sympathize with the mutineers. If it does, then that will set an example for the rest of the trade."

"For, if they support the mutiny," Frederick continued, "then that will lead to other mutinies taking place. The Navy will not allow that, at any costs. Therefore, to expect justice to occur on my side will never be. As such, I have no choice but to remain an exile from my home country and come to visit my parents under the cover of night."

He looked around at the room and then turned back to us.

"I wish that I could take you all with me, to Cadiz. And we could all be happy there. After all, time has taught me, that it's not places that matter, but it is the people that make home feel as such."

Dixon entered.

"Master Frederick," Dixon announced, "your mother is awake again and she is calling for you."

"Yes," Frederick said, "of course."

Jumping up eagerly, he excused himself and dashed off to her room.

Now that Frederick was gone, I could appeal to Mr. Hale.

"You must be happy, sir, to have both your children under one roof."

"Quite so," Mr. Hale said, eagerly. "Quite so. Oh, Elizabeth, I cannot tell you how happy I am now. If there is one thing that can cheer a man from hearing—that his wife is indisposed, this does help. To see one's children again, it helps very much. Mr. Darcy, I am certain that Lizzy knows, but I must ask that you reserve judgment on the matter. My son is a very amiable fellow. He is just passionate. Besides, I didn't raise him to be so inconsiderate of his fellow man to idly stand by and allow abuse to occur. Whatever his actions, they were honorable. Please, do consider that."

"I suppose this is a complicated matter," Mr. Darcy stated, and that was all that he could say. I understood that he didn't fully sympathize just yet. He needed time.

"I see your resemblance in him," I said.

"Nonsense," Mr. Hale said, "he is much handsomer than I ever was."

"Not as much in visage as in spirit. I don't refer to your looks as much as to your nerve and daring. After all, your son risked mutiny to overcome inequality, becoming a deserter. You could not stand idly by and swear to doctrines that you would not adhere to, thus making you a dissenter. Did his courage inspire yours? Or was it your nature working through him?"

His eyes widened at this, which led me to realize that maybe I had taken a step too far somewhere.

"Forgive me," I said, "I was being facetious."

"No, you weren't," he said heavily, "it is just that I never noted the parallel between us before. I suppose, now that I think about it, he did inherit some of my traits—or I inherited his in the reverse. Who would have thought?"

Mr. Hale laughed, sadly.

"Now I wonder that no matter what, we both would have made no other choice. I would still be here, despite any change in past circumstances. The only regret that I have is Mrs. Hale's health being so indifferent. I wish for a miracle, but I know that I do not have the right to ask for them."

"Actually," I said, "you did not need to. I cannot guarantee that a miracle will occur, but we can try. Kitty and Colonel Fitzwilliam have had a remarkable idea. It will require some exertion on Mrs. Hale's part, regarding traveling. But I think, by putting their heads together, they aimed to give you more time with her."

After discussing Kitty's plan to Mr. Hale, we were both surprised that Mr. Hale did not consider any impediment to the plan, nor did anything to consider any complications of the matter. With eagerness, he showed himself amenable to it.

"You all really would assist us in this way?" Mr. Hale asked Mr. Darcy and me.

"Yes," Mr. Darcy declared, "if we write to my aunt, telling her to expect your family, and that Mrs. Hale is an invalid, she can have the rooms prepared in time. She is the sort of woman who will criticize me for my presumptuousness, and in the next moment, will give way to the gaiety of having so many people around her. If Mrs. Hale should survive the journey, Lady Catherine would bring in the best country doctors, as well as provide Mrs. Hale with much fresh air. I think it might assist Mrs. Hale. There can be no guarantee, but only an attempt."

"You would do all that for us, Mr. Darcy?" Mr. Hale asked, his eyes wide with gratitude.

"Yes, I would, sir."

"You are too generous, so very generous. I knew the Bennet sisters would always be there to stand by our family. It is who they are. But to expect such kindness from you and the Colonel, well sir, that is more than I could have hoped for."

Thus was the gratitude of Mr. Hale. Eagerly, he continued to be profuse in his thanks.

All the while Margaret was silent.

When we realized that she said nothing, we turned to her.

"Margaret," I asked, "are you not pleased? This way, you can see us married at Kent, and we can have friends beside us during the happy event, while trying to help your mother."

"I am not against the scheme at all," Margaret said. However, she said it as she often did. Since she combined her strength of feeling with a concealment of her emotions, she didn't indicate too much. "Truly, I appreciate the matter. It is only that this presents the idea of Frederick. Frederick will want to see mama nursed back to health, and I don't think he anticipated leaving too soon."

"Ah, Margaret," I sighed, "always seeing the doomy side of the matter."

Margaret rolled her lip.

"Eliza, you know that I am happy."

"You don't have to be allergic to the idea of displaying it."

Realizing that her love for concealment had stretched too far, Margaret let out a sigh. Finally, she allowed herself to look happy.

"I am happy at the idea; I have just been so used to hearing negative news on mama's health, that I have been told to prepare myself too much, at this point. Give me time to rally. But I just cannot help but wonder if mama will be wishing to be moved, and to consider Frederick in the matter."

"Then perhaps I can propose a suggestion," I said, "if Frederick wishes to join us, then we can easily introduce him as a distant cousin of yours rather than a brother. Anything is possible."

"And," Mr. Darcy continued, "if Mrs. Hale is still of the strength, after our wedding, we can take her to one of the seaside bathing-places. The sea might help her even more. Kent boasts of being one of the most successful places to help invigorate a person."

"When we were in Heston," Mr. Hale said, "Mrs. Hale remarked on loving the sea. On more than one occasion, she even expressed a desire to return there. Let us lead with that. Whatever pain that she is undergoing now, I believe that will persuade her to leave her sickbed and risk anything. But I have a better notion. When Frederick comes down, let us see if he will deliver the news himself. Knowing that she will have him longer in her life might help her rally. Sometimes, positive news can help one's spirit."

When Frederick Hale joined us, we offered the suggestion to him. Despite the dangers of being found out, he considered that being detected was very unlikely.

After all, the Hales had no connections in Kent at all. Therefore, for him to be introduced as a distant cousin seemed to be a likely plan.

Eager to remain in his mother's company for longer, and to become reacquainted with his sister, who he had quite neglected, Frederick submitted to our wishes immediately. He applied to Mrs. Hale for this. With the encouragement of her son remaining with her, of Margaret, Mr. Hale and Dixon being able to return to the South, and to know that she would eventually be able to return to the seaside, was enough to stir some life in her.

Since I was a lady, I was able to visit her in the sickroom. Despite her ill health, she exerted herself enough to tell me to thank Mr. Darcy, the Colonel and Kitty. She expressed happiness in knowing that she would get to see me on my wedding day, and that, if she passed away, it would be around her entire family, as well as among friends. Since she was already dying, she didn't see how traveling could make things any worse.

"And the idea of a house being what makes someone ill does hold some credence," she noted, between coughs. "The Colonel was wise to think of that. At first, I merely thought it was the Milton air and the distress of relocation that affected my health. However, the longer that I have been in this house, the more ill I had become. Maybe there might be a chance. I have my husband, my children, and my friends. If I am to die, let me die attempting to still live."

There, at the darkest hour, Mrs. Hale learned to fight. Just when I thought that I knew her so well...but we humans are forever changing, aren't we?

When Mr. Darcy and I left, we walked through the Milton streets, enjoying the comforts of being alone at last. Arm in arm, we moved through a slight fog that rested in the air. If I were alone, it would be a little daunting. But since I was with Mr. Darcy, it was romantic.

"Do you think your aunt, the great Lady, would really be accepting of this?" I asked.

"Like I said, she would groan at me inviting so many people. But that groaning would give way to boasting of having a large party, a triple wedding to prepare for, and an invalid who she will exert all her powers at healing. Even if all hope is lost. She will complain, while secretly, she will be happy."

"All too true," I said, amused. "From my memory of her, she was a lady who loved to rule those around her. I do not criticize her but merely observe."

"She is that, I do not deny."

"And now, we bring her a whole crowd of people who will be the perfect audience. She can lecture and reign over them with all her delight."

"Yes, she can."

"It will help her overcome the pain of Anne. If that is possible."

"Oh, it's not possible. She will carry that pain for the rest of her life. But we shall prove to be a wonderful diversion, hopefully. Even with the mutineer."

I looked on him, deductive.

"Yes," I said, "that is something that I knew that you needed to talk about. Let us be frank, Darcy, for I am not afraid. You are worried about Frederick and that he might be a rabblerouser."

"I confess that I do. We were not there, on the ship. Therefore, we don't know what fully happened. We could be assisting a man who is a victim of circumstances and was willing to help those who were less fortunate than himself. However, he and the other mutineers could be lying, and gave way to all their rebellious tendencies."

"Frederick does not seem like that sort of man."

"Mutineers are like villains: they never do look evil. Rather, they look like anyone else."

"I know, but until we know everything, let us assume, in this circumstance, that one is innocent until proven guilty. When it comes to the naval forces now, it has often been observed that the conditions can be unnecessarily awful. What if the conditions are still like that and we were not told? So much is left to ignorance nowadays, or indifference. Sometimes, I think that the world functions on us being unaware of the truths to how things work."

"That is the conflict that I fight with in my mind. Believe me, it is an argument that I will have repeatedly. I only gave in to his coming because it might help Mrs. Hale to recover. Being in good cheer can work wonders on a person's health. Attitude does make a difference."

"I am not going to pretend as if you are harsh for considering all matters. I would not have you walk through life being blind to the follies and actions of others. After all, I am not blind to them myself. I just know that Mr. Hale would not raise a bad man."

"Good parents sometimes have no control when their children turn out to be horrid. Just as bad parents can even produce a good child. At some point, there can be a disconnect somewhere."

"Where the person grows and becomes what they wish to become, responsible for who they are," I finished for him.

"I preach at you, don't I?"

"Preach, preach, preach, that is us."

We looked at each other, and our passion was stirred. How well we knew each other and thank goodness we were in public. After all, time proved us to not be trusted.

"It is natural for you to be apprehensive around deserters and mutineers," I elaborated, "for there was always two sides to a story. Since Captain Reed is not here to argue his case, it was only natural for you to be a little dubious. Captain Reed could have been greatly ill-used himself. However, from what Mr. Hale and Margaret have told me about the mutiny, many of the soldiers who were arrested all said the same thing. Of course, their stories could be rehearsed, but I do not think so. They all claimed witness to Reed's abuse to sailors, of him leading to one sailor dying on the rigging, for fear of being the last to finish, and his love for torment. Such men, who seem to take a perverse satisfaction out of punishing others, ought not to be in authoritative positions. And yet, those are usually the ones who are in such places."

"I confess that is true as well."

Eventually, we reached Frances Street and Darcy looked at my house.

"Good riddance to Frances Street."

"Yes," I said, sounding undeniably wistful.

"Why do you sound upset?"

"I have to leave all of this. Even with all the happy memories and the horrible ones. Despite it all, we did make a home here. We had adventures, I found you here, I fell in love with you, and so, despite all of the things that Milton does not have to recommend itself, in a strange way, I shall miss the place."

"I will not deny that, even when there was such doubt and disasters here, it did tug at our hearts. Now we can rest, though. And never fear, since the Hales will return to Milton eventually, and Thornton is still here, we shall return to visit them all. We will return."

"Yes," I smiled, "we will. Smoke and all."

"Cloud and all."

"Oh," I said, "but since even the Hales are leaving now, you have to tell Mr. Thornton this as well."

Darcy sighed.

"Oh, well, this will be the worst leave-taking that I will ever have to offer."

Chapter 12

Strained News

When hearing that the Hales would also be leaving for Kent, it led to three different reactions at Marlborough Mills:

Fanny Thornton was elated. For naturally, despite her affection for Jane, it was not more powerful than her contempt for Elizabeth.

Mrs. Thornton wanted to say, 'good riddance, and don't stumble on the way out of the door'. Despite that Margaret had assisted in ending the strike, her natural prejudice against the family was too cemented in its place and was compiled with her natural disdain toward Miss Hale. She could never forgive Margaret for rejecting her son and could not stand the coquettish manner that Margaret now spoke to him afterwards.

If she were to reject him, then she would do well to let him alone. But that was not the case at all. On the contrary, Mrs. Thornton was unable to ignore how Miss Hale imposed herself more on Mr. Thornton's company than ever. She was not blind to seeing them speaking to each other. And now, her son would be unable to move on, like she had hoped. Her son's sorrow was her own. And as such, it was only proper, only fitting, that she feels Margaret's indecision toward Thornton most keenly.

Regarding Mr. Thornton himself, this was another set of painful news that he had to endure. He was losing too much of the company that he enjoyed. Thus, for Mr. Hale to leave, and take his daughter away, was another weight pressing upon him. And when things were finally turning to the better between him and Margaret... well, why now?

He was sitting in his office, mulling over his account books. But it was a difficulty. Despite his best intentions, his thoughts kept returning freely to the object of his affection: Margaret Hale. With each new encounter, he felt as if their relationship was improving again, and that maybe she wasn't as indifferent toward him as before. She now smiled at him, and they spoke more than ever.

Thus, could it be? Could it be that after two people experience an adversity with each other, it could actually discover a closeness? Perhaps the difficulties that he had with Miss Hale and himself did the reverse than expected. It forced them to be bound together in ways that were unconventional in every respect. And since love was not a conventional emotion therefore, there was no set path for it. Perhaps she could grow to love him. If she did, it was better that way, because it would be real.

The comfort of dwelling in one's dreams shall never last long.

Thornton was driven from his musings when his overseer entered.

"Sir, the new shipment has arrived and is being unloaded."

"Thank you. Oversee the transference."

"Yes, sir." Before the overseer left, he turned back to Thornton. "I've done my best, sir, in telling that Higgins fellow that he is not welcome here, but he remains in the courtyard."

Thornton scowled, confused about what was going on.

"What do you talk of?"

"Oh, no one told you, I see. One of those union men who arranged for the strike is in the courtyard. He comes for work."

"What?" Thornton scowled. But then he recalled the last name that his overseer mentioned. "You said Higgins?"

"Aye, Higgins is his name. That be sure."

"Nicholas Higgins?"

"Yea, that be the fellow."

Thornton stood up, went to his window, and looked down into the courtyard. Near the gate, he saw Nicholas Higgins, pacing back and forth, in wait.

There he was: Bessy's father. Now he had come to him, in need of work. Initially, Thornton felt ill-used that one of the men who had led the strike was now appealing for employment.

But Margaret had asked him, especially, to consider the man.

And in the next instance, he had to recall that Higgins's revolution was not a personal attack against himself. Nicholas Higgins had rebelled against all the factories, out of a demand for higher wages. Wages that the master could not provide, due to how the finances were arranged.

Yet, Nicholas, like the rest of the workers, did not know of that. From their perspective, it was perhaps more complicated on both sides. Thornton's instinct was to be hard and severe, but the man had lost his daughter. Therefore, it had to be considered, that between losing his daughter, Margaret's urging, and his strike being crushed, the man had been punished enough without any effort on Thornton's part. Also, Higgins had never really worked for him, but Bessy had. He could not do anything for the daughter, for she was gone from this earth. But she could do something for her father. Margaret would appreciate that.

Turning back to his overseer, he ordered the man to bring Higgins to his office.

This puzzled his overseer, but he did his duty, went down to the courtyard and summoned Higgins.

Uneasy, Thornton thought it best to sit behind his desk and receive the man with civility, but also with an iron fist. Although Higgins came for work, his recent actions still ought not to be forgotten. Thus, it was better to tread carefully.

Soon, Mr. Higgins was shown into the office, and Thornton looked at him, his expression unreadable.

Both men, so strong and determined, faced each other, and did all in their power to display respect without giving too much ground to the other.

Higgins removed his hat and stood before Thornton's desk.

"Mr. Thornton," Nicholas said.

"Mr. Higgins. I understand that you come for work?"

"Yes, I do."

"Despite that I am one of the 'monstrous masters' that you rebelled against when you organized the strike."

"Between our mutual acquaintances, yer must surely be aware that I did not arrange or encourage the riot that happened on Marlborough Mills. The rule of the union was specifically that there was to be no violence. That was the iron rule. When the workers defied that, they didn't just attack yer, but they done gone an' betrayed us."

"You will imagine that I do not sympathize with your own pains," Thornton continued, "for I was too busy remembering the mob that came down on my Irish and the ladies like a thunderous wave."

"Miss Hale, the Bennets, and Rasby were friends of my daughter, as yer know," Nicholas said, seriously. "When I found out that they were hurt, yer cannot imagine how angry I was. And still am. That was everythin' that I didn' want to happen. I had a dream, yer see? I just wanted a just wage for the rest of us. That was my only intention."

"A just wage?" Thornton rubbed his eyes. "A just wage? Between the rising price of cotton, the machinery, and the mill's maintenance, do you lot ever understand? You can't just put up wages, just like that, and you lot are fools to think you can."

Mr. Higgins opened his mouth, out of defense, but then he thought better of it. He came for work. And as such, he had to keep a civil tongue in his head.

"Sir," Thornton said, "I speak to explain how I feel on the matter, but out of the wishes for a mutual friend of ours, I still am listening."

"I am aware," Higgins said, "that there are two sides to this situation. But if it will help my suit, imagine, sir, that for a second, yer are not a master, but a laborer, a worker at the mill. Year in and year out, yer wages remain the same, while the cost of food be goin' up all the time. And yer be makin' so little, that yer can never set aside anything to save. No chance of advancement in life."

"Mr. Higgins, I *was* that laborer, and my family lived on next to nothing, for years. My mother did the best she could to set aside money that I earned so that I could become the man that I am now. And she succeeded. Therefore, I was you, sir. But worse off."

"Fortune didn' favor yer, but then it did. It's never favored me. I can't even keep a beloved child and the mother who bore her."

When speaking about Bessy and his late wife, Nicholas Higgins blushed and looked down at his hands. The mentioning of his daughter had overpowered him for a moment, and he could not remain as collected as he wished.

When seeing this, Thornton was also a little taken aback. Despite it all, he still could not help but be sorry for the man.

"I am sorry for what happened to Bessy," Thornton said, "she was a dear friend to Miss Hale and the Bennet ladies."

"Yea, she was. I never knew, in all me years, one of my girls would gain such friends. For a second, I could say that my daughter was goin' to recover, and maybe even..." He trailed off, seeing that his dreams were hopeless. "But I was wrong, and life is life. I've got meself one more daughter, and I have to consider that." He straightened himself up and he continued about his errand. "Sir, I was told, by a woman, that yer had a kindness about yer. Yes, I am a committee man, but I'm an honest one who don' believe in deceivin' no one. If I ever were to disagree with yer, I wouldn' be settin' meself up to go agains' yer. I would tell yer things, plain and simple. I'm a steady man, I am. Ask any of the ladies..." he trailed off when he realized that he was bringing the Hale and Bennet women too much into his situation.

Thornton leaned back in his chair.

"Miss Hale was the woman who told you to appeal to me."

Nicholas looked down, rubbing his eyebrow. He didn't want to use Margaret's name, in that degree. But she did give him permission to strengthen his suit, for his sake.

"I'll make a bargain with yer, Mr. Thornton."

"Bargain? With me?" Thornton's eyes grew darker. The nerve of the man.

"I will only agree to admit to such if yer can assure me that yer will not find the lady presumptuous. She did it out of helping me, yer see, and not to put yer in any awkward place."

"I will not think anything lesser of her. Is she the lady?"

"Yea, she'd be the one. And she can tell yer, that when I give my word, I give my word. And I give my word that I am a hardworking sort of fellow, I will not raise word agains' yer without consultin' yer first, and—"

"And what about your union dues? How do I know that you are not just working under me to save up more money for another strike?"

"Ah, I reckon yer heard about how I have not gotten work at other factories because I will not submit to their declarations that we can't pay into the union."

"I have a habit of keeping my ear to the ground."

Nicholas knew that this is where the truth would not help him. But he was who he was, and he knew that he could not lie to Thornton.

"Mr. Thornton, again, for a moment, imagine that yer me, and someone told yer that you could not do what yer wished with yer own money? Is that fair and proper, sir?"

Thornton tapped his desk with his hand, his face still unreadable.

"I confess that it is not, but I don't want to be fooled, Mr. Higgins."

"And yer won't be," Nicholas pressed, "I can assure yer. I will always inform yer about how I feel on such matters before I ever raise a word agains' yer. That's flat. But I cannot tell a lie to yer and may that be proof of civility from me. I will always arrange for union dues among us workers. It's the main freedom that I know. I must be given the freedom to do with my money as I may. For yer would not prefer it any other way if it were yer."

Thornton stood up.

"Margaret Hale trusts you."

"Yea, she does, sir. I should ask that yer be kind to her, no matter what yer think of me."

"I will not blame her for vouching for you. She was merely trying to help." Thornton considered the matter and came to a decision. "I offer you work, but the second that I find you using that mind of yours to stir up trouble, then you shall be driven out. Is that understood?"

"You will let me continue to uphold union dues?"

"I suppose that I have no right to tell you what to do with your own money."

"Then, for all that, I can accept. Thank yer for givin' me work. And that's a great deal, comin' from me."

"You need to start tomorrow. I have many orders that went unfulfilled from the strike. Therefore, you can't loaf about."

"I am my work. Yer don't have to worry yourself about me spongin' on the job."

Nicholas put his hat back on.

"Thank yer again, sir, and I will be on my way."

"One thing more," Thornton said.

"Yes."

"As I understand, Boucher has been given the option of working in London, or here?"

"Aye, he has."

"Tell him that I do this, not for himself, but for his six children. If the Bennets' uncle writes back, with no place for Boucher in his factory at Cheapside, then I will allow him to work. But stress this to him: I do it only out of charity for the wife and children. They saved him."

"Many people save Boucher. He deserves less in life, but he will get more. And for those children, yea, he deserves work. So, thank yer, and I will tell him."

Nicholas Higgins left Marlborough Mills with a lightness in his step. The lightness was invisible because it was an internal sort of feeling. Yet, it was there.

No one likes work, but people also love work. For work occupies them and presents a sort of purpose in their lives. With a man such as Nicholas Higgins, his livelihood was everything to him. Therefore, to be a man of employment again, fulfilled his inner purpose and he found himself both dreading the next day, and looking forward to it. This would bring him closer to his desires, but he also did not know what to expect.

For he was blacklisted. He was a known committee man, and so, he would be potentially met with prejudice on the very next day. But he knew that whatever path that he had to walk down, would never be smooth again. After all, it had never been smooth before.

When it came to Thornton, his mind was occupied in another direction.

While he did not mean to use this new development to

ease his way into Miss Hales's affections, he still wanted to inform her of it.

Of course, when he told her, she would not display much mirth on the matter. After all, it was not her way.

However, he dearly wished to see her face when hearing the news.

Therefore, as a man who accepted the powers that affection made him move, he decided that he would do it. Once the workday ended, he would make his excuses to his mother, visit the Hales and let her know the news, straightaway.

Sometimes, one cannot help themselves.

Chapter 13

Parting News

Farewells are never easy when you have found joy in a place. If Granger Hall had proven to be a place where I had experienced coldness at every turn, then I would be willing to say 'good riddance' to the establishment. However, time and people had been kinder than I expected, and I found much of myself while I worked there.

One could say, that at Granger Hall, Elizabeth Bennet fully became Elizabeth Bennet.

When Charlotte had gone to work that day, I was going to sit with her for her one class and offer my farewell to all the professors. This was one of the few days that I knew they would all be present. For it had been the end of the week, and all the professors had been gathered to receive their wages.

Thus, after the class, I planned to arrange it so that it would be my last day there.

When the moment came, when all the gentlemen were together in the library, I did not know how to present myself. Fortunately, I had a friend next to me.

"You look frightened," Charlotte Lucas said, amused, "never fear, I come to help."

Taking my arm in hers, Charlotte led me forward.

"Gentlemen, there is nothing so hard as losing a dear friend to the place. But I confess that the loss of Miss Bennet is my gain, therefore, I owe her for that."

"What?" Mr. Hunnicutt said, with a raised voice. "What is this, Miss Bennet? Are you fully leaving us today?"

Thank goodness for small miracles. Charlotte and Mr. Hunnicutt had helped smooth the way, as it were, and therefore, I was prepared to speak the proper words.

"It is the worst sort of obligation to finding one's happiness elsewhere," I stated, "but yes. Soon, I am to go into Kent and find the best joy in the world by marrying a man that I love very much. Yet, I leave you now, in the most capable hands of Miss Lucas. Treat her as the worthy employee that you have treated me. Yet I fancy that you shall." I looked at Mr. Dennison. "Or better than how I was treated in some quarters."

Mr. Dennison, taciturn as ever, rolled his eyes.

I looked around at the library.

"I shall miss this place. As well as miss you all."

All the men had been standing in a line, and that made it easier.

Going up to Mr. Hanley, I looked at him. How terribly I felt that I hurt him. I had no choice, for no one ever does when they unintentionally stirred the heart of another.

Worried that he couldn't stand the sight of myself, I was elated when he looked at me with no resentment. Rather his eyes were still stirred with the emotion of his sentiments. How I admired him so.

"You defended me when I came, and that led to me making a life for myself. I shall never forget your kindness, and that you treated me like a friend. But even more, please remember this, I will never forget you. And all that you did for me."

Raising up on my tiptoes, I kissed his cheek. When doing so, he looked on me with misty eyes.

"I could not have done less," he responded, "I knew what I was about. I knew that you were worth believing in."

Tearing my eyes away from him, I moved along the line and stood in front of Mr. Hunnicutt. As was our usual way, I gave him a face and he returned it. After laughing, I kissed him on the cheek.

"You are the kindest man that I have ever met. You are a constant companion. Pray, do not forget me, sir."

"Never, Miss Bennet," Mr. Hunnicutt said, guffawing, "you are quite seared into my heart."

Afterwards, I had no choice but to move down the line and there was Mr. Dennison. Seeing no other way, I offered him my hand to shake, hoping that he would at least stoop to take it.

When looking at my hand, his face was filled with disgust.

"What?" He scoffed. "No kiss for me?"

"When have you ever shown to be the sort of man to want one?"

"I know, but...well, you know... I just—"

Accepting that it didn't do to remember our mutual dislike of each other, I kissed him on the cheek.

After doing so, he looked at me, determined. There was no anger in his face, nor dislike. Rather, he was a little unnerved.

"So, you really are going then?" he asked.

"Are you that eager to see the back of me?"

"It is just... you're a part of the place. That's what I hate about you women: you leave. You always leave."

"You have to forgive us for that, you know."

"I know. It's just that I got accustomed to your face. It's what I know now."

"Charlotte will be a better face to look on than myself."

"I don't like when new things enter. I don't like it."

I didn't know how to react to that, for who could? And what was more was that he looked devastated. Utterly devastated. All that hatred he learned to feel for me, and it had quite betrayed him. Truly, I had never seen anything like it.

"Well," Mr. Hale announced, to sever me from this tense moment, "there you have it, Miss Bennet. You came, you made your presence known and loved, and now we all wish you joy in the next part of your life. Gentlemen, let's wish her well."

As if that lifted the spell, the gentlemen overcame their remorse on my going and decided to dwell on offering me the best chances at my future.

When leaving Granger Hall, Mr. Hale offered Charlotte and I his arms as we walked to the omnibus.

"Dixon is making all the preparations to have us leave when it is time to return to the South," Mr. Hale said, "depend on it."

We spoke of her, but the conversation was strained. Our minds were on the previous scene that we had untangled ourselves from, and not much else. Perhaps Mr. Hale didn't say anything because he knew that it was too delicate a business.

Yet, when Charlotte and I were riding on the omnibus together, I could finally release what I had been feeling.

"Does he miss his hating me?" I asked about Mr. Dennison, "or—"

"If he cared for you all the time, he just was afraid to show it," Charlotte finished my sentence.

"Yes. I knew what each man's reaction would be to my leaving. Mr. Hunnicutt's was the most expected, and we parted as I had hoped. With Mr. Hanley, we parted way better than I had hoped. But with Mr. Dennison, it was the reverse."

"I wish that I could tell you that I understand men like Mr. Dennison," Charlotte said, "but I don't. With him, all I know is this: whether it be love or hatred, he will miss you the most. You gave him something when you came."

"What did I give him?"

"You gave him something to feel. You gave him an emotion. He probably missed having those."

"And soon, he will project that solely on you."

"Yes, he will. Don't worry for me, Lizzy. If I accidentally left my courage back in Hertfordshire, I assure you that soon it will follow me."

Chapter 14

Maternal News

When the workday ended at Marlborough Mills, Mr. Thornton could not contain his eagerness. However, there was the matter of having to inform his mother about where he was going. Of course, when entering his house, he braced himself for all his mother's prejudices and all of Fanny's poutiness.

It was needless to say that he was not left to be disappointed.

"What reason do you have to visit the Hales, pray?" Mrs. Thornton questioned as she arranged her son's necktie. "It is not the day for your lessons."

"Well, yes, but I have grown to sometimes visit the man during moments of leisure. Besides, some developments have changed over the last few days. I do have some news to acquaint the family with, and I would like to do it before they all leave Milton."

Leave.

The very word that Mrs. Thornton had dreamt of ever since Margaret Hale had rejected her son. And could the Hales finally be leaving Milton Common and the North altogether? It would all do well, especially now that what she wished would come true.

"Well," Mrs. Thornton said, with a hint of happiness in her tone, "The Hales are leaving. They might also go back to Helstone."

"No, rather, they only go to Kent and will return. They go there on two counts. First, they will attend the Bennet sisters' wedding, and second, they are hoping that the fresh air might help Mrs. Hale's health. They know that it is very unlikely that she will recover, but they have to try."

"Naturally so," she replied, "the sooner, the better."

Mrs. Thornton sat down and continued about her work. Thornton smiled at her, knowing her true meaning.

"I see what you are about. You are hoping that when they go, may they stay there forever. Eternally banished from Milton, eh?"

Mrs. Thornton scoffed.

Thornton sat down next to her, willing to let her unleash her true feelings.

"I am right, aren't I?"

"Well, yes, if you don't mind. You spend a great deal too much time loitering away with that lot. It distracts you from your real duties. You should have one aim only, and that's to keep Marlborough Mills running successfully. That's the only music that I care about. Besides, this will give you a fighting chance."

"What do you mean by a fighting chance?" he asked.

"You know what I mean, so don't force me into saying it."

"No, I don't know what you mean. And something tells me that you want to say it."

"But you do know. You know very well that you will never recover from your feelings for that Hale girl while she is in your company. It's only natural, despite all things.

When she is gone, that will give you your chance to move on and find a better suit."

Thornton pulled up a chair and sat down beside her.

"Mother," he said, "are you sure that it is her that you despise, in particular? What of another woman? Or any woman for that matter?"

Mrs. Thornton sighed.

"I do want you to be happy," she acknowledged, "believe me, I do."

"I can assure you, that no matter what, I will never stop thinking you are the greatest woman in my life."

Mrs. Thornton stopped her work, and she remained silent. It was already difficult for her to reveal her feelings about anything, but when it came to her son's affections, it had no choice but to affect her.

"Mother," he assured her, "there is no need to ever feel threatened."

"I just... I cannot help it. You must understand, John, that you are a very good son. Not many mothers can boast of having a child like you, but I can. I can claim that I have the greatest son in Milton. When in such a position, no mother can help it."

"I know."

Since they were revealing and exposing much to each other, Thornton had to inform his mother about the rest of his heart.

"Mother," he said, "I have to tell you that I still love Miss Hale, more than ever."

"Why?"

"Do you still love father?"

When hearing mention of her unfortunate and late husband, Mrs. Thornton's security was shaken. Indeed, it was enough to rouse every feeling that she had for the late Mr. Thornton.

"I fancy that you still do," Thornton answered for her, "despite all things, you do."

"I have no choice. He gave me you. But that is the wonder of it. When he killed himself, I hated him. When he allowed himself to be swindled, I hated him. When he left you alone, with Fanny, and did not give you any other choice but to suffer for his actions, I hated him. But then one day, the love returned. It all came rushing back to me in a day that overwhelmed me, and I did something that I had not done in so long."

"What?"

"I cried." Mrs. Thornton took in a deep breath, feeling so terribly exposed. But there was nothing for it. "I cried so hysterically. And that was when I knew, even if some man was to fall into my life, willing to marry an old and taciturn widow with two children, I could never accept him. Poverty and all. Because no matter how much I deserved a bit of happiness somewhere in life, I could never be." She chuckled sadly. "It's a bitter thing, you understand. To know that paradise, romantic paradise, will always evade you. It's not meant for you, because you were cast out of the shades of it long ago. I was cast out, John, never to find my way back. Your father was the beginning and end for me. Then again, all things must end. Mustn't they?"

To know the depth of a parent's heart.

Thornton had never asked his mother about Father's lingering effect on her life. First, he never had the time, and second his mother was not the sort to talk of her emotions. It was not her way. Ergo, since there was neither room nor willingness to discuss the matter, he was overwhelmed. After all these years of knowing his mother, he still did not know her.

For, despite the vastness of Milton, people do change so frequently, that there is always something hidden...some part of them that they have not revealed for many years.

All these years later, and now he knew the woman who bore him. He knew she was capable of deep feelings, of clandestine desires, but he could only guess. Now, he knew.

With all the strength of feeling, he reached out and touched her hand.

"You know what I would have you do?" Thornton asked.

"What, John?"

"I would have you smile again. Laugh. And be happy. I know that it's not your way and habit, but I remember that you would do so when father was alive. When he died, the laughter in you died. The music in you died. But I want to believe that you can find it."

"Do not fear, son. It did return. When I saw you fight to keep our family alive and well, it returned. And then, when you succeeded at paying off all your father's debts, you established the Thornton name, and you achieved so much, it was an added elation. I do smile and laugh, in my heart. But you must understand, John, that I must be hard, to keep you so. I cannot break in any way, or I will not be your support. That is why I do not prefer a woman like Miss Hale. I don't think she has the same interests as you and can therefore support you properly."

"You and father were different."

"And look what he made of himself."

"Do you regret my existence, or Fanny's?"

"Of course not."

"I am the product of that union. Therefore, mother, I cannot begrudge the difference between you both when it led to my creation."

"And that is the great gift. One of the best of my life."

Mrs. Thornton sighed. "You will probably propose to her again. Won't you?"

"I have no choice."

"I know."

"Differences be damned."

"Very well. But if she rejects you a second time, I will do everything to make sure that you never see her again."

Thornton smiled.

"I know, but there is no cause for alarm, on that score. I will only propose when I am certain that she might favor me. Darcy may leave Milton, but he promises to be a loyal correspondence with me. And Miss Elizabeth tells him everything. He will inform me if my behavior will be welcome to Miss Hale. This time, I will tread carefully. I will not make an offer unless I can be sure that I am receiving encouragement. Maybe, if I am lucky, absence might make her heart grow fonder towards myself. Or forgetful. Now that will be a scary prospect."

"If she does not choose you, promise me, John, that you will try to release her from your heart? I would like for you to rally from this."

"I will."

"Very well," she said, kissing his forehead. "Give Mrs. Hale my regards, and that's the only kindness that I can exert."

"I know."

Thornton left the parlor to prepare to leave. As he retrieved his hat, he saw a shadow on the upper landing. Looking up the steps, he saw Fanny Thornton huff as she was about to go to her room.

"Were you listening in?" he asked, calling up to her.

"It's not my fault," Fanny replied, "you were speaking loud enough for me to hear."

"Well," Thornton said, resigned, "now you know."

"I always knew," Fanny pouted, "even when you both didn't think to speak to me about it all."

"Fanny..."

"What?" she asked, coming down the stairs. "Is Fanny not to know anything? Must Fanny always be left out of such discussions? Oh, yes, she must be."

"And you wonder why?" he asked. "Fanny, look at you. You speak of my affections so openly on the stairwell. Can't you see that no one wants to feel so exposed?"

"How am I to ever feel any sort of freedom when I am always being stifled?"

"What do you want, Fanny?"

Once more, she huffed. "What a mean thing to ask."

"How so?"

"You sounded so cold when you asked it."

"I just want to know what makes you want to talk about it. You often have reasons for why you speak thus."

"I was just being a little sister, wanting to know something about her older brother. But go on, do as you do. Do as mother does. Leave Fanny out of it all."

"Don't do this now."

"Do what?"

"Make yourself out to be the victim of this case."

"But I am. I can't talk in this place, and I feel stifled all the time. I feel the limits of being so very powerless, and not in my own family's confidence. You are mother's favorite. I am no one's. But I tell you this now; I have my chances. Mr. Slickson is now showing particular attention to me. And I will have my happy life, where I run the household. I will have my family. And it will not be like this. I have a voice, and they will appreciate it."

Thornton did not respond, but not out of vexation.

Although it was not the conversation that he wished to have, he did understand what she was feeling.

"We do love you, Fanny."

"Yes, you do. But you all do not like me."

"Fanny, be honest with me now. Are you upset with us, or are you upset with what your heart is going through? I am not insensitive to your past affections for a certain gentleman."

When hearing him reference Mr. Darcy, Fanny tried to remain strong, but her eyes quite betrayed her. Rather there was a flash of heartache that dashed across them, like lightning out of a clear blue sky. Thornton noted it, even if she didn't want him to notice. Or maybe she did want him to notice, despite herself.

"I am right, aren't I?" he asked.

"I don't care for him. Not anymore."

"That is good. But if you are not telling me the whole truth, then I can tell you now, Fanny, that you were not in any error for favoring him. He is a worthy man, to be sure. It displayed your good taste. What you must remember is that he arrived here, in Milton, with his heart already given to another woman. You are not wrong, or defective in any way, because you could not secure his heart. No one is ever defective simply because someone did not choose them. It is the way of the world for rejection to occur, even at the best of times. But if you are using this new romantic avenue to recover from your damaged heart, then I would advise against it. It can always lead to placing affections in a forced way."

Unable to hold in her grief any longer, Fanny began to weep, uncontrollably.

At first, Thornton worried that a servant would see, but he knew that there was nothing for it. It rendered him the right to be there for his sister. Going up to her, he held her as she collapsed into his arms and let her weight rest on him.

"Why me?" She wept. "Am I so ugly?"

"No," he assured her. "You are not. Please, believe me, Fanny, that one day the pain will lessen, and you will recover. This is just a part of the way of life when one grows up. Eventually, innocence dies, and we are exposed to the difficulties of the heart. You have now experienced those difficulties. And you shall come out, on the other side, and be the better for it."

"I feel like I am being torn inside out."

"Yes, it does feel like that. But soon, one day, you will rise above it all. And it will be another story to tell. We all need to have stories. That is what renders us fascinating. You will gain perspective from this and become a whole new woman. But please, Fanny, don't let your heartache make you desperate to offer your heart to another man too quickly. I don't want you to make that mistake. Believe me, you will be the better for this all, and we will be here for you."

Fanny continued to weep into her brother's arms. But it was not just general sadness. She needed someone's affection in that moment, as well as the warmth of being enveloped in their embrace. Her brother had never hugged her in such a way.

Therefore, her sentiments took advantage of this opportunity, and she allowed herself to be coddled.

Out of the side of his eye, Thornton spied a figure watching them from the bottom of the steps. He knew the look from the gown. It was their mother, watching her two children as they showed sibling affection.

He did not look at her and see that she was a mixture of emotions.

She was both prouder of him, for he offered Fanny advice that she could never fully give herself.

She was also annoyed that her children gave such outward displays of emotion.

It was vulgar.

But it was also beautiful.

Such was the mind of Mrs. Thornton; a woman torn between the logical platitudes of life and the affections of a maternal outlook.

Chapter 15

Revealing News

After comforting his sister, Thornton wondered if he still had time to visit the Hales. He was spared from being torn, fortunately. After her feelings quieted down, Fanny excused herself and retired to her room, to enjoy the solitude of it all.

Once she was safely attended to, Mr. Thornton was able to depart for Crampton, feeling a variety of things. He hoped his presence would not disconcert the Hales, for it was a sudden decision of his to come. But he was certain that if Miss Hale was not happy to see him, Mr. Hale's general cheer would be enough to offer recompense.

Therefore, he sojourned to Crampton, with the agonies of not knowing how well he would be received when he arrived there.

And there he stood.

At the Hales front door.

Now all that it took was for him to knock.

He raised up his hand, balled into a fist.

And he froze.

He couldn't understand it. Margaret and he had

achieved a beautiful sort of move toward true friendship, so why was he nervous? Perhaps it was because he was coming to deliver good news, and so he wondered if it would make him more endearing in Margaret's eyes. Perhaps, perhaps, perhaps! That was what stirred in him. He had entertained that idea called 'possibility', or the word 'maybe', or the word 'perhaps' itself! It was altogether too much for him.

How could he face his hopes rising again? He had begun feeling for her, genuinely, and was knocked down. He didn't think he had the ability for his heart to be torn out again. Naturally, it was not a sensation that he wished to repeat.

Suddenly, the door opened, and Margaret Hale faced him with a shocked expression. She had her coat, hat, and gloves on, indicating that she was about to go somewhere. When seeing the disappointment in her eyes, Thornton immediately shirked inwardly. Evidently, she had no desire to see him whatsoever.

"Mr. Thornton!" she cried.

"Miss Hale," he said, removing his hat. "Forgive the intrusion, but—"

She looked behind her, quite distracted. Rather, she was looking up at the steps, as if she worried that someone might be behind her. When she looked back at Thornton again, her cheeks were red from shock.

Thornton was no fool. Quickly, he deduced that there was something that she was worried about him seeing. Or something had happened to one of her parents. Instinctively, he stepped more towards her, unconsciously making it impossible for her to move forward and close the door, barring the sight of what was behind her.

"Has something happened?" he asked, reading her expression. "Is it your mother? Or has something happened to Mr. Hale?"

"No!" she uttered, but it accidentally was too sharp, and he blinked. "Oh, pray, forgive me, nothing is wrong. You came to visit Father?"

Even though it was a simple question, her face still looked alarmed. There was something else wrong, but he had no right to pry into her affairs, no matter how much he wished to.

"I was merely on my way to visit the Bennets and tell them about a letter we received from Mr. Bell," she declared. "Come, let us walk together. They would like to see you."

This startled him, because she not only had never invited him to accompany her in such a way, but she was moving to push them both forward, to close the door behind her.

He stepped backwards, willing to accept. Just as he did so, and she was about to close the door, a young man came down the stairs.

A young man whose features were like a mixture between Mr. and Mrs. Hale.

"Sister!" he called as he came down, "Mama is calling for you, and—"

He cut himself off when he saw Thornton standing in the doorway.

On his face was alarm.

The same alarm that Margaret had when she faced Mr. Thornton at the door.

In a quick two seconds, Thornton pieced together all that he had heard. For the mind races quicker than the speed of light and sound.

Sister? This man called Margaret his sister.

And mother? He was evidently referring to Mrs. Hale.

This could only mean one thing.

Thornton had come face to face with Margaret's brother, and Mr. and Mrs. Hale's son.

But Mr. Hale had never mentioned having a son before. If he did, surely, he would have told Thornton. Therefore, what was the meaning of this?

Then he saw both Margaret and this man's faces. Shock and embarrassment were etched across their features.

All of this, he saw in the matter of ten seconds.

The three of them stood there, with Thornton at the door, Margaret in front of him, and Frederick Hale in the middle of the stairs.

All felt mortified in one form or another.

Thornton was the only one who was ignorant on why he felt such a way, but with the others, it was obvious to them both.

They had been discovered.

A door opened from downstairs, and this had the desired effect of lifting them from their frozen spell. They all started, their nerves were filled with a manic frenzy, and they all turned to the sound of the door. It opened to see Dixon enter, with some medicine in her hands. When she saw Mr. Thornton, her eyes filled with an immediate anger.

"Oh, dear god!" she uttered, groaning inwardly. Being the only one who knew what she was about, Dixon dashed forward and began to make excuses.

"Mr. Thornton, sir," Dixon said, walking toward him, "you come at a time where we are looking to hire another servant for the household. This is Mr....Jenkins, my brother. He's come up to the North, looking for work. If you both wouldn't mind, I need to show him more of the house. Go upstairs until you are needed."

"Yes, sister," Frederick said, going upstairs with alacrity. When he disappeared, Margaret looked at Thornton. Somehow, she was able to read his expression very well.

"How much of that did you believe?" she asked, whispering to him.

"None," he responded, his voice equally as low. "He was referring to you when he said sister, didn't he?"

Margaret breathed inwardly and looked down. But her silence was enough.

"Miss Hale and Dixon," he said to both women, "help me to understand."

Margaret looked at Dixon and they both looked so downhearted.

Margaret stepped aside, to make way for Mr. Thornton.

"If you will step inside, sir, will you give me leave to explain everything?"

Mr. Thornton did not respond but only entered.

When he entered, Thornton removed his gloves, hat, and handed them to Dixon. Resigned, she took them and stored them away while Margaret removed her coat and hat.

"Well," Margaret sighed.

"Yes?" Mr. Thornton said.

Margaret opened her mouth but was too overwhelmed to speak at first. From behind, Dixon watched them by way of reflection in the mirror. Instinctively, she regretted what this all had led to. With great care, she had done everything to avoid Frederick being detected, but this was what fate called an unlucky turn. There was no way in which she could have predicted this scenario. Showing just how much was out of her hands in life.

"Mr. Thornton," Margaret said at last, "forgive me, but I wish to speak to you in the strictest of confidence. Do you mind if we speak in the kitchen?"

"The kitchen!" Dixon exclaimed.

"Yes, Dixon."

"I understand," Thornton responded, "secrecy might be vital in this case, and kitchens are very good at being a place where there are no spectators."

"Thank you for understanding me."

Margaret escorted him there, and half a minute later, Dixon returned, bringing in some chairs. When they both sat down in a corner by the fireplace, naturally, they expected to be alone. Their surprise was a little roused when they saw that Dixon had moved toward the cutting table and began to roll some dough.

When they looked at her, she gave them a shaming look.

"If you both think I am leaving either of you alone," she stated, "you must be outside of your right minds."

"Yes," Margaret said, "thank you, Dixon."

"My pleasure."

Dixon gave Thornton a 'I will kill you if you spread any rumors' look, hitting the dough against the bake board. Thornton found that his familiar scowl did not work, in this instance. Especially since he realized, in that moment, that he was afraid of Dixon. Perhaps he had feared her for quite some time and had never acknowledged it till now. Therefore, he swallowed his insecurities and looked back at Margaret.

"Forgive me," Margaret said, "I ought to offer you some tea."

Margaret stood up to prepare it, but Thornton grabbed her arm, to stop her.

"You do not need to supply me with refreshment. I know that you might prefer to get to the heart of the matter, and I can assure you that I am willing to hear what you have to say, with discretion."

Margaret sighed, exhausted.

"Thank you. I know that you would."

"Then," he said, taking Margaret's hand, instinctively, "sit and tell me all."

When seeing Thornton's hand on Margaret's, Dixon picked up a knife and pointed at Thornton.

"Don't get familiar," she declared.

Without a second thought, Thornton removed his hand from Margaret's.

"Yes," he responded, "quite."

Margaret couldn't help but smile. Despite all that had fallen apart, she was amused. Seeing her smile, Thornton felt the right to note it.

"You smile about that?"

"Yes, I suppose that I do."

"You like seeing me get chastised? Is that funny to you?"

Despite herself, she let out a chuckle.

"I'm sorry," Margaret said, then she let out a burst of giggles. "I'm so sorry."

"You're sorry?" he said, then he found her gurgles infections, because he began to chuckle himself. "Perhaps it is comical, from your perspective."

"Yes, it is."

Somehow, they began to laugh more freely, and openly. They didn't know why, but it just felt right.

They were so preoccupied in their mirth, that they didn't notice Dixon.

Over her shoulder, she looked on them and rolled her eyes.

One had discovered a secret.

The other had revealed a horrible secret that could ruin their family.

And they sat there laughing.

'Honestly? What was the world coming to?' she asked herself.

When their laughter came to a very natural, but awkward end, Margaret realized that she had to finally explain everything.

The serious cloud returned over them, and she had to hope that Thornton was the sort to truly keep a secret. When she realized that he was the perfect sort to do so, she finally began to convey the truth.

"Mr. Thornton," she said, "I know that you can be trusted, and I know that you are a man of your word. Whatever our past, I know that I can trust you, as well as I know that you care for my father. Therefore, I must ask you this, that what I tell you now will be of your strictest confidence. Please, sir, promise me that you will tell no one of what you saw here today."

She was trusting him. The sentiment was keenly felt and so was flattery. Naturally, she had no choice but to tell him everything that would explain what he saw. However, to hear that she trusted him. That was so lovely that he felt that they truly could rise above their past and both were now made anew. Their disagreements were officially over, and now a new chapter in their lives began. It would be a chapter where both would no longer be plagued by a rift caused by misunderstandings, tenseness, pride, or prejudice. No, this was something altogether perfect for them. This was a definite and new beginning of better things on the horizon.

"Miss Hale, I promise that whatever you have to tell me, will die inside of me," he assured her, "and believe me when I tell you that I respect your family. Always have. I admire your father, for he has become one of my best friends. I will never do anything to harm him. Or your mother."

Margaret looked relieved, abandoning all emotional concealment.

"I know. You are a worthy man. I do value that about you, Mr. Thornton. Whatever I have said before, I acknowledge that I didn't appreciate that about you until now."

Now she was fully complimenting him. His spirit rose within him, and he was more enthralled with her than ever. Her kind words were like food to a starving man.

"The man that you saw," Margaret said, "is my brother, Mr. Frederick Hale. He is my mother and father's firstborn."

"But I don't understand why I have been in ignorance of the matter. What I refer to is, I never knew that Mr. Hale had a son. He never mentioned him."

"It has nothing to do with our father's lacking any pride in Frederick. Even with all that has happened, he is fond of his son. The only reason that you never learned of him is because my parents had no choice. My brother has been living in Cadiz, Spain, these last few years, because he cannot return to England. He is here because I sent for him, so that our mother might see him one last time, in case she took a turn for the worst. Therefore, he came to Milton under the cover of darkness, and is here, in secret."

"Why can't he return to England?"

"Because my brother—he is a deserter."

"He is?"

"Yes, and more than that. He is also a mutineer."

Margaret told him the whole history of Frederick's past with the law. When she finished, she thought it was needed to excuse Frederick, but Thornton was not judgmental at all. Despite not being there to witness what Frederick had witnessed, he still could very well believe that Mr. Hale's son could be anything else but obliged to take his course of action. Since he knew the father, he was willing to offer comprehension to the son's character. It was only natural that he could not foresee Mr. Hale having raised anything else but a moral man, who would only turn mutinous if he had no other choice.

Therefore, Margaret was elated at knowing that, if someone were to accidentally stumble on the truth, it had been Mr. Thornton who had done so.

"I suppose," Margaret said, when she finished, "that it is time for you to face the family now. Would you be willing to meet my brother?"

"I would be delighted," he said.

Dixon looked between the two of them.

"Is that a good idea?" she asked.

"Dixon, it's the *only* idea," Margaret said, realistically. After all, she could not have Thornton leave without seeing Mr. Hale introduce his son, first. Seeing her father's love for his son, it would only enhance Thornton's wish to maintain Frederick's secrecy.

Before they even stood up, he heard Mr. Hale cry down the stairs.

"Margaret? Where are you?"

Giving Thornton a look, Margaret stood up and he followed her out of the kitchen. When he did so, they both stood at the bottom of the steps. When seeing Thornton beside his daughter, Mr. Hale's eyes widened, and he removed his spectacles.

"Father," Margaret said, "we have a great deal to tell you."

When Margaret explained how Thornton accidentally discovered Frederick, and how she felt obliged to tell him the truth, Mr. Hale was not upset. On the contrary, his natural preference for Mr. Thornton, his holding his pupil in high esteem, and respect for the man, actually made Mr. Hale relieved. If there was one man that he would like for Frederick to meet, it would be Mr. Thornton.

When accepting that his secret was out, but only to a man that his father and sister trusted completely, Frederick welcomed Mr. Thornton and did his best to be cordial and good company.

Mr. Thornton's belief in Frederick's good character was cemented. For, despite the foolishness of judging a book by its cover, he could not help but trust Frederick Hale. The man had open and pleasing looks, a sincere smile, and he didn't appear to be a hotheaded sort who would resort to mutiny blindly and because he took sport in it.

And, since he felt obliged to tell his own story about the events, Frederick elaborated on his experiences in the Navy. Thornton was a man of the world, and he was aware that some men achieved their captaincy through connections rather than qualifications. He had heard many a woeful tale of some abusive superior that an officer had to serve under, in one time or another.

"If I knew that there was any justice in the law," Frederick told him with finality, "I would stay and have it out. But there is no hope for it. Whatever can be said of me, I face reality and not fantasy. Some of the men who assisted in the mutiny pleaded their case, but they were hanged anyway. That is the problem with living on a ship; the abuse is hidden, away from the eyes of any who can sympathize. Anything can happen on a ship and the rest of the world is none the wiser."

"So," Thornton said, "you cannot remain in England, for fear of your life. And your freedom."

"And now also for love."

"My son is married," Mr. Hale boasted.

"Yes, I am," Frederick said, blushing. "My perfect love is in Spain now. She understood, however, that this was something that I needed to do."

"But what of the wedding?" Thornton asked. "Will you leave when your family goes down into Kent?"

"He is going to go with us," Mr. Hale said.

"I am hoping to see if the country air will help my mother recover," Frederick said, hopeful. "I know that it might not be possible, but we have to try."

"Understandable. You only get one mother."

"Yes, you do. And our mother is a great one."

"Mr. Thornton understands," Margaret added, "His mother stood fast to him when their family needed a strong matriarch. He understands how you feel, Frederick."

When hearing Margaret mention Mrs. Thornton's virtues, Thornton's heart warmed. He was prodigiously proud of her, more than she could ever know.

After sitting with the family a while, Thornton knew that it was wise to take his leave. After all, Frederick would want to spend as much time with his mother as possible, should the worst ever happen.

Margaret offered to see Thornton out, and it suited Thornton to the fullest.

When they went downstairs, Dixon had walked past them, to light the candles in the house. When seeing Thornton, she huffed and walked away.

"What is that look for?" he asked Margaret. "Is she still upset with me for getting too familiar?"

"It's more than that," Margaret said. "She still remembers when scandal followed me from when I tried to save you from the mob."

"Oh." That was all that he could think of.

They walked down the stairs, and Margaret retrieved Thornton's hat and gloves. As she did so, Thornton remembered his reason for coming. He had been so wrapped up in the events that he still had not mentioned his discussion with Nicholas Higgins.

As he put his hat on, he informed her that he had offered Nicholas Higgins work, and that if Boucher did not get work in London, then he would consider taking him on.

"I admit," Thornton acknowledged, "that I have hesitancy in seeing Boucher return to my service."

"On account of events that took place at the riot," Margaret surmised.

"Precisely. I cannot forget that he was the one that led the crisis that almost took your life and your friends."

"He has repented and truly does feel sorry for what had happened. Besides, I cannot help but wonder if maybe, when a set of individuals turn into a mob, it's like they seem to lose all perspective and sense. It's as if their minds become like that of one collective."

"It makes sense. How else have monarchs been able to mold men into armies? A rational person would stop and see the futility of engaging in a battle where certain death is almost imminent. But when a part of a crowd, they will rush into anything, no matter how fatal."

"The powers of people when they all get it into their minds to not think as one among many, but as one in total.

But then, we must remember that they were starving and driven to act like wild animals."

"Do you still blame me for breaking the strike?"

With a heaviness, Margaret had to accept that she had been too severe in her assessment of things. Of course, Thornton would do everything in his power to keep his business running. She had not considered his perspective on the situation.

"No," Margaret said, "I suppose that I do not. You are a businessman, and you had a right to maintain your work. Especially with so many orders coming in, it must have frozen so much of your profit."

"It still does," he answered, with much weight behind it.

"Your work really did suffer, didn't it?" Margaret asked, truly curious. Despite her desires, she could not help but care for this man who she was obliged to admit that his character was raising in her eyes.

"Yes, it did."

"You are...you are not in any danger, are you?"

"Not yet."

Those two words, to her surprise, filled her with an inner sense of dread.

"There was a heaviness to that word 'yet'."

"You read my mind," Thornton said, "Miss Hale, truly, things are difficult. I am fighting to catch up to the orders that we were not able to fulfill."

"I am afraid that I do not know what to say. I cannot help you in any way, therefore, my condolences for how things are progressing will sound useless. I do not know what I can say, because I accept that there is nothing that I can say. I feel like a dead weight."

"I do not find you to be so. Whatever sympathies that

you can offer, will be genuine, for your opinion is so rarely bestowed, therefore it is more worth the earning."

"Then I am sorry for what has happened. And I believe that you will recover very well."

"Miss Hale?"

"Yes."

"Am I going mad, or are you beginning to respect my work?"

"I...well, I had not considered it so, but time is teaching me to appreciate industry and the role that it plays in English society."

When hearing this, Thornton couldn't help but allow his chest to swell with pride. Thankfully, it was invisible, therefore, he was happy that he did not appear to strut about like a peacock who was putting his plume of feathers on display.

"That means a great deal to me," he professed, staring at her intensely. Unable to help himself, he studied all of Margaret's figure, and he was left to only marvel at the finesse of her facial features.

Margaret, realizing that she was being scrutinized by a man who might still be in love with her, blushed and looked down at her hands, that were folded and rested on her gown.

Seeing her cheeks turn red increased Thornton's passions, and he could not help but slip into the world of his daydreams, where he still encompassed herself into him.

For two to become one. He could see her fitting in his arms most naturally, giving into the caresses of affection, and the truths that they always shared.

Between them, there was always veracity, be it pleasant or unpleasant. Since Margaret and him had gone through the abyss and back together, it only added to her charms, rather than detract from them. After all, she had seen the best and worst aspects of himself, so there was nothing left to fear.

Whether Margaret liked it or not, there was a connection between them that could not be denied.

There was heat between them.

Thornton knew that heat. He felt it.

Margaret might perhaps need more time to discover it herself. And, unfortunately, she never might. That was a fear that he had to consider might be the death of his heart. What if she never recognized the tenderness between them? He would be left, in a deranged sort of limbo, forever.

"When you leave with the Bennets," he said, "I must ask if you will take leave of my mother and sister?"

"I would like to, however, I have to consider something, for their part."

"And what would that be?"

"That I might be the last person that they would wish to see."

Mr. Thornton raised an eyebrow.

"You noticed that?"

"Yes," Margaret answered, with no pain, "I did. I could not help it."

"I prefer that you do not choose willful ignorance, just because the truth might not be easy to see."

"You need have no fear for me. I shall do it, but I know how it is going to end. It will end with your mother and sister being very cordial to me but never wishing to remain near me ever again."

"I cannot explain why they look on you in such a way."

"It is their choice, but yes, I will go and take leave of them before we go down into Kent."

"Thank you."

Thornton put on his hat and gloves.

"Unless we shall run into each other on the streets, I shall see you when you all depart."

"You will be meeting us on the railway station?"

"Yes, I shall."

Margaret turned sheepish once more.

"I shall tell my mother. Thank you, Miss Hale, for being understanding."

"It is no trouble on my behalf. Be safe, Mr. Thornton."

"And you as well."

With that, he left, with both in a state of inner turmoil.

Chapter 16

Relocation News

On the eve of the Bennets and gentlemen's great journey back to the South, there was a letter by way of express.

For the happiness of all, it was from their Uncle Gardiner, who had written back his reply.

"Luck has found our way into Milton!" Jane said as we were packing our things, to prepare for tomorrow.

"What is it?" Kitty, Rasby, Charlotte, Maria, Margaret Hale, and I said as we read the letter over her shoulder.

"Uncle Gardiner has recently lost two workers. They were brothers, and their uncle died, leaving them a farm to inherit. Since they have given notice of quitting his factory in two weeks' time, he will be in need of another laborer who is accustomed to factory work. Since we described Boucher's history with being a miller and spinner at a cotton factory here in Milton, he is eager to find a replacement. As long as Thornton sends down a reference, he will accept Boucher for employment."

"And there's more to it," Kitty observed, overjoyed, as she pointed to another part of the letter. "Since those same brothers must leave London to collect their inheritance, they would prefer to get new tenants to take over their establishment, so that they do not have to argue with their landlord of their vacating the premises sooner than expected. For another family to come in and take the residency will smooth the way."

"Now, when has fortune ever been that lucky and convenient?" Charlotte asked.

"I'm sure that I do not know," I replied, amazed. "All things are coming together in a way that it feels like it is too much to be true."

"The only thing that is left to wonder is if Boucher is willing to accept it," Rasby said.

"Only one way to find out," Kitty said, snatching the letter from Jane.

"Last one there is a rotten egg," Rasby cried as they both dashed out of our house and ran to the Bouchers.

Maria watched them as they went.

"Who would have thought that this is the girl that Kitty turned into?" Maria observed.

"I never would have seen it myself," I said, "she has enhanced her principles, but still has maintained her lust for life. She found the best of both worlds. More for her, I say."

Margaret looked at me.

"Did any of us take the time to say farewell to Nicholas?"

"We wanted to," Jane said, "but he was still at work."

"I'll go and see if he is home," Charlotte Lucas said, leaving to go and inquire after him. Her sudden ability to immerse herself into these new situations made me proud. She and Maria had accepted this lower station in life with such a degree of sense that I wondered how much the laziness of country-life perhaps felt too stifling for them for longer than I was aware. How can you live next to someone for so long, and then suddenly, they could surprise you?

———

Charlotte returned, but this time, she was not alone. Nicholas Higgins had come with her. When he entered and saw all of us there, he removed his hat, looking on us all with gentleness.

"Ladies," he said, "I was told that yer lot were leavin' tomorrow."

"You came to offer us a good journey," Jane said.

"Right yer are there, I was."

"We heard of your recent hiring at Marlborough Mills," I said, "congratulations."

"Thank you." He looked around and saw that someone was missing. "Where is Miss Kitty? Or is she off with Rasby?"

"She went to the Bouchers," Maria said, "for there was some news."

"News? About Boucher gettin' work?"

"Oh, Nicholas, you would not believe it all, even if we told you," I said. "Have you ever known Boucher to be lucky?"

"Never in me life," Nicholas responded, sitting down at the table. "There were even times where I believed that he was brought into this world to bring us all down."

"Oh, Nicholas, you didn't say that to Boucher, to his face, did you?" Margaret asked, concerned.

"I could not help it. He ruined the strike, ruined our chances for a better life, and all that. I was angry, yer see? And heartbroken."

"We know," Jane said, taking his hand. "But it's time for you to make peace with all that."

"Besides," I elaborated, "there is no chance for you to worry about his company, or any stain that you think he caused. Our uncle is giving him a chance to work at his factory in London. If Boucher accepts, then the whole family will be uprooted to the South, where he can start again."

"Maybe, when I see him at such a distance, I can move on," Nicholas admitted.

"You are being too severe, sir," Margaret said, "especially on our last day of seeing you for some time."

"*Some* time?" he repeated, his countenance becoming a little fidgety. "Does that mean that you will all come back?"

We all looked in between each other. But the truth is that many of us would probably not be able to return to Milton for quite some time.

"Well, naturally we must return to make sure that our friends are still well," I said, "but I suppose that the truth is that we will be back down in the South for quite some time. Does this mean that you will miss us?"

"I... I, well yer gotta understand, yer were my daughter's friends. Yer were there for her and everythin'. What father could forget that? From what I believe, every father likes to see the idea of his daughter bein' loved, or maybe even a little popular. A man can't help it. When yer love someone, yer want the world to love them as well. Yer loved my poor Bessy. So, I suppose that I grew accustomed to yer faces. It's hard for me to know that I can walk down the street and not see yer lot passin' by at all. It will be no more Bennets on Frances Street. No more Hales at Crampton either. It will be strange. Hard, hurt a bit—but I'll bugger on. It's what I do."

We both sat there, feeling the heaviness of his words.

"Well," Margaret Hale assured him, "take heart,

Nicholas. My father, mother and I go to visit Rosings Park, and the seaside. But once our mother's health shows any signs of recovering, we will return to the North. For my father still has his pupils and might wish to keep up his practice."

When hearing this, Nicholas was enlivened.

"Yea, that's a happy thought. The way that I look at life, everythin' gets taken away from all of us eventually. But the way I see it, is that if everythin' were to be taken from me, then it ought to be taken slowly. But when it's all taken away so quickly, I can't bear it very well."

"It's natural," I said, offering solace. "Nicholas, wherever we go, we will never forget you. And we miss that you will no longer be a part of our everyday lives."

"I know the feelin'," he said, "so thank ee' for sayin' that."

The scene was going to continue to take a morose turn, to my sadness. After all, I wanted our farewell with him to be jovial and bittersweet. This was not so, but rather, it was like that of a slab of stone pressed on us. I wondered what I could say to offer levity, but my work was done for me.

The door opened and Rasby and Kitty entered.

"He accepts!" Kitty cried. "Boucher accepts the new commission."

"He is eager for you to all write his confirmation to Mr. Gardiner," Rasby said, then she saw Nicholas. "Oh, Nicholas!"

"Nicholas," Kitty laughed, going around him, and wrapping her arm around his shoulders, hugging him from the back. Their sudden entrance brought excitement in, and it was just what we all needed. "We will miss you, you stodgy old codger!"

Feeling Kitty's excitement, Nicholas laughed and held her arms.

"My dear, Kitty! Yer not goin' too, are yer, Rasby?"

"Not yet," Rasby said. "If all goes well, you still have my company for a few more weeks. But if it does not go well, then you will have no choice but to have me in your life."

"Well, I'm a sour wuss puss, and selfish sometimes. I hope yer stay."

"Our dear old badger," she said, kissing his cheek. "Oh, and Boucher will come and offer his thanks when they finish their supper," Rasby explained to us. Then she turned to Nicholas. "Think you can be nice to him if he comes?"

"I'll leave before I see him again," he said, standing up. "I'll be nice to him when he leaves."

"Still angry, eh?" Kitty asked.

"Sometimes, I man cannot be moved, no matter how much he wishes for the reverse."

Going to the door, he took one look on us all again.

"Yer lot was Frances Street's pride and joy. We boasted about havin' all yer ladies here."

"Promise to take care of yourself?" Jane said.

"I will, tha's flat."

"Then you will make us still proud of you."

Smiling once more, he left.

When he closed the door behind him, I took advantage and pursued him.

"Nicholas!" I called to him as he walked back to his house.

"Yea?"

I walked up to him, offering him my hands. He took them and I began my plea. "I must ask you for a favor," I said.

"A favor? From me?"

"Yes. You have the ability to offer them, you know?"

"Ah, yer bein' witty at my expense, aren't yer?"

"Yes, I am. I need you to inquire after the Lucas sisters. They may wish to remain here, but they still will need some sort of protection. Can you make sure that they are always safe and well? And, if your other daughter ever wishes for a friend, they might help her on. They are just as willing to be amiable and social neighbors as we were."

"I promise yer, I will look after them. The whole street will, yer will see. Nothin' will happen to them."

I smiled.

"Thank you, Nicholas. Till our roads meet again."

"Yea, till that day."

We parted as friends.

Soon Boucher did pay his respects, and for the first time in so long, I could boast of saying that Boucher was happy.

Never before did his smile reach his eyes.

But today, they did.

He had his chances for a new life now. Often, one does need to start again.

Chapter 17

Informative News

Since Boucher had confirmed that he wished to take his family to London, in hopes of a new life and chances for his children, Thornton had to be informed of the news.

Feigning a sense of it being an obliged duty, Margaret Hale offered to go to the mills and tell him about Boucher's decision. Elizabeth and the others took her reluctant tone as being kind and considerate, but no more than that.

Internally, it could not have been more different. Secretly, she was feeling desirous of seeing him and this was the perfect sort of excuse.

Therefore, as she walked toward Marlborough, alone, she preferred it that way. Whenever Thornton came to her mind, heat began to rise within her body. She felt a tremor radiate in her stomach. It was both painful and pleasurable.

For a while, she could not account for her sudden alteration towards him, nor fathom when it had occurred, or what had brought it about. Yet, the facts were the facts. As such, it could no longer be denied, and she felt the words rise to the forefront of her thoughts.

'I like him.'

Those were the three hardest words in the world to hear her utter to herself!

The revelation proved so intense, so overwhelming, so upsetting, that she stopped where she stood and clutched her stomach.

Is this what falling in love was like?

Since the sensation was new to her, she did not know if she was right, or if she was mistaken. All she knew was that this could neither be hatred nor indifference. Perhaps it was a mere bit of fancy passing through.

Although, that could not be right. Margaret prided herself on not being the sort to have passing affections, so she wished that she was not succumbing to such tendencies now.

But she also was not the sort to have such feelings as she was undergoing now. Indeed, she felt somewhat mortified because she worried that it would show all over her face.

Sensibility was not what she wanted to display.

She wanted to run away, but she wanted to walk onward. For the very notion of not seeing Mr. Thornton, of not being in his company, felt like agony to her. To want to look and not look all at once. These sensations were not only novel to her, but very provocative.

Her feet carried her onward, with the courage that she lacked. When she arrived at Marlborough Mills, it was as if her body was controlling her more than her mind.

As she entered the courtyard, moving around all the workers, it was at the precise time that Mr. Thornton had exited his factory, and was going to his office.

There he was.

What could she do?

What was there to say?

She remained there, rooted to the spot, in a state of indecision.

Out of the side of his eyes, Thornton saw her, and her presence was now known.

Turning, he saw her and stopped where he was.

Instinctively, Margaret smiled, raised up her arm and waved to him. Embarrassment took her immediately, and she wondered if that made her look foolish.

When seeing her civility, he changed his course and walked directly toward her.

"Miss Hale?" he said, "you come to the mills sooner than I expected."

"I do not mean to interrupt your work at all," Margaret assured him, "in fact, I come with a business matter of my own that will make you happy."

"Will it?" he asked. "Come to my office and we can discuss the matter further."

Margaret was all too happy to obey because she didn't want anyone to overhear their conversation. And, even more to her perturbation, she found that she enjoyed the notion of being alone with him.

They went to his office, and he removed his coat.

"Forgive seeing my shirtsleeves," he said, rolling up his sleeves. "But I was in the factory, and the action there made me overheated."

"I am not offended. It is merely forearms. I do not get offended by seeing a man's forearms."

He smiled.

"Thank you. There are some habits that can come across as being too strict sometimes."

"I can understand."

At first, they merely looked at each other. Margaret remembered herself, blushed and she looked down.

"You look happy," he noted.

"I suppose it is because I come with good news that I know will ease some of your burdens."

Thornton lifted an eyebrow.

"You do? Pray, tell me it at once. I need a little cheer today."

"Is the day going ill?"

"No. It just feels longer than usual. Help me gain relief from it."

"The Bennets uncle, Mr. Edward Gardiner from London, has offered to employ Boucher. Boucher has accepted and he will uproot to Town. You do not need to worry again on that score."

"Really? This all has been arranged."

"Yes, it has."

"That is wonderful. I am glad to hear it. Boucher might fare better in the South. Life moves slower, and he might need that pace."

"Precisely. Now you are free from that experience. And I..."

"Yes?"

"Well, I was hoping this all can be viewed as the last great chapter to a tumultuous time in your life. And now a new chapter can begin for you."

"A new chapter?" he asked, leaning forward.

"I just thought this last event might help you to move on from it all, and now you can look to the future."

"I aim to."

"Good."

"Good."

"Thank you."

"You are welcome."

"Yes."

"Yes."

They sat there, in awkwardness.

The awkwardness had reached such a pitch that Thornton felt compelled to speak.

"Miss Hale," Thornton shrugged, "I do believe that we wish to speak to each other, but we still have no notion of what we are about."

"I suppose that we are. But sometimes silence does not have to indicate discord. Silence can be a good thing. It shows comfort in another person's presence."

"Yes, it does. You and I are both of a reserved manner, unwilling to speak unless we have something to say. Don't we?"

"Yes, we are like that," Margaret observed.

"Well, I am glad over that. I like that you and I are at that place where we can do so. But I still feel like we need to say something. Not because of the silence, but because it seems like we wish to speak of such things."

"Yes. It is only that I do not know what to speak about."

"Are you excited for going into Kent?"

"Yes, I am. But it's not only that, but since the weather might be agreeable, I also look forward to sea-bathing."

"I have never sea-bathed."

"Nor have I. But if I go to one of the bathing places, like we wish, then it will be my first time."

"I envy you."

"Thank you. But I wish for you to know that I do not do it for myself. But rather, my mother might benefit from the sea air, and maybe even partake in it herself. The wonders of nature. I have been without it for..."

"For so long?"

"Yes. Precisely. I am not saying that I despise Milton, truly, I am not."

"I know. I understand. I appreciate that you have grown to see the value of industry, but you shall always be a creature of nature."

"Even when I was in London, I still felt provincial life call out to me. But today, I learned something."

"Did you?"

"Yes. It was when Nicholas Higgins came to take leave of us. Even though we are the ones who are taking the leaving. He said something."

"What?"

"That he would miss us. He felt that we had become so much a part of this place, that he could not see us leave Milton Common."

"This is probably the first time that Mr. Higgins and I agree on something."

"Truly?"

"Yes. I have grown accustomed to having so many friends close by. I suppose, perhaps, I might have taken it for granted. I feel that, when you all leave, I shall take to feeling a great loss."

"You will?"

"Yes."

"Even with me?"

Such a direct question. It made Thornton feel utterly naked, before the cold light of day and the truth that Margaret Hale always preferred.

"Yes," he answered simply, "especially with you."

Margaret blushed and began to fidget with her fingernails.

"You asked," Thornton replied, trying to regain his defenses.

"I am not angry for you saying it," Margaret rushed out, "for as you said, I did ask. It is merely that I wonder why. I know that you have never sought any sort of revenge on me for our past disagreements, but I wonder that you should not wish to see the back of me—to the point of wishing me only to not stumble on the way out the door."

"You really think that I would ever wish that?"

"I know that you do not and never have. What I will always be confused of is why? Why don't you?"

"You are asking me questions that I am willing to give answers to. Those answers will either cause you pain, or it will disconcert you and make you wish to turn away from me."

"I am not afraid. You were right."

"Was I? About what, pray tell?"

"That I should have at least tried to understand you. Well, I am trying now. I realized that maybe you needed to say those things to me, because it would hurt you to keep it concealed. Did you wish for me to hear those things, for fear that you might burst?"

Thornton's eyes widened, and without being aware of himself, he took a step toward her. She was letting him in. In full and without any awkwardness or sense of rejection. She reached a point where she did not fear his love for her. On the contrary, she was asking about it, showing the keenest interest.

"Yes," he said, his tone soft, but firm. "That is precisely how I felt. Margaret, I just felt compelled to tell you."

"But there is one thing that I do not understand."

"What?"

"Why did you prefer me to begin with? After all, we had been constantly in disagreement with each other. All we did was speak in a way that gave the other pain, in one form or another."

"I know. And yet, I fell in love with you anyway. That was the wonder of it. Also, it was my fault that we began so wrong."

"Have you overcome your anger? I know that you will always have a temper. Between the struggle in your past, and the way that life is here, perhaps you are bound to have such. After all, it seems wrong to show weakness here, of any kind."

"I cannot be seen to be anything else but as a leader, Miss Hale. Margaret. Might I call you such?"

"You may."

"Thank you. I must be hard and strong, or others shall walk all over me. If that be the case, then everything can topple all around me. I have many people to save."

"It is strange that, to save all, you must also be hard on them."

"Yes."

Margaret sighed.

"I do not think that I will ever grow accustomed to the ways of industry. I tried, as you can imagine, but I never fully wrapped my mind around it."

"Does that mean that you feel that you can never grow accustomed to my sort of life?" he asked.

Now that it was Mr. Thornton's turn to ask a direct question, Margaret was left to feel the heat of his query under the neckline of her gown.

"I don't know," Margaret answered simply and honestly.

"You don't?" he asked, his tone not desperate or urgent. Rather it was merely a little wistful and his eyes were soft.

"Mr. Thornton, you know me; lying is not a skill that I acquired. If I were to do it, I would probably make terrible work of it. Therefore, you know that I mean as I say. I wish, very much, that I was determined and had quite made up my mind. But, over these last few weeks, I have been thinking and rethinking. It has left me altogether confused."

"Confused?"

"Yes. Confused. I dislike being in such a state, but there it is."

"I suppose that you have no choice," Thornton said, getting closer to her and sitting on his desk. They were not too close to each other that he was pressing any sort of advantage. If two lookers-on were to glimpse them, it would just be of two individuals who were interested in what the other one had to say.

"You have been a child of London and Helstone," he elaborated, "And now you are a woman in Milton. Maybe being torn between three different locations influences one's temper and findings. You cannot help but be torn in your own way."

"Yes, I suppose that is it. I wish I could make up my mind. To not know what side one is on, is not a very pleasant experience. I feel as if I am in some strange sort of limbo, going from one intense viewpoint to another. And now my opinions have taken the same turn. I cannot deny that the South is my home. It calls out to me, and I feel its call."

"And does it call to you stronger than this place?"

"Have you ever gone to London before?"

"Yes, I have. It's a marvelous place."

"But if you were to fall in love with a lady of the South, and her family wanted you to remain in London, would you? Milton is your home. You have made a life for yourself here, and to leave it all behind—no, Mr. Thornton. No love could tear you away from the industry here, the mills, the factories, and even the people. If you were taken from Milton, and brought to a paradise, you would soon grow tired of the perfection. You would antagonize all the paradise-dwellers around you, then you would rant and rave. They would fling you out of paradise and you would fall back to Milton, over-joyed to see the cloud, and sounds of the machinery making cotton. And you would look down on what you see, thinking that there was never a better place on earth."

"Perhaps I would, but there is one thing that you are forgetting."

"And what is that?"

"That I did fall in love with a woman from the South."

Ah, once more the two of them danced around the subject, then drove right to it.

"Yes," Margaret acknowledged, no longer looking away from him. Rather, she looked him straight in the eye. "Yes, you did."

Her direct look back at him, without fear, shame, or annoyance, stirred his affections even more. Her look was strong, it was bold—and she was beautiful.

"You do not look at your hands when you say that," he observed, "nor look away from me. You look directly at me. It is a steadfast look."

"I am not afraid of you," Margaret said.

"I know. You never have been, and I will live my life making sure that you never have reason to be. But such a look. Such a steadfast look makes me wonder. It makes me wonder about you. Margaret, what am I to feel?"

"I cannot determine how to have you feel."

"Very well. Then how does this conversation make you feel? Evidently, you are not angry with me."

"No, I am not."

"Then what are you?"

"I am doing as I always do, without giving anything away."

"You can trust me," he assured her, "but as you are not afraid of me, I am very afraid of you."

This confession surprised Margaret.

"You are afraid of me?"

"Yes."

"Why? When have I ever hurt you?"

"Not hurt me of body, but of mind and heart, yes, I am greatly terrified of you. When a woman has found her way into your heart, she can hurt your sensibilities. She can break your spirit, for the spell has been cast."

"I never meant to stir your feelings," Margaret stressed, "please, do not make me appear to be some sort of conjurer."

"I do not. Please do not be offended. I merely say it as a choice of words, to help you understand."

"Yes. I see. I was being a little extreme there, wasn't I?"

"Never fear. I know your mind, even if I don't know your heart."

"But now," Margaret said, "I know yours. Are you still deeply attached to me?"

"Yes," he answered simply, "I am."

"I do not want you to be afraid of me. I am not here to hurt your heart. If you like, I shall write to your family when I am away. It will drive your mother to distraction, and your sister will not want to read it, but I am certain that my father will welcome the correspondence."

Thornton did not smile, but his eyes did.

"You would write to me?"

"Yes, I would. Through my father, of course, but yes, I will. And you can tell me how things are in Milton. You can confide anything to me, as I have confided in you. You know our family's darkest secret, therefore, you can believe that I will always hear anything that you have to say without me exposing any feelings that you may have on any matter. Well, I admit that I will inform my father about it, but I believe that you will understand why."

"I will. I should appreciate the correspondence."

Margaret smiled gently.

"I ought to take my leave now."

———

Now that it was the proper time to depart, Margaret stood up.

When seeing her leave, right when they were in the middle of their achieving such connection, Thornton could not help but cling to this interaction, like that of a drowning man clawing to the surface of the water.

"Must you leave?" he asked.

"Must?" she repeated. "Mr. Thornton, I have been here for so long already."

"I know, it is just..." he began, holding his hands together, "I will not see you for quite some time. It might be months, depending on how circumstances unfold."

"Aren't I taking you from your work?"

"Yes," he recalled, "you are. But what I abandon now, I shall make up for tomorrow."

"I shall not be used as a reason for you to begin to abandon your work. I will become a bad influence."

"You will not. I assure you. Just spend a little longer with me."

Margaret sighed.

"Very well," she said, sitting back down, "but I will not stay more than half an hour. That's the furthest that I would be a bad influence."

"You are not a bad influence."

"Well," Margaret said, "at least this will give me more time away from considering how to take my leave of your mother and sister."

"Oh. Oh!" When imagining the situation, he laughed.

"Yes, you may laugh," Margaret allowed, "because it will surely be a comical experience from your point of view. But from my viewpoint, it's going to be an awful business, all around."

"Yes, it very well might. Would you like me to come with you? To help smooth the way, as it were."

"No, you need not trouble yourself."

Pause.

"On second thought, never mind my last response. Yes, you can join me. I am not afraid to have any sort of ally when I am with your mother and sister."

"There's no shame in it."

"She knows that I refused you, doesn't she?"

"Yes, she does."

"Good lord, she will never forgive me, will she?"

"You want the truth."

"Why not?"

"She will despise you till kingdom come."

Margaret sighed.

"Even if I had accepted, I get the feeling that she would have despised me anyway. I cannot help but assume that she will always believe that I am the one who is not good enough for you."

"Mothers usually think that way."

"I do not think you are beneath me, Mr. Thornton. We are equals."

"Yes, yes we are."

Mr. Thornton sat down near her.

"Margaret, can you possibly call me John?"

"Really?" She asked, her eyes widening.

"Well, yes. Why did your eyes widen when I said that?"

"Well, it just seems so very strange calling you anything else but Mr. Thornton."

"Give it a try."

"John. John." Margaret threw up her hands, in defeat. "Forgive me, I cannot do it. But what about simply Thornton, and not Mr. Thornton? That's the furthest I can go."

"Very well. Thornton it is. But I still get to call you Margaret?"

"Yes," she assured him, "you can. I will never revoke that right."

Now that he had the assurance of calling her by her first name, once more, Thornton felt as if he was given the deepest chance to find his way into her heart. Despite that he was pushing his fortune, he decided to press the matter.

"Margaret," he asked, imploringly, "I ask one thing. And one thing only."

"Are you about to ask me something that will cause tension between ourselves?"

"I promise, what I have to ask will be entirely for you to decide. Only give me the right to ask it."

Gently, Margaret nodded.

"I know that you do not feel for me in the same way that I feel for you. But I only ask that you grant me this one wish. Might I request a courtship from you? This is neither me pressuring you, nor pressuring you into any sort of choice that you do not want. After all, you shall be so separate from me for as long as your family will remain in the South. But as you are in Kent, will you be willing to allow me to court you through our correspondence? And if you feel that you can never reciprocate anything that I feel, then you may break off the courtship. You can send me away at once, and I will not attempt to convince you of anything. I just ask for permission to try and win your heart. But if I lose it, I shall not complain, nor will I turn vicious. I will let you go."

Margaret breathed in sharply. This sort of talk was taxing to her, while also being surprisingly welcome.

Why did she want to say no?

But why did she also want to say yes?

"Margaret," Thornton said, "are you confused again?"

"Yes," Margaret answered, "you must understand that I respect you, but I am so used to being my own person, that I cannot fathom the idea of letting a gentleman into my life."

"As I am not accustomed to having a lady in my life. It is daunting, isn't it?"

"Yes, it is."

"That is why I tell you now, Margaret, that I hold you to

nothing. You are not bound to me in any way. I am merely asking for an attempt. No more and no less."

"I do not know why I am so terrified right now," Margaret said, "not of you, but of this strange emotion called affection. It is such a difficult thing to understand, even if one is feeling it. I do not deny that I find you very agreeable now. I find myself to be proud of you, I respect you, and I have grown very accustomed to your face in my life."

Thornton waited for her to finish. Every compliment that she offered was like music to his ears. Her words were spoken with such sincerity that he knew it was all real. She merely was like him: love was whole new to them both, and it was more daunting for her, because it threatened her autonomy, her sense of self and all that she had wanted to be, perhaps. But what was even more flattering was the fact that she was showing signs of considering him, in a way that she had never considered another man before. It was terribly gratifying.

"And do you promise that there are no proverbial strings to this situation," Margaret stressed. "That I will not be pressured in any sort of way?"

"No, you will not be. I prefer not to be under anyone's power. But in this case, I am entirely under yours."

"Very well. I confess that I am frightened under the weight of my feelings and what they could grow into." Standing up, she walked to the window and looked out of it. She needed her courage, now more than ever. Bracing herself, she delivered her answer.

"Yes," Margaret Hale confirmed, "I shall allow a courtship between us."

Thornton's body, heart, and mind exhaled.

He knew that this was not a confirmation of Margaret's heart, but it was a tremendous start.

"Oh, Margaret," he said, stepping forward. However, Margaret was so overwhelmed by her offer, that she took a step back, away from him.

"Pray, forgive me," Margaret said, "it's not you, I promise. This moment is just so overpowering that I need time to settle it into my spirit. It is so alarming to me."

"I suppose that you need time."

"Yes, I do. Do not be offended. I am not going to revoke my assurances. I said it and I meant it."

Thornton couldn't help but be happy.

"Well, this is a joyous day, isn't it?"

His happiness did not unnerve her but only solidified her.

"Very well," Margaret said, "we are in agreement. Now, I suppose it is time to escort me to your family. I feel my courage returning to me and I can face anything."

"Yes," Thornton said, confident. "I am sure that you can."

Together, they walked to Thornton's home and called on Mrs. Thornton and Fanny. They received her peacefully, and Fanny was more sedate than usual.

Margaret asked for them to be open to calling on the Lucas sisters when they were away or inviting them to Marlborough Mills. The mother and daughter were amenable to the idea because they approved of the Lucases.

Thornton was steadfast and remained near Margaret the whole time.

Now that Margaret's nerves had quieted down, she could sit near him and speak to him evenly.

Thornton, having enjoyed their afternoon together, was very amiable and verbose. Margaret sat by the window with him, speaking equally as much.

Years later, they would declare that *that* was one of the best days of their lives.

Chapter 18

Arrival News

All had been prepared, and the days had arrived at the time for departure to Rosings Park. All items had been loaded and taken to Milton's railway station.

Since so many were leaving, Rasby and Thornton felt the need to see us all off.

"I feel like we shall never meet again," Rasby said to Kitty as they hugged.

"We shall, Rasby," Kitty cried, "all is looking upward, I can feel it."

Mr. Thornton was the most surprising. Out of the corner of my eyes, I spied him and Margaret speaking in confidence, with her hand placed in between both of his. They were speaking in hushed tones and Thornton's eyes looked kind.

The conductor announced the departure, and we all filed into our car, looking out at the window.

As the assistants arranged our luggage, I overheard Mr. Hale behind me, talking to Margaret.

"Margaret," he whispered, "I saw you and Mr. Thornton part in so friendly a manner, that it makes me wonder if you both have finally gained a friendship in between you both."

"Father," Margaret answered, "there is very little that I can say about things, but I can confirm that yes, you are right. Mr. Thornton and I are friends now. And I do believe that we shall be so, for a very long while."

"You have made me so glad, Margaret. I told you he was a good man. Did I not tell you? He is a good man."

"Yes. I daresay that he is."

Turning to her, I gave her a 'told you so' look out of the side of my eye.

Good-naturedly, she rolled her eyes at me.

When we sat in the car, a few of us looked out of the car's window, and we saw Thornton and Rasby wave to us from the train platform.

As the car took off, soon, they disappeared along the smoky fog that was on the tracks.

"What are you thinking?" Mr. Darcy asked me, holding my hand.

"That lord knows when we might meet them again."

"We may yet, Lizzy. We may yet."

"Either way," I said to him, "I am glad that you are with me. Arm in arm, sir?"

"And hand in hand."

"Let us walk down the same road together, till the end of our days."

"Even after the end of our days. Eternity will not be long enough, but we shall walk it together."

Standing on the platform, watching the train depart, Rasby and Thornton just stood there until it disappeared out of Milton's station.

"Well," Rasby said, "they are gone."

"Yes," Thornton said, "they are."

"I am so scared. What if I never see Kitty again? What if I never see any of them again?"

"I want to believe that we will," Thornton responded. "It is hard when you lose such friends. It seems like all lights go out."

"And never to be warmed by the fire."

"They will come back. I have to believe. They will come back."

The train arrived in Kent and there were a series of coaches waiting for us. Fortunately, the train ride did not affect Mrs. Hale in any negative way. While she was still sickly, she managed to not only survive the journey, but she found some joy in knowing that she was returning home, in some way. During the entire ride, Frederick Hale remained in our compartment, to avoid any sort of detection.

When I saw the carriages waiting for us, I smirked.

"Courtesy of our future aunt," I said, as the stablemen put our luggage on the rooves.

"I feel like she will not like me," Kitty said, "and then I realize that I am being paranoid. Or maybe I am not."

"My love," Colonel Fitzwilliam said, "I love my aunt, and now I am about to give you some strange advice."

"Will this advice help Lady Catherine like me?"

"It might."

"Then I don't care how strange it is. I'll take any advice

where I can get it. I want this wedding to run smoothly, and besides, I have a friend in the North that I have to convince your aunt to be my companion."

"Flatter my aunt. I know it may sound false, but flattery helps smooth the way."

"She will not find me to be obsequious?"

"Not in the slightest."

"Thank you, dear. I can build on that advice."

"I was wondering," Mr. Bingley said, his voice low, "that when it comes to Rasby, maybe it would be best to have Lady Catherine invite her, and you not tell her what Rasby fully is. If the great lady will be upset when you see her, she might be too much afraid of her image to send her away. After all, our Queen and sovereign, right now, has taken in a negro girl, therefore, it would not be fashionable for Lady Catherine to reject Rasby when she is here."[1]

"That is a happy thought," Kitty realized, "after all, it is better to beg for forgiveness rather than ask permission, sometimes."

Kitty looked at the rest of us before we entered our carriage.

"What do you all think? I like Bingley's plan."

"We will discuss it later," Mr. Darcy said, "but it does seem like a promising idea. That was clever, Bingley."

"Why do you sound as if it's the first clever idea I've ever had, Darcy?"

"Do you really want me to answer that?" Darcy asked, amused.

"Oh, shut it, man."

---

1. This is historic fact. Queen Victoria did indeed adopt an African English girl for a time.

Our carriages traversed along the Kent countryside, and we all marveled at what we saw. Even though the land was foreign to us, it was still familiar in that it reminded us of the land that we used to live on.

"Even though we are not going home," Jane said, "I feel as if we are still coming home."

"Yes," I professed, "I feel the same. Well, this is a joy. A true joy."

Soon, our carriage drove passed Hunsford Parsonage. I knew it because Darcy explained it to me.

"So," I remarked, "that was the one-time parsonage of our cousin, who took our home from us. I suppose the house should not be considered ugly because it once was occupied by him."

"I have some sad news, Lizzy," Darcy said.

"What?"

"The new parson is as stupid as your cousin."

"Truly?"

"Yes."

"Well, your aunt seems to prefer a trend."

"The more that I think of it, I think that she prefers them to be idiots. The more foolish they are, the easier that she can control them."

"Well, I've met many a wealthy person who prefers a gentlemanly idiot any day, over a smart person. I will say this for your aunt: she understands that idiots are harmless."

"Yes, she does. And you are not an idiot."

"Oh, I know what I am walking into. She did not like me then, and she will not like me now. Only this wedding will pave my way, I suppose."

We rode onward, and soon, we rode along a set of lovely

trees. When we reached the end of them, Rosings Park unfolded itself before us. We all gasped at the grandeur of it.

Rosings Park was a large home, was very well situated and was on rising ground. Every park has its beauty, its prospects, and I saw much to be pleased with.

Naturally, every single boast that Mr. Collins had made of Rosings Park had come to mind. I could not help but smile at such a happy memory. After all, my parents were still alive at that time.

When our carriages stopped in front of the house, there were many servants who met us on the steps of the hall.

Colonel Fitzwilliam immediately ushered in assistance for Mrs. Hale to be brought to a room to rest and have Mr. Hale join her.

"Remember when Mr. Collins said that the house had sixty-four windows to it," Kitty remarked.

"Yes, I do remember," Jane said, "all of his praises came to mind when we first saw the house."

"As did mine," I said, "and the fireplace that cost eight hundred pounds?"

"Oh, yes," Kitty said, groaning, "he talked of that for more than five different conversations. How did we bear his company, I wonder?"

"I have no idea," Mr. Darcy acknowledged. "I could not withstand more than one conversation with him, myself. Ergo, I could not imagine living with him for a fortnight."

"Mr. Collins really counted the windows?" Margaret asked me.

"Yes, he did."

"Did he like a good view of nature?"

"No. He was simply enamored with the money that was behind it."

"Ah. The plot thickens."

"But," Kitty said, going to the Colonel, "it is a lovely house, Richard. I am proud of you."

"I am not its master yet."

"No, you are not. But I believe that you are the responsible sort, who will do right by this place."

"This is our home now, Kitty. I am happy that you like it."

We all complimented the house, expressing our joy in Colonel Fitzwilliam's new inheritance.

At last, we were able to enter, have our things taken, and the housekeeper informed us that, due to our journey, we were given the option of being shown to our bedrooms, where we could freshen up.

This was readily agreed to, and we all were shown to our bedrooms, which were all grand and had been laid out for us. Since Rosings Park was such a vast home, it was made to house large parties of company, therefore we could all be accommodated very easily.

"Mama misses Dixon," Margaret said as she and I were helping each other dress. Since we had been so accustomed to looking after ourselves, we got used to getting dressed without many servants to attend us. "I wish she could have come down, but she had to remain behind to tend to the house."

"One thing that I recalled about Lady Catherine is her attention to the ill," I noted. "Your mother will be nursed well. And when Dixon has finished closing the place, she will join us before we leave for the seaside. So, what do you think?"

"You look lovely."

"I meant the house."

"Oh, it is so beautiful. It reminds me of Aunt Shaw's house in Harley Street, but instead in the country. But I will reserve judgment for now, because it is not places that matter, but people. When I meet your future aunt, Lady Catherine, then I will judge the house in full."

"Wise. Margaret?"

"Yes."

"You parted ways with Thornton very amiably. That is good. You have a friend in him."

"Eliza, I need to tell you something."

"Yes?" I asked, pointedly. The way that she spoke, it sparked my interest.

"It is a delicate thing. You cannot tell anyone about this."

"Very well, I will not. Of that, you can be certain."

"I have found myself in a very interesting situation."

"Really? What about?"

"Well, Mr. Thornton and I are now courting."

I almost fell over.

"What?"

Margaret unfolded everything to me. The more she did so, the more amazed I was. She had not told me about her changed feelings for Mr. Thornton until now. I was desirous to know everything, but there wasn't time.

The servants came to assist us and were surprised to see that we had already changed our own clothes.

"We are definitely talking more about this after dinner," I told her.

"Yes," Margaret said, "I suppose that I have more explaining to do."

"Yes, you do, you little minx."

"Who are you calling little?"

When all had dressed and were now presentable enough to stand amidst such a great lady, we all had assembled and followed the servants.

They led us to an antechamber, and finally to the very room that Lady Catherine was sitting.

It was a remarkably handsome room and Lady Catherine sat there, aware of her magnificent presence. Her ladyship, with great condescension, rose to greet us.

She was precisely as I remembered her. She was a tall, large woman, with strongly-marked features, which might once have been handsome. Her air was not conciliating, nor was her manner of receiving us, such as to make her visitors forget their inferior rank. She was not rendered formidable by silence, but whatever she said was spoken in so authoritative a tone that it marked all her self-importance.

Because of her strong presence, I had to remind myself that she had recently lost a daughter. Then again, from what I recall of her nature, she was not the sort to display any sort of weakness. Therefore, perhaps she was strong on the outside, but was cracking from within.

The first thing that she did was look at Mr. Darcy and Colonel Fitzwilliam. They both went to her immediately, and she received them with a generous amount of familial affection. Colonel Fitzwilliam was very profuse in his thanks to his aunt for her extraordinary kindness.

"Your kind words are appreciated," Lady Catherine replied, "but I will make sure that you will repay it with actions."

"Oh, believe me," Colonel Fitzwilliam replied, teasingly, "I did not forget. And I can assure you that I am as eager to learn every corner of this house, from top to bottom, at the soonest opportunity. Whatever my faults be, disappointing you is not one of them. Now," he said, "might I have the honor of introducing you to our lovely set of ladies, and one of the lady's cousins?"

Lady Catherine looked at us all, but it was me most

directly. This made all the sense in the world because I was the only face that she was familiar with.

"I am well acquainted with one of them. Miss Elizabeth Bennet, you found your way to my home."

"Indeed, I have, your ladyship," I responded, "but when it comes to good fortune, I can easily declare that I didn't land on Kent. Rather, it landed on me."

"Ah, still very decided in your words, despite your youth. I remember your verbosity, and it's nice to see that the North has not swallowed it up."

"I do not think any part of England has the ability to do that, your ladyship."

"Quite so." She looked at the other women. "And two of these are your sisters, and one of them must be a friend."

"They are, Aunt," Colonel Fitzwilliam responded, "This is Miss Jane Bennet, Miss Kitty Bennet, my fiancée, and Miss Margaret Hale. And this is her *cousin*, Mr. Frederick."

All us ladies looked at each other and curtsied together. We had been practicing it before we left Milton, in hopes of giving a good first impression.

When seeing us move in unison, Lady Catherine could not help but look on us fondly.

"Well done," she said, "charming. Very charming indeed." She looked at Miss Margaret and Frederick.

"And you are the Hales daughter, and cousin."

"I am, your ladyship," Margaret Hale said. "Thank you for welcoming me to your home. My father is not present and perhaps is not aware that we are meeting. Shall I retrieve him?"

"His removal from this company is solely because I had our doctor waiting in the kitchens before your arrival. The second your mother was placed in bed, I had her attended to. Your father remains beside her. And you, Mr. Frederick, were you visiting them in the North when you joined our party?"

"Yes, I was," Frederick responded, giving into the lie. "It had been years since seeing this part of the family, and when hearing they were in Milton, I felt compelled to visit them, since I felt a deep affection for the family."

"Well, I am glad of it. You have a pleasant and stable look to you. And people always need more family beside them at times such as this, when one in the family is ill." She looked at Margaret Hale and then us Bennets. "Well, you four are a lovely, genteel, and prettyish set of ladies. When first meeting you, Miss Elizabeth, I was unaware that your sisters shared your looks." She looked at Jane. "You appear to be the handsomest of the lot, and Mr. Bingley?"

"Yes, your ladyship?" Mr. Bingley said.

"I congratulate your conquest."

"Thank you, your ladyship."

"All of our ladies are equally handsome, I believe," Mr. Darcy said, eager to stand by me and not have my features belittled. Secretly, I thanked him for that.

"Quite so," Lady Catherine responded, "no need for defensiveness, my nephew, for I was merely beginning." She turned to me. "Miss Elizabeth, your looks are more handsome than beautiful, and nothing less will do for Darcy. You must be strong for him, and I know that you will be." Then she turned to Kitty. "And this is the one who will one day take my place as mistress of Rosings Park?"

"I confess, your ladyship," Kitty began, "that I do not seek to supplant you. I merely come to the match with the happiness of being the Colonel's wife. Yet, I will do my best to attend to your teachings. But I would much prefer if you were to remain running Rosings while I focus on learning how to be a proper wife."

"Do you speak the truth, or were you instructed to say that?"

All our eyebrows raised. Yet, why was I surprised?

"Aunt Catherine!" Colonel Fitzwilliam uttered.

"I ask because I must," Lady Catherine said.

"Thank you, Colonel," Kitty said, "but I understand why you ask that of me, your ladyship. After all, much of life is pretense, isn't it? And I might very well be the largest pretense of all. And when your nephews' happiness hangs in the balance, it can lead to protectiveness. Well, Colonel Fitzwilliam can tell you that I do mean to give a good first impression, but I am not false in what I say."

"Well, you also give your opinion very decidedly."

"I thought that you would admire that about her," I supported, "after all, if she is not outspoken, then how can she be a proper mistress?"

"My sisters have all the abilities of being leaders in their society," Jane supported. "Surely, Rosings Park would like to have ladies with such confidence, would it not?"

She looked between the three of us.

"Well, you three speak very frankly. Not that there is not a great deal of sense in what you all say." She looked at our fiancés. "Well, you three have brought me three very interesting brides who know their own minds. I think you have set yourselves up to have a very unique life. And so, there is nothing for it but to have an interesting wedding."

"We hear that you have made many preparations for our most fortunate day," Kitty noted.

"I have. You will love how the church looks, all the arrangements, and the social scene that will take place for the engagements. All the respectable houses in the counties have already invited you all to dine, and I have accepted all of them. I do hope that you have brought your best gowns in your trousseau, and if not, then we shall have to enter the village to have some gowns made for you. You may choose your gowns, but I have made some selections, and I do believe that you will like some of those options."

Lady Catherine then went on to speak about all the plans she had for our wedding day, and how she had set up quite the whirlwind of parties and events that we would attend. It reached such a point that we would barely have time to sit down at Rosings Park for more than one day after we married. It became very evident that she was determined to show us off to every respectable family in her county and the neighboring ones.

I had grown accustomed to her lectures, where she loved to speak and seldom cared for a response. Jane naturally was accustomed to it, because the serenity of her countenance left her naturally amenable to others being chattier than herself. Darcy and Colonel Fitzwilliam also knew not to be unnerved by it. Kitty seemed to have been properly warned as well, because she only answered questions when she was given a long enough time to answer. Unfortunately, Margaret and Frederick were not so very used to this and accidentally would speak when Lady Catherine did. Of course, she would just talk over them, and I had to show empathy with my expressions.

Eventually, when the discussions on the wedding were exhausted, she directed her attention to Margaret and Frederick.

"So," she said to Margaret, "your mother was born and raised in London, then you all lived in Hampshire, where your father was a vicar."

"He was, your ladyship."

"Did he retire? Is that what took him to the North?"

"No, madam. Rather, he changed professions and left the church."

Lady Catherine raised an eyebrow, her face became shocked, and she leaned forward.

"Your father left the church?"

"Yes, he did. Of his own choosing. Then he took us to the North, and got work there as a professor, teaching pupils and classes."

"Then your father is a dissenter."

"Yes, he is. But it was a matter of conscience, and he was right to trust himself."

"Well, when your father comes, I will advise him in the precise way I advise you now: taking a delicate southern lady to the North was the main source of her illness. From going from one climate to another, can be detrimental."

"I am well."

"And so am I," Frederick stated.

"Yes, but you have youth to help you. Your mother is not so fortunate. And in life, one cannot be too careful, as I have learned. Our Doctor Carney is most extraordinary. He has a plethora of medical treatments, which I will list for you. In the meantime, here are the best foods to provide for an invalid. Due to my late daughter's ill health, I procured an invalid's chair, and I believe that fresh air will do your mother good. I instruct that you and your cousin must make a mission of this every day, to give her some brief walks about Rosings grounds. Nature will do Mrs. Hale as much good as medicine."

"We thank you, ma'am," Frederick responded, feeling quite out of his element. He had never been accustomed to a woman with authoritative and demanding tones, and therefore, he had no choice but to be a little intimidated. Margaret merely sat there, motionless, which might be precisely what Lady Catherine would have wished. Lady Catherine often boasted of ladies who had such elegance.

Lady Catherine did as she promised and began to list all the foods that Mrs. Hale should eat while she remained with us.

The dinner was exceedingly handsome, and there were all the servants, and all the articles of plate which Mr. Collins had boasted of when he visited us at Longbourn. Jane and Frederick complimented her on the meal, and Mr. Bingley was also very profuse in his flattery. Lady Catherine seemed gratified by their admiration, and gave most gracious smiles, especially when any dish on the table proved a novelty to them.

Lady Catherine instructed food to be sent to Mr. and Mrs. Hale in their room, so that the delicate lady could rest properly. Then she proceeded to boast of her ability to tend to the sick, and of all the poor in the neighborhood that she sent foods to.

This part of her talk did not upset me very much, because it wasn't just a matter of selfish praise, but merely an establishment of identity in the world. Time taught me that charity was what made up the wealthy. Their money was a praise in a village because they felt obliged to be kinder and considerate of the poor around them. The destitute were low enough to be within a great lady's notice, and thus providing for them was precisely what the wealth ought to do.

As we sat to eat together, I was not seated next to Mr. Darcy. Sitting next to one's fiancé was not how Lady

Catherine had arranged it all. Therefore, Darcy and I were obliged to exchange quick glances with each other, whenever we wished to be in each other's confidence.

"Well," Lady Catherine declared, "onto the matter of the wedding, I can declare that it is considered not only an excitement here at Rosings, but all the village is in excitement with the news."

"The village?" Mr. Darcy asked. "They know of our engagement?"

"Naturally," Lady Catherine declared, "you cannot imagine that I was going to host a triple wedding and let all the parish be unaware of it all. They haven't had such news in so long. Naturally, this is agreeable to you?" Mr. Darcy was about to open his mouth to object to our ceremony being made popular, but Lady Catherine overrode him. "Yes, I am certain that you do." She looked at all of us Bennets. "As I understand it, you two are the eldest sisters, but you, Miss Kitty, are the fourth daughter, with one in the middle."

"You refer to our third sister, Mary," I said, "yes, she is the middle sister."

"And is she to be soon married?"

"No, she is not. She was living with our aunt and uncle Gardiner, in London. Yet when Mrs. Collins passed away, she was invited to Longbourn, to help Mr. Collins with his child."

"What?" Lady Catherine asked, perplexed. "Your sister lives with Mr. Collins?"

"A visit, merely," Jane answered.

"And since we were the original residents of the place," Kitty added, "Mary is being most obliging to him."

"Being a widower now," I added, "Mr. Collins finds that looking after his child is too much for him, and he needed a woman to assist in looking after the baby. Mary has always been the most dutiful one out of the five of us, and therefore—"

"Yes, yes, yes!" Lady Catherine snapped. Margaret blinked at her rudeness, but I was not offended, because I was used to her temper. "My surprise is not about your middle sister's situation, but of me being wholly ignorant of the matter. Mr. Collins never wrote to me of these recent developments. This is extremely vexing."

"I am certain that the man meant no offense," Frederick inferred. "In fact, he probably did not want many people to know of it."

His sudden remark made Lady Catherine raise an eyebrow and turn to him critically. It was obvious that Frederick Hale then regretted that he ever spoke. He swallowed, insecure.

"What do you mean, Mr. Frederick?"

"Well, if a man feels a deep affection for his wife," Frederick assumed, "and he loses her, he is not in a proper state. I have some experience on the matter, in befriending men who have lost their wives. Usually when that is the case, part of themselves unravel, and they fall away from society. They want to be alone. But when the woman leaves a child behind, not all men know how to take the responsibility of both mother and father at the same time. In fact, I have noticed that fathers are not always so able to be a parent without a wife, sometimes. And it seems like such in this case. This Mr. Collins probably came undone when he lost Mrs. Collins, and therefore, he forgot to write to his particular friends."

"Well, that must be surely the reason. As a woman who has recently lost a loved one, I can see the inducement of wanting to fall away from the eyes of the world. Even when he became the master of Longbourn, he still wrote to me of his situation. Therefore, this reason makes all the sense in the world. Though, he ought to remember what he owes to Rosings Park. Miss Bennet?"

"Yes, madam," Jane said.

"You will write to Longbourn tomorrow and tell your sister to order Mr. Collins to write to me of his recent developments. Since I can empathize with his tragedy, I could offer far superior advice than anyone else in Hertfordshire. And I will advise your sister on how to look after an infant. The servants at Longbourn might not be as experienced as I am on such matters. Write the letter tomorrow and I will have it sent by express. Even when letters are not of emergency, I still prefer them sent as quickly as possible. I despise having to wait for news, nor for having it sent."

"Very well, ma'am," Jane said.

"But as for your younger sister, Miss Mary, as much as I prefer the eldest to be married before the younger ones are, I can make an exception in this case. In fact, I am quite certain that Miss Kitty will do very well for you, Colonel Fitzwilliam, but I still remain steadfast that the eldest ought to be married before the younger sisters are out."

The next thing that I was about to say was going to provoke her, and I welcomed it.

"Actually, we are not the first to marry. Our youngest sister, Lydia, was the first to marry."

"What? The youngest sister married first of the five of you?"

"Yes," Kitty said, "she married an officer, named Corporal Denny. They are a striking couple."

"What were your parents thinking?" Lady Catherine stated. "The youngest married before the eldest? Truly, I cannot understand your mother at all."

I took one look at Mr. Darcy, and he was offended for me.

"Sadly, she can never be present to give her explanation. Lydia married after our parents died. Therefore, our parents never had time to see her, or any of us, marry. She did so after Longbourn was entailed to our cousin."

"Oh, well, that is natural, I suppose," Lady Catherine had to acknowledge, "as I have said before, I have never seen the necessity of an estate being entailed solely to male heirs. Sir de Bourgh never thought it correct to entail Rosings to anyone else but myself and my poor Anne. But, if one were to lose their home, then marriage is the natural step to make. I wonder that you never thought to do it yourselves as opposed to traveling all the way to the North. Yet, fortune worked for you."

Mr. Darcy and I looked at each other.

"Yes," I said, "I daresay that it did."

Chapter 19

Sister-in-law News

"Lizzy and Margaret!" Kitty cried, running into my room. Margaret and I were sitting there, where she was telling me everything about her recent development with Mr. Thornton, when Kitty knocked on the door. This annoyed me, because Margaret had still not reached the point yet of when she had begun to admit that she was beginning to feel for Mr. Thornton, and what she said to him, when the most unwelcome intrusion burst upon our door.

"Hold that thought," I informed Margaret, "Don't lose your place."

"I won't," Margaret said, "not in the slightest. I am just as eager to talk of this as you are to hear it."

I grinned.

"Now this is a changed Margaret indeed."

I opened the door and Kitty was standing there, her cheeks red.

"Kitty," I said, "you do realize that you have interrupted me during a very vital part of my education."

Kitty looked between Margaret and me.

"I doubt that."

"Perhaps I was exaggerating. Now, what do you huff and puff about?"

"She is come!"

"Who has come?"

"Georgiana Darcy, of course. Her carriage has just arrived, and she is soon to enter the house."

My eyes widened.

"Georgiana Darcy is here?"

"Yes. Now make haste. You don't want to be absent when your future sister-in-law enters and we make introductions, do you?"

"Oh dear!"

Margaret and I raced around the room, pulling up our stockings while Kitty grabbed our closest set of shoes. We dashed around the room, putting our things on, getting arranged, then we both raced to the mirror and checked our appearance.

"My hair," Margaret and I exclaimed since a few strands had fallen.

"Kitty," I said, "help us."

"Don't worry, I know the routine."

She dashed around us and pulled the strands back into our hair knots, clasping our hairclips back on properly. While Margaret and I tidied up our fronts and made sure that no lent was on our dresses, out of the corner of my eye, I noticed two figures grinning at us.

I turned my head, sharply, sending Kitty into a fit, when I saw Mr. Darcy and Colonel Fitzwilliam smiling at us.

"Mr. Darcy and Colonel," Margaret uttered.

"How long have you two hobbyhorses been standing there?" I asked.

"For quite some time to see the entire show," Colonel Fitzwilliam laughed.

"You cannot blame us," Darcy added. Though he did not smile, his eyes twinkled. "We came to inform you that my sister, Miss Georgiana Darcy, has arrived and that she is already in the sitting room, awaiting an introduction."

"Brilliant," I declared, rolling my eyes. "The first time that I meet your sister, and I have done it entirely in the wrong way. Is this a bad omen, I wonder?"

"And as for me," Kitty said to the Colonel, "I will come rushing in to meet your cousin and charge with rosy cheeks, and behind the first sister who already feels incorrect."

"It is not your fault, we assure you," Darcy coaxed us. "She arrived two hours earlier than expected, and since Lady Catherine has been tending to Mrs. Hale, even she was not prepared."

"Where is my brother?" Margaret asked. "We both went our different ways when Lady Catherine ushered us out of my mother's room and would not let me be nurse to her."

"Do not be offended by my aunt's strong will, Miss Hale," Colonel Fitzwilliam said, compassionate. "I just think that... well, I think my aunt needs to pay attention to an invalid right now."

"I know," Margaret said, eyeing me, "I suspected that she might."

"When last I checked," Kitty said, "Frederick was taking a tour of the stables. A servant will call him in eventually."

"Then where is your sister now?" I asked, going up to Mr. Darcy and taking his arm. "She is not alone in the drawing room, is she?"

"Not at all. Miss Bennet and Mr. Bingley are with her."

"Oh, Jane is the one to make the best first impression," Kitty sighed, "why must it always be her? Her ability to always be in the right place at the right time will baffle me."

"Some people paint," Colonel Fitzwilliam responded, by way of explanation.

"Yes," Kitty cooed, "and I can't do that either."

"If it helps, I can't draw, sing, play, or cover screens."

"Good. We can be mediocre together. I adore you."

"You better do so."

Darcy and I looked at each other, while Margaret gave us space, walking behind us.

"Your sister plays well," I said, "and I do not. What will she do with me?"

"Love you."

"I know that *you* do," I said, grinning, "but hopefully, so will she."

When we walked into the drawing room, Lady Catherine had beaten us there. Jane and Mr. Bingley were sitting down, listening to Lady Catherine talk about Mrs. Hale's condition to a young and delicate-looking young woman, who I could only surmise was Miss Georgiana Darcy herself.

When seeing her, my nerves rushed over me. The one and only benefit to Mr. Darcy's and I both being orphans, was that there were no parents to object to his union with me. Naturally, a sister did not hold precedence over his heart, but it still would help if she liked me.

A person's relatives can have a great effect on one's domestic happiness, of course.

When looking between Georgiana and Mr. Darcy, I saw very little family resemblance. This left me to assume that Georgiana looked similar to her mother, while Mr. Darcy must have resembled his father.

Miss Darcy's figure was formed, and her appearance was

womanly and graceful. She was less handsome than her brother, but there was sense and good humor in her expressions. From the little that I had seen, her manners were perfectly unassuming and gentle.

"Ah," Lady Catherine declared, "now our party is at its proper size. Georgiana, here is your brother, cousin, and their fiancées."

Georgiana turned to us, and her expression was obviously bashful.

"Cousin!" Colonel Fitzwilliam cried, going up to her. His exclamation was followed by Mr. Darcy, who also approached her.

"Brother and cousin," Georgiana said, as they eagerly hugged her. "How long it has been."

"I know," Mr. Darcy said, "and it will never be so long in parting again, I assure you. Georgiana, it was not my intention to be away from you for too long, but I had business in the North that I needed to attend to."

"I know," Georgiana assured him, looking at me over his shoulder, "Your letters said everything."

"Yes," Darcy responded gently, "I did, didn't I? For the first time, I probably wrote more words than usual."

"Yes, you did. I understood. Truly, I understood." Then she looked at Colonel Fitzwilliam. "Your business kept you away, but you also found your happiness as well."

"Yes, we have," Colonel Fitzwilliam replied, "and eagerly, we would love for you to meet our future brides, and their friend."

"You fit the role of master well, nephew," Lady Catherine said, "but till then, I still make the introductions."

"Of course, aunt. Forgive me."

"Naturally. You were just excited. Georgiana, these are Miss Bennet's younger sisters: Miss Elizabeth Bennet and

Miss Kitty Bennet. This is their friend, Miss Margaret Hale. Ladies, this is my niece, and Mr. Darcy's sister, Miss Georgiana Darcy."

We all curtsied together, and I felt that we had begun the conversation awkwardly.

"Do sit down," Lady Catherine said, then she turned to a servant, "call in Mr. Frederick from the stables, so that he can pay respect to my niece."

"Miss Darcy," I said, as we exchanged glances, "it is a pleasure to meet you. I've heard a great deal about you, but I feel as if I know you already."

"And I about you. My—brother—has written to me... a great deal about his adventures in the North. I was—wondering—if we would ever meet."

She turned to Kitty.

"And you are to marry my cousin—and—be the mistress of Rosings Park."

"I believe that title will remain with your aunt for many years to come," Kitty responded, "but yes!" Her last word spoken was loud and sharp, and it made Georgiana's eyebrows raise. "Oh dear, I said that loudly, didn't I? I did. Good gracious."

"It is well," Georgiana said gently. When she did so, Kitty's eyes became discerning.

"I am nervous," Kitty rambled, "I suppose that I cannot help it. But then, so are you, aren't you?"

Jane and I exchanged an apprehensive glance, worried that Kitty was beginning this in a strange way.

"Miss Kitty," Lady Catherine said, "you are being impertinent."

"Forgive me," Kitty said, "but I just thought I'd say what we were all feeling in case it might help."

"You are nervous as well?" Georgiana spoke, and that

was the loudest she had ever been.

"Yes, I am. I cannot help it. I want you to like me, because my fiancé has said that you are quite the paragon, but I worry that I will say the wrong thing."

"My cousin flatters me greatly, to the point where he speaks more highly of my qualities than I deserve, but yes. I am worried that I might say the wrong things as well."

"Then we are all equally nervous?" I questioned. I turned to Jane. "Are you nervous?"

"Well," Jane blushed, "since we are all admitting it, I confess to being a little so as well."

"And what about you?" I asked, turning to Margaret. "Are you nervous?"

Margaret half-smiled.

"I have the benefit of not being engaged to anyone that Miss Darcy is related to, so my apprehension is less so. But I confess to the very same nervousness that is attached to every new introduction to a lady that you want to impress."

"There is no need to impress me," Georgiana said, her voice cracking a little. "I can assure you."

"Then it is settled," I determined, "we are all equally nervous, and therefore, we have all the chances of going forward, because we already began backwards."

"This conversation has begun all wrong," Lady Catherine determined. "Ladies, decorum, please."

"Of course, your ladyship," Kitty said, "I just think that we needed to establish that we were all equal in our anxiety. Sometimes," she said, looking compassionately at Georgiana, "it can be nice to be kindred in that way."

"I do believe that the ladies have the right way about it," Colonel Fitzwilliam said, "Sometimes, what ought to be discussed cannot be discussed too quickly."

"I confess," Georgiana said, "that this did make me feel

easier. If three of these ladies are to be my future sisters-in-law, then maybe their honesty will—work—in the present. Ladies, you must forgive me. It is just... that I am known for my bashfulness."

"There is nothing to apologize for," I said. "We are not ogres. We will not judge you, but accept your habit, if you will be so kind as to accept that you have three very voluble sisters in your hands."

"I welcome conversation from others, when I am not able to supply it myself."

We were interrupted when Frederick Hale entered. Introductions were made on his part, and soon after, he asked if he could bring his mother outside, due to the fine day.

"Forgive my presumptuousness," Frederick said, "but I was wondering if maybe, I could bring my aunt and uncle down to meet Miss Darcy, and then I can take them along the grounds. The air is so fine that I am certain it may do my aunt some good. If your ladyship is not against the idea, of course."

"That is a perfect suggestion," Lady Catherine said, "and it shows familial consideration." She ordered a servant to retrieve Mr. and Mrs. Hale.

While we waited, Lady Catherine asked Georgiana very direct questions about the time she spent with her friends in Scarborough. Georgiana's answers were brief, but it was no matter. Lady Catherine filled up most of the space with the advice that she offered about Scarborough not being the ideal place for anyone to live, due to the terrain. Then she advised Georgiana and the rest of us what to wear whenever we would face areas that produced such harsh winds. Since I had never gone to Scarborough, I had no opinion of the weather conditions there, but I doubted that it was any different than the rest of Southern England. In that duration, we learned a little of Georgiana's friends, but not enough for us to be aware of her preferences regarding companionship.

What I did learn of her was that she was naturally shy.

This reminded me of Mr. Wickham's description when I first asked about Miss Darcy. His explanation only indicated just how deep was his level of deception.

Gone forever were his 'when she and I were children, we were great friends, and I spent hours and hours devoted to her amusement. But alas, she has grown up to be very like her brother. Very proud!'

And then, in its place was Miss Bingley's description of Miss Darcy.

'Mr. Bingley is much engaged in town with Miss Georgiana Darcy, who there is no equal to her, regarding her nature and accomplishment. I flatter myself that I am not wrong for not only hoping, but easily predicting that soon I shall call her my sister, eventually. For my brother is much struck with her charms and always finds a keen interest in her company.'

It was truly all lies.

Instead, in its place was the actual reality. Mr. Wickham would have it that Georgiana was proud.

But he was the one to lure her into an elopement, to steal her money when he had squandered his fortune away in months.

Miss Bingley would have it that Georgiana was intended for Mr. Bingley.

But now Mr. Bingley was engaged to my sister.

I never believed Miss Bingley's findings, so I didn't feel shame on that score.

But that I had once believed Mr. Wickham. Good lord, what could I have been thinking?

Miss Darcy was shy, single, and seemed to have no interest in Mr. Bingley whatsoever. There was no hint of jealousy in her eye when she looked at Jane with Mr. Bingley. There had never been any affection between them. Once more, this reinforced me to only ever make my determinations on what I saw for myself, and not for what others told me.

Soon, Mr. Hale came down, wheeling Mrs. Hale in the room in her invalid's chair. While Mrs. Hale's skin was still pale, her eyes were opened widely, and she smiled when she entered.

Even if she was very ill, she seemed to have more life in her than her last few weeks in Milton. I suppose that she was happy to be back in a world that she thoroughly understood. When she was a beautiful young woman, she would often stay in homes such as this. Perhaps the effects of falling back into the past couldn't help but make her rally from the pain she was experiencing.

Immediately, Frederick and Margaret went to her.

"Are you well, mama?" Margaret asked, kneeling in front of her.

"I am well enough, my dear," Mrs. Hale said. "And I believe that I am greatly looking forward to conversation and company. Lady Catherine, once more, I cannot thank you enough for inviting me and my family. There is a decided magic to this house."

"You speak well of something that I have always believed," Lady Catherine said. "And your cousin could not have been more correct about you needing some fresh air. The air today is very fine. I recommend that we all take a walk about the grounds, and I will give you history of much that has happened here."

"I can take the reins from you, *cousin*," Frederick said to his father, as he took control of his mother's chair and rolled her further into the room. "I prefer to be of service."

"The children in my family are so very good," Mrs. Hale said, referring to her two children. "Always wishing to nurse me."

"As children ought to," Lady Catherine said, standing up, "let us all gather our things and meet in the vestibule. A day without storm clouds and fine weather cannot be the day to remain inside."

"Are you tired from your journey?" Mr. Darcy asked Georgiana. "I would prefer you to join us, but I do not want you to overtax yourself."

"I am not tired," Georgiana said, "since I was in a carriage, I actually would prefer to walk a little, and I would like to hear more about my new family. Especially since the wedding is soon approaching. I want to know as much as I can, since I have new sisters in my life."

"That's right," Kitty acknowledged, "you have never had a sister."

"Just like you have never had a brother."

"Yes. Our lives are different. How brilliant, isn't it?"

Georgiana smiled at her.

We all began our walk about the grounds. Since the green was very even, it was easy for Frederick to roll the invalid's chair along the grass, and Lady Catherine was on full display of showing us most of the enhancements that her gardeners had made to the landscape.

We complimented when we were given the chance, and it was all genuine, for the scenes before us did show great advantage to nature.

"How do you feel?" Mr. Darcy asked as we walked along.

We had a certain amount of privacy because Georgiana

remained closer to Kitty and Colonel Fitzwilliam, with Lady Catherine closer to the Hales, talking to Mrs. Hale the most.

"I feel happy," I said, turning to him, "and as if I have fallen in love with these woods and hills, and then I remember that we are still not at Pemberley. With you there, I think only then will I be happiest." I blushed. "Am I being too flowery in my words?"

"No. I cannot wait to take you to my home. All the places on the grounds that I know of, so intimately. There are miles of land that many do not walk upon but are lovely beyond comparison. It is nature at its most intensely serene, and we would be away from all prying eyes." He turned to me. "I will show you those places. We will get lost within them, and when we do, our thoughts and feelings will turn in a true union. Adam and Eve will have never experienced the bliss that we shall share when we are in those spots, and you and I will let all strictness fall away. The things we shall do, the way in which I will do it to you, will be something that the graces of heaven will smile on, for it is love, at its purest."

I knew his meaning. The winding path of his passions were neither foreign to me nor unwanted. I feared none of it, but was willing to tear down decorum, to shed propriety and to not pick it up if it were to lay by the wayside. I would hold nothing back.

"To Pemberley," I declared, "we must go. And when you go to those intimate places on your grounds, you will find me there, you will love me in them, and you will take me over and over—and I will be your wife repeatedly."

He swallowed deeply.

"Thank god we shall marry soon."

"I know. This waiting is always the hardest part."

I looked ahead at Georgiana as she laughed at something that Kitty said.

"If your sister knew what we were speaking of now…"

"She must never know."

"She will not. But I must allow her to know that I love you very deeply."

"That, you can talk to her about."

"And I will."

"But for now, what do you think of her?"

"I think that I shall live my life trying to be a good sister to her, because she deserves it."

"I know you will," Darcy replied, his chest swelling with pride. "I know that you will."

We continued to walk around the grounds for an hour, then we entered when it was time to dine.

Chapter 20

Matriarchal News

I n her bedroom, Margaret was composing a letter to Mr. Thornton. Each time she wrote a sentence, she jotted it out, for fear that it would sound imprudent, and that her father might see it. Since her letter was going to be sent through his, her tone had to be sanguine and simple. But she wanted Thornton to know that she did not have a cold tone when writing to him.

Therefore, dipping her pin in the ink, she did her best to write about the events that were occurring since they arrived, their meeting Miss Darcy, Lady Catherine, and how her mother was regaining her good cheer, despite everything. Every now and again, she expressed a desire to know how he fared in Milton, and that she wanted to make sure that he was happy, well, and that the factory was running success-fully. She said, in the only way that it could be said, 'that I am now taking an eager interest in all the dealings in your life, for now I see the importance of it'.

She wished she could say that she missed him. But that was not proper.

And even more painful—it was true.

She missed Mr. Thornton. Every day she was in Rosings Park, she found that she was always turning her thoughts back to Milton and wondering what he was doing there.

What a shocking blow it was! All that time she spent in the North, wishing she could be thrown out of it and returned to the beloved South. And now she longed to return to her friends in Milton, and to see a man that she despised for so long. It was too much.

Would that she could release him from her mind!

He was slowly winning her heart, but she at least wished that she could maintain her self-control.

She went to her father and handed him the letter, since he was composing some of his own.

"You write to Mr. Bell?" Margaret asked as Mr. Hale was composing his missive.

"Yes, I am," Mr. Hale answered, "he writes to tell me that there is to be a reunion at Oxford, of all my school friends. He was wondering if I could attend. I would like to, but right now, your mother shall need me. If it would take a turn for the worst, then I don't want to miss a day with her."

"I understand, father, and so would Mr. Bell. Tell me that I offer him my well-wishes, and that we miss him."

"I shall."

I looked around their bedroom.

"And where is mama?"

"She is with Lady Catherine. They are speaking in the breakfast room, I believe."

Margaret squinted.

"Why do you look that way?" Mr. Hale asked.

"It's just strange, that's all. First, Lady Catherine will not let me nurse my mother, but always sends the doctor at all hours, and then she also is taking up much time with her.

Even Lizzy remarks on how the two of them speak together very often."

"It makes all the sense in the world to me. They are two ladies nearing the same age, who are from the same time and level in society. Do not be offended for Lady Catherine not wishing for you to spend so much time tending to your mother. First, you are young and should enjoy yourself. Second, this is doing your mother a world of good. She often returns to me, telling me about something that Lady Catherine said, and she does it with such animation! Oh, Margaret! The best thing was for us to come to Rosings Park. Who would have believed it?"

Margaret smiled gently at him.

"Yes, who could have?"

Despite her father's explanation, Margaret's mind was still not rested.

Lady Catherine's growing relationship with her mother was curious to Margaret Hale, who did not understand how such a bond could have occurred.

Her ladyship was such a fine lady, of an elderly age, who had an estate to run, a triple wedding to plan for, many young people under her care and company, and a new heir to help adjust to the estate. Despite all this, she still found time to sit with Mrs. Hale and tend to her, even dote on her, in a way that Margaret and the Bennet sisters could not help but observe. This marked attention made it impossible for Margaret to ever be offended at Lady Catherine's impertinent questions directed toward herself, her occasional offensive remarks, and her voluble behavior.

Every now and again, Lizzy and Margaret made their assumptions about what the reason for such marked attention was, especially since Lady Catherine had so much to do, but they had only theories.

Finally, Margaret's curiosity ate away at her so much that she finally approached her mother about it when they were alone in her room.

"Actually," Mrs. Hale said, "when you think about it, it makes a great deal of sense that she and I have formed a friendship, even if it will not be a long-lasting one."

"Truly?" Margaret asked, confused. "You must help me, for I cannot get on at all. You both are such different sorts of women. You are slight, quiet and delicate, and she is more robust, talks a great deal, and is larger."

"Similarity of characteristics does not always mean friendship, nor do differences cause discord. You forget, Margaret, that Lady Catherine and I are the same age, and grew up in the same sort of society. We remember the same fashions, the same historical events, the same sort of romances and balls that we experienced—but yesterday, we spent a whole three hours talking about the lace that our dressmakers used to put on our clothes." Mrs. Hale leaned back and smiled warmly. She had looked better than she had in weeks. "Sometimes, Margaret, when you reach a certain age, you want to remember those days when you were young, the world was before your feet, and you thought that you would live forever. That's what it means to be young, you know: it's to burn so brightly, and even though it's fleeting, it's beautiful. We both had those times, those experiences, and so we understand each other. Also, we are two women who have a daughter. Mine is still here, and hers is gone."

When hearing her speak like that, Margaret was even more humbled than ever. On top of that, she also was moved by her mother's serene expression. In her mother's eyes was the memories of the social scene that she experienced when she was a young woman thrown into the pleasures of London society.

"I told her about how I sent you to Harley Street to be your cousin's companion. She scolded me for spending so much time away from my own daughter. Her exact words were 'time with your child is a treasure', and you don't know that it is, until it is too late." Mrs. Hale turned to Margaret, repentant. "I should have kept you by me, Margaret, and not been so ashamed of my situation in life. I should have given you the choice and have been the mother that you wanted. Lady Catherine was right. I should have spent more time with you," she said, taking Margaret's hand. "My dear and wonderful daughter. If I have not said it before, I am so proud of you."

"I know that you are, mama," Margaret said, holding her mother's hand. "You did what you thought was best for me. While I would have preferred to be near you and father much more in life, I did not hate my life. I loved Edith and Aunt Shaw. I did have happy moments there, even if London society did not agree with me. You are telling me now, and that's what matters."

"She misses her daughter," Mrs. Hale continued. "She misses Anne very much. Yet she knows that it does not help to talk about it to you all, because she understands that this is her nephews' time for happiness with their brides. She does not want to dampen their experience with her tales of woe. But those tales need to come out somewhere. I know that her manners are strong, and her tone is intense, but always indulge her, Margaret. Tell the Bennet sisters to do this. I know that you do this already but continue to. When it comes to a person who is suffering in the way she is, attention is what they need. Attention. And I give her that. Sometimes, she spends hours talking about her poor Anne, and I sit there, interested in everything that she has to say. No mother should have to lose her child. It would be agony, you understand. Always remember, she is a woman who lost her baby. That is not fair."

"I will not forget. I am happy that you both gain a great deal by being in each other's confidence."

"Also, I think it's more than that. I am an invalid, and I think that Lady Catherine needs to feel like she has the possibility to save a life. I feel terrible that she might not succeed."

"You are looking better."

"And I feel it, somewhat, but the fact is that I am aware of what will happen."

"Yes, it may, but mama sometimes the mind can do powerful things. If you tell yourself that you will die, of course you will. But if you tell yourself that you can live, and you fight to do so, then maybe you might. Of course, God will take you when he will, but please, try. For me. For father. For Dixon. And for Frederick. Please try."

Mrs. Hale looked at her daughter, sadly.

"Margaret, just for you, my dear. For you, and for Frederick. I will fight."

Chapter 21

The-Night-Before News

On the night before our wedding day, we all were invited to a dinner party at a neighboring estate, called Granwell Abbey.

The Darcys, Lady Catherine and the Colonel were well acquainted with the family, but for most of us, this was our first time meeting them.

Their family were the Howards, and they were a pleasant sort of people that Lady Catherine had arranged to be one of our final engagement dinners.

Fortunately, there was dancing there, and we were able to enjoy the experience. Only the Hales had not attended, except Frederick, because Lady Catherine expressly ordered that Mrs. Hale should still rest and that meeting new people could be exhausting for her.

"I want to thank her ladyship," I said to Darcy as we were at the party, "for all that she has done with Mrs. Hale and how well she welcomes that family. But each time I approach her, I don't know how to approach the subject."

"There will never be a perfect time to do it," Mr. Darcy

said, "all you can do is find your nearest opportunity and strike when the proverbial iron is hot."

"You, good sir, are talking through metaphors. I like it."

"Oh, then the trick is if I can do it while dancing."

He turned to the dance floor as Mr. Howard called up any couples who wished to dance.

"Well, Miss Bennet, will you do me this honor?"

"With all my heart, all my arms, and both of my legs," I replied, placing my hand in his as he led me to the dance floor.

While we stood there, facing each other as we waited for the music to begin, I admired my partner in full.

To my right, Kitty stood up with Colonel Fitzwilliam, to my left, Jane stood up with Mr. Bingley. Next to her, Frederick stood up with Georgiana.

When the music began, Mr. Darcy took me in his arms, and we began to dance.

"Do you know what?" I asked.

"What?"

"I could do this for the rest of our lives."

His eyes looked on me mischievously.

"Oh, but there is one activity that I will teach you to like more than others."

"First," I said, whispering frantically. "You wicked creature. And second, you forget, I already like that activity."

"Oh, tsk, tsk, tsk. You have seen nothing yet. Or rather, you have experienced nothing yet."

"You make me impatient to know what that is."

"You will not have long to wait. For tomorrow, the knot will be tied, and you will experience all the luxuries of being Mrs. Darcy."

"And I will teach you the pleasures of being *Mr. Bennet*."

At first, he looked at me confused as we turned, but soon, he saw the joke that I made.

"Oh," he replied, comprehension dawning over him, "you imagined a reality where I took *your* last name."

"What are the chances, I wonder, that one day, that will happen? When the man takes the woman's last name."

Mr. Darcy chuckled.

"That is a dream, if I ever saw one. You and I both know, Lizzy, that *that* will never happen."

"Yes, it might. Oh well, a dream is a dream."

"I am sorry that Margaret cannot be here."

"She is fine being at Rosings with her parents. But I must ask you something?"

"Yes?"

"Have you received a letter from Mr. Thornton at all?"

"No, not as of yet. But then, I have not written to him. I didn't think to do so until we are married, and I had something of note to write about. Don't worry; he knows that I do not neglect him. He and I are just the sorts to not be casual about our writing. Thornton and I don't have the habit of writing unless we have something of import to tell the reader."

"When you are a lady of leisure, as I have been for most of my life, you often learn to write letters of pleasure, as opposed to letters of business. But when it comes to letters of business, tsk, tsk, tsk! Miss Bingley always felt: how odious I should think them!"

"Yes, she did say that while I was writing to my sister! She really didn't see all the harm she did, while she assumed that she was strengthening her image in my eyes."

"And soon, I will have no choice but to see her. That was the one benefit of no longer being in the South. Oh, but then I remember Fanny Thornton."

"You really never stood a chance no matter where you went, were you?"

"No, I was not. From one woman to the other, I seemed to suffer under the wrong side of their intended romantic plans. No matter how far I run, I seem to end up in the same place as I had begun. Now I have learned not to run away, but just to *walk* away."

"Is there a difference?" Darcy asked, amused.

"Oh yes, a very great difference."

"But why did you ask me about Thornton?"

I looked down at the floor as we danced.

"No," he pressed, "do not do that, Lizzy. Do not entice my curiosity, and then send me away, leaving me in wonder."

"No, I should not do that, should I? Well, I will do it every now and again, but only if I mean to torture you. But right now, I do not. I have been taken into Margaret's confidence, so I cannot give much away."

"You know something of Margaret's heart? Does it relate to Thornton?"

"Yes, it does. I will not tell you of any set intentions that she may have, but I know that, when they parted, Margaret indicated that she appreciated his affection for her."

When hearing this news, Mr. Darcy's face underwent a major transformation. His face tensed up and then relaxed.

"Lizzy, is this true?"

"Yes, it is." Taking in his expression, I was most amused. "You look happy about this."

"Well, Thornton and I are friends. I want him to be happy, and the more that I consider the matter, the more I must take his nature into account. Margaret is his first large love, you see? Thornton spent so much of his life helping his mother climb out of the hole that his father placed them in. As such, he never had time for love. Now he does, and when a man has his first grand affection, it is like he is hit by a lightning bolt. Margaret struck him; he will be in love with her for the rest of his life. Also, with the strike and all the rest of it, he needs some comfort right now. If Margaret left, giving him some assurance that she was grateful for his regard for her, it will be like a balm on his wounds. He will carry that with him as well. Do you... never mind, it is not my place to ask."

"We are getting married in the morning; ask it or go to the devil, sir," I teased. "Paradise is overpopulated anyway."

"I just cannot help but be curious. She is grateful for his feelings for her, yes, but does she feel anything in return?"

"That is a bold question, and I will only tell you the answer if you promise to keep it between us. It must strictly be in each other's confidence."

"You know that my mouth is like a steel trap."

"Yes, I do. I just needed confirmation. Well, the truth is that...she is indeed beginning to feel for him. In a romantic sense as well as in a friendly way. She is growing fond of him."

"Well, now, is that not altogether wonderful?"

"Yes, it is. I am happy for it. I wanted Margaret to gain more friends. Now she has one, in the man that loves her. There is nowhere for them to go now, but forward."

"And they really ought to go forward now. All we can do is wait, can't we?"

"Yes, we can."

"Now that I know, I shall write to Thornton. Maybe he wants someone to talk about it to and doesn't know where to turn."

"Write to him," I said. "At this difficult time, his close confidantes are gone, and he needs someone to confide in. Write the letter tonight and have the servant send it before our ceremony."

"I will," Darcy said, his eyes gentle, "now, to marriage."

"Yes, sir. To marriage we go!"

When we returned to Rosings Park, we were all exhausted. The gentlemen bid us a goodnight, and we parted from them longingly, knowing that tomorrow could not come sooner.

We inquired after Mrs. Hale, who had retired to bed, by the time that we returned.

Mr. Hale and Margaret sat up, waiting for us. Lady Catherine explained our evening to them, in incredible detail.

She listed every dance, and who danced with whom. In that moment, I had the knife of nostalgia digging into my stomach. After all, that was how my mother always talked of our assemblies when we returned from home. And if father did not attend, she would explain the events with immense detail.

Mrs. Hale listened with animation, and Mr. Hale just sat there, quietly, happy that his wife had been receiving so much attention.

The only time he spoke was when I sat down next to him and observed that Mrs. Hale was looking happier. Even though she did not necessarily look healthier, she did not look any worse.

"Yes, she is," he replied to me, keeping his eyes on his wife. "Some people believe in a theory, mind over matter. That a person's attitude toward illness can help the illness on. Of course, none of us want to be sickly, and I am aware that death is quite beyond our power. Ultimately, death always wins, and no medicine can prevent it. But sometimes, a positive disposition can increase a person's chances of survival. If the spirit fights, then maybe our constitutions will fight alongside us." He looked at me hopefully, and then his face transformed into embarrassment at his own folly. "Naturally, I know what might ultimately happen. I do not pretend that we humans can always defeat serious ailments, but I have to—"

"Hope?" I finished his sentence. "Yes, you do. You must hope, even when reality looks bleak. Hope is often all we have."

I knew that I might have been giving him dangerous advice. After all, when you give someone hope when that hope very well might not come true, the aftermath can be detrimental. Widows and widowers have often fallen apart when their hope led to unrealistic expectations.

However, I could not tell him the truth. Because, quite frankly, sometimes the truth is not good enough for some circumstances. Sometimes, being wholly honest is the most erroneous thing you can do. Once more, the gray of life decided to paint its color of my situation.

Dream on, Mr. Hale. Dream on about Mrs. Hale recovering. Of her remaining by your side for longer and walking beside you till the end of your days. Dreams are important. I would know.

I was interrupted from my musings when I overheard Lady Catherine boasting about Frederick's success at the dinner party.

"You should have seen your cousin," Lady Catherine said to Mr. and Mrs. Hale. "He, along with my nephews and

Mr. Bingley, were quite admired in the set. If you didn't have that wife in Spain, Mr. Frederick, I daresay that Miss Howard and her little sister would have been quite taken with you."

"You flatter me, your ladyship," Frederick responded, "but if you saw my wife, you would understand why I could never choose another in the world. I think you would like her very much."

"Well, when you come to England again, you must bring her with you. I believe that she would not be happy until she has seen Rosings, for I can boast of my estate being one of the grandest in the country."

Frederick blushed under the weight of the invitation. The poor man! To have finally reached a point in his life where he received special attention and he could never accept the offer. He knew, after this visit, that he could never return to England. For our company shielded him from any suspicion. No one would doubt the deception he placed on himself, because he had Mr. Darcy and Colonel Fitzwilliam to vouch for him.

However, even he knew that his days of bliss were limited. For, despite the joys he found here at Rosings Park, he could not remain, since he was still a wanted man.

I could not imagine being exiled from one's own home-land. Yes, people matter more than places, ultimately. But home is still home. Hence why patriotism is almost an obligation of the human will.

"Well," Margaret said, watching Lady Catherine with her family. "What do you think?"

"I think this is one of the happiest days of our lives. I met new people, and you still have your family."

"Yes, I daresay that it is." She gave me a look out of the

side of her eye. "I do not mean to be pessimistic, but I do not think we shall ever have moments like this again, shall we?"

"You might be right. But I will choose to believe opposite if you don't mind."

"No, I do not mind at all."

"Now," Lady Catherine bellowed. "It's time for everyone to retire for the evening. Tomorrow is the happy day of three couples' lives, and I will not have it ruined because we stayed up too late. Miss Hale and Mr. Frederick, take Mr. and Mrs. Hale to bed, and make sure that they receive the proper comforts."

"We will, madam," Frederick said, still beside him, "you may depend upon it."

Walking up the stairs to retire, Mr. Darcy and I were the last. Together, our arms almost touching, we walked slowly.

Looking longingly at each other, I remembered all the possibilities of intimacy that we would share in the future.

"What are you thinking of, Mrs. Darcy?" he asked me.

"You would call me wanton."

"I want you to be wanton. Now tell me, or I shall burst."

"I am remembering when you and I were at Frances Street, and we let our passions get the better of us. I want to make sure that we do that on our wedding night. But this time..."

"No interruptions?"

"Yes. No interruptions."

"There will be none, I assure you." He leaned into my ear and whispered. "When you wake up after our wedding night, you will have a hard time standing up. That is how much my passion shall shake you."

I shuddered, for I knew that he could make it so.

"I will eagerly await you."

"Yes, you shall."

We stood on the landing, and here is where we had to part ways. But, by the will of Morgan le Fay, we could not move, so much enraptured with each other's gaze.

But naturally, we had a chaperone over my shoulder... again.

"Lizzy," Jane said, "it is time for bed. We marry in the morning. You can see Mr. Darcy then."

We both looked at her, and Jane shocked us both. Once more, gone was the serene and gentle sister. Instead, it was replaced by a woman with a firm gaze and a power to intimidate—in the most subtle way imaginable.

Again, Darcy and I were shamed.

How did Jane do that? Truly! When did she acquire this power?

Darcy and I breathed in deeply, bade each other goodnight, and we parted ways.

"Jane..." I whispered to her.

"Do not even think of getting angry with me, Elizabeth," Jane said. "It will do no good."

"No, I am not angry. I just never knew that you possessed subtle resonance."

"Oh, I have been like this for quite some time. I just never employ it unless I have to. In life, one can be intelligent, or kind. I choose to be kind. But if my intelligence is needed, I shall produce it at the opportune moment. Mark my words."

"Consider them marked."

We parted ways and I retired to my room. A servant helped me undress, and I prepared for bed.

Tomorrow was to be the best day of my life.

There were no other impediments. No other misunderstandings where life got in my way, or I got in the way of myself.

It would be the happiest day.

Please, I prayed all that controlled it, let it be so.

Chapter 22

Matrimonial News

"Girls!" Lady Catherine bellowed, "you must not fidget about."

It was our wedding day.

Each of us ladies awoke early. Not just for the ceremony, but also because of pure nerves.

Every single part of me felt like pins were sticking into it. And I was evidently not alone. Jane and Kitty were also filled with such energy that when our baths were drawn, we plopped right into them, splashing water on the floor.

Soon after we bathed, we immediately set out to get changed into our wedding clothes.

We'd fully dine when we returned from the ceremony. Until then, tea and a little bit of toast and cheese was brought to us.

Since it seemed proper for us all to get assembled in the same room, the servants brought all our items to Jane's bedchambers, and we assembled there.

Throughout all this, Lady Catherine was moving around us with such frantic energy that I could swear that she never had been happier a day in her life.

At this point, we all had grown accustomed to her demanding ways, and decided to judge it as her being affectionate toward us. Interestingly enough, I think we all liked it —because Lady Catherine might not know this, but she now was acting like the closest thing to a mother hen that we would ever have.

This led to her ladyship being fully in her element. Even though we had servants, Lady Catherine was taking it upon herself to make sure that our gowns were properly fastened, that not one strand of our hair was out of place, and that our wedding veils had no ripped seams.

"I can't explain why," Kitty said to Margaret Hale as Mrs. Hale sat in the corner, "but I just can't stand still, for the life of me. You don't think the Colonel will meet me at the altar and then change his mind, do you?"

"Never," Margaret assured her. "I've never seen a man more determined to get married in the whole of my life." She held Kitty's shoulders, and they looked at each other in the mirror. "Besides, how could he walk away from this? He will never see anything more beautiful in the whole of his life."

They continued talking, but my attention was seized when Lady Catherine came up to me and inspected my gown.

"Oh, there is a loose thread here in the back." She turned to one of her servants. "Elena, cut it, and then make sure that it's not going to tear apart."

"Yes, ma'am," Elena replied, and she turned to the back of me.

"Well," I said to Lady Catherine, "other than the rebellious loose thread, how else do I look?"

She looked at me and crossed her arms in front of herself.

"Once more, I believe I have proven to be excellent in my choice of gown. I know that you all wished to have a say in the design, but in truth, young ladies never know what looks best on themselves. An elder woman's hand is always to be preferred."

"Yes, you may be right," I said, looking in the mirror, and then at my sisters. "You really did choose some of the loveliest gowns that I ever saw. Thank you, Lady Catherine."

She looked in the mirror, behind me.

"When I got married, my wedding gown was yellow."

"Yes, my mother told me that wedding gowns were usually all sorts of colors back then."

"Then Queen Victoria came along, had a white wedding gown, and began the trend that might last for a millennia. Well, every monarch ought to be known for setting some sort of trend. Womanhood will probably be thanking her for many years to come."[1]

"What was your wedding like?"

Lady Catherine looked away from me.

"In truth," Lady Catherine confessed, "it was a busy day. Nothing about it felt special."

"Really?" I asked, amazed. With it being Lady Catherine, I never thought she would say anything else but that it was the best day of her life. Even if it wasn't true, I still thought she would say that.

"Yes. My late husband was not the most romantic about it, and, for the first time, I felt like it was more of an alliance than it was a wedding. I wanted different for Anne. But that proved to be impossible."

"I really am sorry for your loss."

"I know. Everyone is. I cried, and I cried, and I cried. But now I must stop crying and look to the future. That is the

---

1. The white wedding gown tradition began with Queen Victoria's wedding in the early-mid 19th century.

main thing I have left," she said, looking at Kitty as Margaret checked her hair.

"My sister has a good heart," I stated, "and she respects you. She wants, so very much, to be right and do the right thing."

"There is no need. She is healthy and I foresee that Rosings will have a future with her and the Colonel. The sooner they have children, the happier I will be. Colonel Fitzwilliam is like a son to me. Therefore, his children will be like my grandchildren. That will be a great comfort to me."

"I believe they shall."

"It's no delight—to be so very alone, when one is not used to being so."

At first, I didn't know how to answer that. Being born to such a large family, often I sought solitude, to be free of the noise. But Lady Catherine had the reverse sort of life. Now it all made sense!

For Lady Catherine was the sort to talk so often because, if she didn't, she might burst. She actively sought company because she, perhaps, was terribly lonely. That loneliness was a shocking blow to a naturally talkative creature, and it manifested into an overbearing character. Her fate was inevitable.

Without thinking, I spoke. The words came out even before I thought about it.

"Thank you," I said, "for everything. When our parents died, we had no mother to help us through such a time. With you being here, to guide us, it feels like she is still here."

When hearing that, Lady Catherine's eyes brightened up.

"Oh!" She gasped. For the first time, I thought that she was speechless. She did not expect me to have said such a thing. "Well, that is... I..."

Overwhelmed, she turned away and excused herself from the room. Everyone watched her depart, and then they turned to me.

"What did you say?" Kitty asked.

"Kind. I said something kind."

"Yes," Elena the servant said, "and it shocked her to her very core."

"I don't understand," I said, "she has been complimented many times before. Why is she so unnerved now?"

"Because your compliment was real. Now she can see the difference than all those other times before."

I looked in the mirror.

Truth on a wedding day.

When it was time to leave for the church, there was a misunderstanding, and the carriages did not arrive at the correct time. There were three coaches, for us brides and bridesmaids, the grooms, and the Hales with Lady Catherine.

On the contrary, the gentlemen did not arrive at the church before we did but rather arrived at the same time.

We descended from our carriage first, with Margaret and Georgiana stepping down with us, in their bridesmaid dresses.

The men's carriage arrived behind ours and the door opened.

All of us ladies stood in a line, aware of the momentous event that would occur. Our future husbands were in there, about to step down and see the three of them, dressed in their best apparel.

The first to exit was Mr. Bingley, who was naturally the

most eager. When seeing us, his eyes lit up, he turned and spoke to the gentlemen within. Then he stepped down, his eyes fixed on Jane, who looked radiant.

Afterwards, the Colonel practically jumped out and landed right next to Bingley, eagerly searching for Kitty. She laughed at his buoyant behavior.

Then, Mr. Darcy emerged, his serious mien giving way when he saw me. The tenseness of his scowl had fallen to the wayside and gave way to a look of reverence when he saw me.

'I love you,' his eyes said.

'And I love you,' my eyes said in return.

Suddenly, I was stricken with an intense desire.

I knew what I needed to do. And even when I knew that I was going to get scolded, I chose to do it anyway.

"Run," I declared.

Jane, Kitty, Margaret, and Georgiana looked strangely at me.

"What?" Georgiana asked.

"Who cares for normal anymore?" I asked them. "When has 'normal' ever given us anything?"

For some reason, Kitty knew precisely what I was feeling.

"Yes," she confirmed. "Let's run mad!"

With a smile and nod to Darcy, I began my rash act.

Kitty grabbed Georgiana's hand, I grabbed Margaret and Jane, to encourage them to run, and then I began to sprint across the grass, toward the front door of the church.

As I began to run, with Kitty doing it as well, and the others easily feeling persuaded to follow us, I turned to the men, and for some reason, they were not perplexed or disturbed. On the contrary, they began to run as well.

It became a race.

Both brides, bridesmaids and grooms were racing toward the church's front doors, just as the reverend emerged to greet us.

"Oh, good god!" he cried, recoiling. "What is happening?"

How shocking it must have looked to him. To see three brides, three grooms, and two bridesmaids racing towards him.

Behind us, I heard Lady Catherine shout, horrified.

The first of us to arrive was Kitty and I, who were used to running. The next to arrive was the Colonel, then Bingley, and the rest arrived at the same time.

Naturally, running in corsets was the worst thing ever.

"Oh dear, we cannot breathe," Jane cried as we began to gasp for air.

"Never fear," Bingley said, taking her fan and fanning her. The other gentlemen did the same with the rest of us, and slowly we stopped gasping.

"Well," Lady Catherine chided, "it serves you right." She rolled her eyes. "I do not know what you all were about. But depend on it, all of Kent will be talking about this now. Now get yourselves in." She turned to the reverend, who was standing there, stricken to the point of being frozen. "Don't just stand there, man! Get to it."

Her sharp order awoke him from his stupor, and he ushered the men in, when we women were arranged to stand and wait for our time to walk down the aisle.

I regretted nothing.[2]

---

2. This scene is inspired by the wedding scene in D. H. Lawrence's novel, Women in Love.

Since our father was gone, and our uncles were in different counties, Mr. Hale had to perform the chores of groomsmen, as well as the chief parent for us all.

He committed to his task with fervor, the bridesmaids walked down the aisle, and soon, it would be our turn.

As Jane, Kitty and I stood in a line, with our bouquets in hand, we looked in between each other.

"Now is the hour of our content," I said, deliberately misquoting the phrase.

"We are here," Jane said, "I cannot believe it. We really are here."

"Yes," Kitty said, "I suppose we three shall just have to be content with being far happier than we ever thought we would be."

Yes, we were and would be.

At last, it was time for us to walk down the aisle.

Bracing ourselves, we took one step forward, then another and another.

The altar was before us.

The reverend stood at the end.

And our three grooms were there, looking at us with even more reverence than before.

Was this wedding day finally here?

After all that we had endured.

That we had underwent.

And all of it was leading up to this one moment. This one defining moment. There is something altogether bewitching about finding one's second self in another person, and we had found ours.

No man and woman could be closer to their loved ones, than the three couples who were marrying this day.

We were of the same mind, flesh, and feelings.

Our feelings were real.

Our hearts were true.

At last, we reached the altar, and each groom went near his prospective bride. Darcy, slowly, walked up to me and I looked at him.

'Dearly beloved,' the reverend said, "we are gathered here today to join these three couples into holy matrimony."

That was the last thing I heard from him because I spent the rest of the wedding with my mind astir.

I was marrying Mr. Darcy!

I, Elizabeth Bennet, had fallen in love with Mr. Darcy, and he loved me in return.

Kitty had fallen in love with the Colonel, and now she would be another Lady Catherine.

Jane had chosen her heart.

The reverend's words continued to wash all over me, I lost all sense of time, of space, and all that mattered was Darcy and me.

After a while, the church service was nearing an end, rings were exchanged, the reverend asked if there was any impediment to our being bonded in holy union, and no one came forward.

All was allowed and granted.

"I now pronounce you husband and wife," he said to Bingley and Jane. Next, he turned to me. "I now pronounce you husband and wife." He turned to Kitty and the Colonel. "I now pronounce you husband and wife. You three gentlemen can now kiss your brides."

"Now," Mr. Darcy whispered to me, "Mrs. Darcy, you are all mine."

"Arm in arm," I said, "and hand in hand. Forever."

Leaning forward, Darcy and I closed our eyes, and we kissed.

Now, I found where my road led to.

Now, I felt the peace of all that we had struggled to find. Here, in the depths of civilization and nature, I had found the grandeur of life, saw the breaths and beauty of it, and now our perseverance had become the ultimate reward.

We were now Mrs. Darcy, Mrs. Bingley, and Mrs. Fitzwilliam.

Love was to burn, to be ablaze with one's passions. For no love, no matter how pure, could be without troubles ahead, without doubts and difficult situations arising to engulf. It is to know these things, to see the conflict, and then, with our hands united, to sojourn onward, even when the conflict proved torrential. It is to walk through the fire and know that getting burned is part of the bond that you share.

Mr. Darcy and I would walk through that fire, and it might burn us, from time to time, but we would come through it in the end. Maybe with a few scars, but all the stronger for it. For the first time ever, I could raise up my arm and shout about love, the complexities of it and that all the labors that we had endured had been beaten, bested, and won!

But of course, it was merely the calm before the storm.

End of Book V[3]

---

3. There is an Afterword behind this that I promise will amuse the reader.

Afterword

Reader, thank you so much for reading Book V of the series. Naturally, this book was meant to be the conclusion of the saga, but things took a little turn, and it proved to be the book before the finality of it all.

I am quite certain that you were expecting it to be the end, and all I can ask for is your patience, and I will explain why.

First, I had originally intended that the wedding would not be the end of this entry, but merely the middle, and I would write all the aftermath and the conflicts that led up to the conclusion. But soon into writing it, I realized one chief thing:

The wedding ought to receive more pomp and circumstance.

The fact is that, as I wrote, I realized that the triple wedding was important and was worth building up. Originally, I was not going to have much notice for it, and it would be a part of the rising action that led to the climax. But then, I began to realize that would be a very stupid thing to do.

This is a grand moment that the readers would naturally want to have more time to spend with and want to view it as what they wished to close with. Each entry has progressed from a graver tone to a lighter one.

Book 1 ended with emotional turmoil.

Book 2 ended in violence.

Book 3 ended in tragedy.

Book 4 ended in a chance for a brighter tomorrow.

Ergo, it seemed that Book 5 ought to end in utter bliss.

It just seemed like the audience deserved one that leant itself most prominently toward optimism and ecstasy.

As such, to have the wedding, and Margaret's newly discovered affection for Thornton, be the primary focus on this chapter, made more sense.

So, I would save the conflicts and drama for another conclusion, and hope that the reader still can forgive me. But believe me when I say that I thought of the respect for the reader's pleasure. There's more to the story, but for now, let happiness be the primary focus.

This new development also gave me the chance to develop Margaret and Thornton's relationship further, because I didn't have to worry about rushing things just to have the novel written in a proper amount of time.

It also gave me the chance to change my mind.

Originally, when I went into writing this book, I was going to have Mrs. Hale die before they went to Kent. Because I changed how the book was to end, it led to me changing my mind about Mrs. Hale's survival. This led to Mrs. Hale and Lady Catherine becoming friends, which I didn't foresee occurring until I had written it.

Therefore, cutting up the events of this book for a later entry saved me from making another stupid decision.

The third foolish decision it saved me from is from making the decision of having Frederick leave Milton before he was detected, which was another of the original choices that I was going to make. Yeah, that was dumb as God knows what!

In Mrs. Gaskell's original book, Frederick's quick entrance and exit made all the sense in the world. Frederick had no choice but to enter the tale when his mother was at death's door, to see her once more. But his swift departure (and Lenniard's sudden appearance) also made sense because it put Margaret in the place where she had to lie to protect Frederick. This lie made Margaret realize that, when in a difficult situation, she was just as capable of deception as any other. This humbled her, making her appear as erroneous in Thornton's eyes because of said deception, and it knocked her off her high opinion of herself—in the same manner that Darcy's letter humbled Elizabeth. Frederick's quick entrance and exit served a great purpose to the narrative.

However, it would not work for a reimagining. To have Frederick enter and exit very soon looks uninspiring, flat, unoriginal, and tedious. And since I had every intention of making Mr. Thornton aware of Frederick Hale already, Frederick was not going to be used as a means to humble Margaret. For she was already widening her views toward Mr. Thornton.

Now, you see...how close us writers come to easily making some of the dumbest decisions in the world. Often enough, we are saved by our own instinct and betray ourselves if we overthink. The choice to have the primary focus of this book be the buildup to Colonel Fitzwilliam's good fortune, Margaret developing more feelings for Thornton, and the preparations for the triple wedding, were ideas that were stumbled upon organically. Whereas my original ideas were forced. I hope that my instincts were correct and were what the reader was looking for.

The Final Exit of Mr. Hanley

Reader, this hurt. I loved writing Mr. Hanley, Hunnicutt, and Mr. Dennison. The dynamic between them and Elizabeth was always very stimulating for me, and it gave me more chances of what to write. As perverse as this sounds, I was looking forward to when Elizabeth had to confront Mr. Hanley about her true affections. Then I reached the point of writing it, and I almost cried. I liked Mr. Hanley. So, to have him receive rejection of any kind was a little alarming. I did the best I could with it and only could find a way to wish him well.

Purity vs. Passion

Remember when I said that it might interest you to read this particular Afterword? Well, it is for a good reason. When it comes to writing the last entry to this series, I am open to advice on how best to proceed.

There has always been a sort of joy-stigma relationship when it comes to sensuous scenes in Jane Austen re-imaginings. I admit that much progress has been made, where previous fanfiction writers have paved the way for the rest of us, over the years. Where they have traversed that very same dilemma. Some have written about the intimacy of love, while never showing any passionate scenes. Others have dared to bring them into the narrative.

I have always understood both avenues that writers took.

I understood the writer who didn't wish to include sensual scenes, and others who dove into those sensuous scenes with gusto. I suppose it is because I have always considered the connection between purity and passion to not be as distant as they are usually considered. Sexuality and sensuality are something that I learned had its own sacredness and spirituality to it, especially since the human soul cannot fully exist without them.

Since many of us variation authors have already dared and sojourned forth, confronting the sensuous side of Darcy and Elizabeth's relationship, I think the reader knows what to expect it.

That only leaves the matter of Thornton and Margaret Hale. With the way that the narrative is going, there was an instinct in my mind to consider a romantic and sensuous scene between them in the next and last book of this series. But then, I am also aware that maybe it might not be what the reader wishes.

Based on reviews from the original first edition of this book when it was released, I have relied on previous reviewers to give their advice.

Yes, I do sometimes, read reviews. Usually, I do not read them, for fear of it influencing me—a negative review can knock one's confidence off and you end up making choices that only make things worse for the readers who already were interested. Originally, I did read them because I got fortunate in receiving kind and open readers. Yet, over time, I knew that my writing style was not for everyone, because nothing can be. But in that time, when a reader gave me good advice, I was not against being a little dependent. After all, dependence works sometimes. You just must remember to be independent again, later. So, for the last book, some parts of it were suggestions from a reader who left a review. I just wished to make sure that reader knows that I still respected her ideas and appreciated her feedback.

The next time you pick up this series, it shall be the end. And that shall be a conclusion that, I hope, I shall see you there.

— Ney Mitch

THANK YOU FOR READING

Did you enjoy this book?

We invite you to leave a review at your favorite book site, such as Goodreads, Amazon, Barnes & Noble, etc.

DID YOU KNOW THAT LEAVING A REVIEW...

- Helps other readers find books they may enjoy.
- Gives you a chance to let your voice be heard.
- Gives authors recognition for their hard work.
- Doesn't have to be long. A sentence or two about why you liked the book will do.

About the Author

Ney Mitch has been a long-standing Jane Austen enthusiast, having written forty novels that were inspired by her various works. Since stumbling on Miss Austen's books after graduating from college, she has always dabbled in Austen inspired literature, ranging from writing works for teens to adults. Originally, her desire was to adapt Jane Austen's writing in a way to help young adults connect with her, however over time, she has spread her aims to other genres and styles. Having received her BA Degree at Desales University, she is a writer, both literary and dramatic, as well as being a Historic Reenactor.

facebook.com/courtney.mitchell.589

x.com/CMMitchelPsyche

pinterest.com/shebaanna

Also by Ney Mitch
with Satin Romance

Austen Gaskell Series

Curiosities & Contemplation

Resolved & Resigned

Triumph & Tragedy

Woes & Worries

Love & Labors Won

Economy & Ever After (Coming soon!)

Kitty Bennet Adventure Series

Vanities and Vexations

Forms & Fashions

Romance & Recklessness

Nuance & Novelty

Doubts & Difficulties

Follies & Forgiveness

Joys & Judgements

Romance & Revolution Saga

The First Impression

Chances Fade

Chances End
